To my daughters, whose strength and spirit shine brighter than any star.

Sirum em qez'

Dakken Haes

Dakken LLC

ISBN: 979-8-9940286-0-5

Cover design by: Steven Haaes

Library of Congress Control Number: 2018675309

Printed in the United States of America

Chapter 1

The Worst of Times

The quiet moments before events are always the most extreme.

Tonight was no exception.

No noise, no wind, no movement. Just the shallow rhythm of a sleeping household in southern Tehran.

CRACK.

Not thunder.

Wood splintering.

Hinges shrieking.

Shadows moving fast.

Two

No, four

No, six men.

Six black figures pouring in like liquid darkness.

Guns drawn. Faces obscured by helmets and beards. Boots stomping across the tile, shouting filling every corner.

The house was suddenly ablaze with noise—screaming, shouting, muffled cries, furniture toppling, glass shattering.

Nare Darya, who had been wiping down the kitchen counter, dropped the cloth just as a rifle butt smashed into her shoulder. She crumpled. Her hands searched the tiles, but all she found was dirt and blood from the cut on her cheek.

"Where is Maryan? Where is Maryan?" the men barked in Farsi. "She is under arrest!"

Upstairs, Maryan Darya, eighteen years old, stirred from uneasy sleep.

Boom.

Her bedroom door was blasted open. Splinters rained across her blanket.

Men with flashlights, guns, and thick beards swarmed her sanctuary. Before she could even sit upright, hands were on her arms, her hair, her clothes. She was yanked upright.

"You whore!" one of them spat, his breath sour with cigarettes and rage.

Maryan, just 18, still half asleep, blinked at him in disbelief.

A whore?

She, who had never so much as kissed a boy?

She almost laughed at the absurdity but thought better of it.

She just mumbled something to herself about his intelligence but thought best to let it go.

These were FARAJA, more commonly known as NAJA, Tehran's police force. Clad in black, helmets strapped tight, weapons gleaming. The sight of them in your home was the beginning of ruin.

And with them, unmistakable in their posture and their shrill authority, were members of the Guidance Patrol—Iran's morality police. The same unit that had haunted every street corner of her life, that could stop her at any moment for showing a strand of hair or wearing jeans too tight.

Maryan's heart pounded, but her face remained still. She wanted to scream, to hurl every insult she knew, but her sister's sobs and her father's pleas filled the hallway. To fight now would only fuel the storm. She swallowed her words.

The Guidance Patrol—how her mother loathed them.

Nare often told stories of the years before 1979. Stories that felt like myths to Maryan, as distant as fairy tales.

"There were no dress codes then," Nare would say while folding laundry. "I wore skirts to university. We had women in parliament—eight at once. Do you know how many American women had sat in their Senate before that? Only three, total."

"Women were powerful, full of pride, full of love for Iran."

"Iran the most beautiful country in the world", her mother would say.

Maryan had memorized these lines, repeated over countless evenings. She could see the glow in her mother's eyes when she remembered. "Education was free. We were encouraged to lead, to create. We had dignity. Do you understand? Dignity."

But dignity had been stolen.

With Khomeini's- the self-appointed messenger from Allah - came new decrees:

- Marriage age lowered to **nine.**

- A woman's testimony worth half a man's.

- Nurseries closed, because women belonged at home.

- And worst of all—the **mandatory hijab**.

The hijab was said to represent honor, respect, purity. Maryan only ever saw chains.

Before the hijab women had rights, women were leaders, turning the country into a dream that not even the United States could comprehend

While women in the United States, were struggling to get bank accounts and credit cards, the women of Iran were leading the country.

But like the entry into her room, the unwanted leader Khomeini who wanted babies to marry at nine, new laws were mandated and forced on the women of Iran.

Although looking from outside the Hijab, may not seem the worst law in Iran, to the women of Iran, the hijab was the regimes symbol of control over them.

The hijab, head coverings worn by Muslim women. It was supposed to signify not only the act of covering but also represent honor, respect, and moral purity in Islam.

To Maryan it was funny the hijab was supposed to symbolize respect, as she had never seen respect, not for women rights that is. Not in Iran anyways.

Neither respect nor honor. Never once as a woman was her wishes honored.

A slap brought her back.

One of the officers had struck her across the temple. Stars burst in her vision. Her ears rang.

Her father let out a sharp gasp. She turned in time to see him struck with a rifle butt, his forehead splitting open. Blood spilled down his face, bright against his gray hair.

Her mother screamed, crawling toward him, but a boot met her ribs and sent her sprawling.

The soundscape blurred—shouts, crashes, sobs, each noise sharper than the last until they all bled together.

Another slap to Maryan's head.

"Answer!" a voice barked. But she hadn't even heard the question.

She didn't need to. She knew the real reason.

It wasn't drugs. It wasn't treason.

It was art.

It was protest against the Hijab.

A small gathering, hardly worth the word. A few hand-painted signs, some chanting, graffiti that she had drawn herself. A swirl of faces, women and men, tired but defiant.

And her. Eighteen years old, armed only with markers and courage.

That was enough to summon the black demons into her home.

Maryan dizzy now unable to grasp the movements suddenly understood.

"Here I am sitting here on my bed, while the black robe bitches, search my room, all for not wanting the hijab." thought Maryan.

Her dresser was overturned. Clothes, sketches, books, pens—all dumped on the floor like garbage.

"Tell me what you are looking for?" she asked in a voice dripping with disdain.

Another slap. Then another.

That was a two-slap question. She thought bitterly.

The room was unrecognizable now. Her safe haven had been reduced to rubble in minutes.

Through the broken window she saw neighbors' curtains twitch. Eyes peering out, quickly vanishing. The whole street was awake, yet no one would come. Everyone had learned: survive by silence.

Maryan was not sure what the specific charge was, but unofficially she knew attending a protest against the Hijab, was the reason for the black demons being in her house.

Then suddenly engines roared. Tires screeched. And just like that, her family was dragged out into the night and scattered to dark places.

Silence returned, thicker than before.

Maryan now trembling, sarcasm gone, pride gone.

A minute ago, she had been brave. As long as her family was near, she had armor. Now, stripped of them, she was prey.

Her hands shook. She could barely breathe.

She knew what came next. Every girl in Iran knew.

Rape was not a possibility—it was a routine. A weapon sanctioned by the state.

Maryan's mind reeled with the stories she had overheard: girls assaulted on the way to prison, women brutalized in cells, virginity stolen as state policy.

She thought of Hussein Mortazavi Zanjan, infamous head of Tehran's Evin Prison, who had decreed that virgin women must be raped before execution—because virgins went to heaven. And the regime could not allow that.

Even the presence of female officers offered no safety. Some participated, others turned away.

Tears streamed down Maryan's face. She pressed her fists to her eyes, willing herself not to scream.

Her lips trembled. Her lungs felt crushed.

On the bed that no longer felt hers, in the room that was no longer hers, Maryan closed her eyes and prepared for the worst.

Chapter 2

Dreams in Iran

Lying on her bed, held down unable to scream Maryan felt all life leave her. The smell, the yelling, the screaming, the crying, it all became quiet.

Just five years ago Maryan had made up her mind to become a doctor.

Understandable it was not easy to be a woman in Iran now, a country once seen as the cutting edge of women's rights.

Maryan was born in July according to the western calendar, a good month, if you believed in month seven in the west. But in Iran it was different, it was the lucky month according to a many Iranian people.

Iran actually has two main calendars, which always confused Maryan.

The Western Gregoran calendar for dealing with the world and the Islamic or Hijri calendar.

The Hijri calendar is a lunar calendar, and lunar calendars are always approximately 11 days shorter than our Gregorian (solar) calendar. Year 1 in the Hijri system roughly corresponds to the year 622 in Gregorian dating, the year that the Prophet Muhammad undertook Harjan fleeing Mecca to take up residence in Yathrib. This is considered the foundational event in the origins of Islam, analogous to the birth of Christ in the Christian tradition, hence its identification with year one of the new calendar.

Maryan's birth was also seen as a blessing to Maryan's mother, who always said Maryan was born lucky, and she would become the world, a phrase Maryan still thinks about.

Maryan's mother, Nare Darya, was born as an Armenian Christian. To an outsider this might seem odd, being born a Christian in a Muslim land, but in reality, there were about 300,00 Christian left in Iran, and each generation prouder and louder to be Christian.

Nare was a true Armenian beauty, beautiful even at 52, she was easy on the eyes. She studied linguistics and languages, and speaks nine languages, including Farsi, Arabic, French, English, and Hindi. Her job was translations for a large multinational firm in Tehran, a job she was very good at.

Maryan's father, Sahar Darya, was an architect and artist in Tehran, who helped design many city buildings including taking part in the design of the Central Library of Semnan. Well known in Tehran as an artist. He is a practicing Christian, and a strong supporter of women rights in Iran, which was reflected in his underground art, that hund in secret around Tehran.

Art, once highly censored after the 1979 revolution, was now allowed and especially classical art, which Sahar practiced. He practiced in most mediums, but large wooden art as well as canvas classical were his preferred formats.

It was odd, Sahar always said, that art, the expression of feelings, was looked at negatively in Iran, but a lot of people, when the world at large treated Iranian art as masterful. In fact in 1931 Time magazine called it 'Persia in Piccadilly', when the Irian art exhibition traveled to Europe. An exhibition so well received that Winston Churchill invited Aga Khan to walk with him through the exhibit.

Art in all forms, from poetry to canvas was Iran, an Iran that seemed to be forgotten, like women's rights.

But Sahar had not forgotten,

Often times, he was called in to review classical art, to ship off for shows in the west. But his real passion was his daughters, and the rights they have lost under the Islamic revolution.

This fight, the fight for women's rights caused him to lose jobs, and caused mocking from his neighbors, but as a proud father of two girls, he had no choice but to fight for the country he previously knew and loved.

Maryan's sister Marineh. At 14 strong and beautiful, dark brown hair and brown eyes. A lover of traditional Iran poetry, who often quotes ancient authors, could now be hear screaming as they loaded her into the van. '

Maryan's father and mother no where to be heard or seen, were for sure now off in a van headed for a room at the police station or worse.

Why, why, why did she participate in the hijab protest. It was nothing elegant, it was a simple march, a few chants, no media, no press, just some kids letting off steam.

Lying on her bed, held down and unable to scream, Maryan felt all life leave her. The smell, the yelling, the screaming, the crying—it all became quiet. It was like the world had sunk beneath water, where pain echoed through her whole being.

Just five years ago, Maryan had made up her mind to become a doctor.

Understandably, it was not easy to be a woman in Iran now, a country once seen as the cutting edge of women's rights. Once, Tehran had rivaled Paris in fashion. Once, women had filled the lecture halls at the University of Tehran. Once, girls had walked with confidence through the bazaar without a hijab or chador. Now, all that seemed to belong to a past as unreachable as the moon.

Her mother always told Maryan, she was born lucky.

Maryan was born in July according to the Western calendar—a good month if you believed in month seven. in Iran, It was the lucky month, according to true believers it was a time when fate smiled.

Iran, with all its complexity, had two main calendars, which always confused Maryan. There was the Western Gregorian calendar for dealing with the world—for embassies, imports, and internet dates. Then there was the Islamic or Hijri calendar, a lunar system that danced eleven days shorter each year than the Gregorian solar one.

Year one in the Hijri system corresponded to 622 AD, the year the Prophet Muhammad undertook the Hijrah, fleeing Mecca to settle in Yathrib, later Medina. This was considered the foundational moment of Islam—analogous to Christ's birth in the Christian tradition.

Maryan's own birth was also seen as a foundational moment by her mother. "You were born lucky," Nare Darya often whispered. "You will become the world."

That phrase—you will become the world—lodged itself deep in Maryan's chest. What did it mean? A burden? A destiny? Some days it gave her strength. Other days, it felt like a curse.

Nare Darya had been born into an Armenian Christian family in Tehran. To an outsider, it might have seemed odd to be born Christian in a land so strongly identified with Islam. But Iran had always been home to diversity, hidden and whispering though it may be.

Some 300,000 Christians remained in Iran, each generation prouder and louder. Nare was one of them—a woman of knowledge, elegance, and quiet defiance. Even at 52, she drew attention when she walked into a room. With cheekbones like a sculpture and hair the color of chestnuts, she commanded presence without ever demanding it.

She had studied linguistics in Tehran and could speak nine languages: Farsi, Arabic, French, English, Armenian, Russian, Turkish, Hindi, and a smattering of German. She worked as a translator for a multinational firm in Tehran, decoding diplomatic jargon and corporate reports with the precision of a surgeon.

Maryan's father, Sahar Darya, was an architect and artist. His works were all over Tehran, though many bore no signature. He had helped design the Central Library of Semnan, a gleaming structure filled with hidden references to pre-Islamic Persia. He was known in Tehran's underground art circles—quietly, carefully—for his wooden sculptures, which breathed fire and grief.

Sahar was a practicing Christian and a fierce believer in women's rights. That conviction cost him commissions, friends, and once, a close brush with the morality police. Still, he persisted. "Art is our resistance," he often said. "Art remembers what law forgets."

After the 1979 revolution, art had been censored, redefined, muted. Yet classical art—Persian miniatures, floral calligraphy, Safavid-style sculpture—had made a cautious return. Sahar operated in those shadows, threading his real beliefs in double meanings and layered allegories.

It was odd, Sahar always said, that art, the expression of feelings, was looked at negatively in Iran, but a lot of people, when the world at large treated Iranian art as masterful. In fact in 1931 Time magazine called it 'Persia in Piccadilly', when the Irian art exhibition traveled to Europe.

An exhibition so well received that Winston Churchill invited Aga Khan to walk with him through the exhibit.

Art was Iran.

He liked to say it was ironic: that art, which was once declared haram by fanatics, was now hailed as part of Iran's proud heritage by the same regime. That the West treated Iranian art as masterful, while Iranian children were being arrested for painting slogans.

Maryan grew up surrounded by brushes, pigments, poetry, and purpose. Bookshelves towered in every room, sagging under the weight of volumes by Rumi, Forough Farrokhzad, and Gibran. Her sister, Marineh, four years younger, could recite Hafez by heart.

Marineh. Fourteen, beautiful, sharp as a knife. Always quoting ancient poets as if they were TikTok stars. She had dark brown hair, brown eyes that burned when she was angry, and a tendency to correct adults with unnerving confidence.

Her sister, her friend, where was she now.

Was she meeting the same fate?

Was she alone with the black robe bitches?

Was she ...

It was all too much.

The last thing Maryan remembered hearing was her sister's scream.

A scream that no child should use.

A scream that pierced the night.

They had come at night. Vans without plates. Men in black who shoved her father into a wall. Her mother crying, arms outstretched. Marineh fighting, kicking, shouting, as two men dragged her by the wrists.

Then black bags. Cuffs. Shouts. The slam of a door.

Why?

Why had she participated in the protest?

It hadn't even been a protest, not really. More like a gathering. A march. A few chants. No media. No press. Just students, girls mostly, letting off steam. Angry about Mahsa Amini. About the others. About everything.

Maryan hadn't planned to go. She was studying for her anatomy exam. But then she saw the flyer, the scrawled words: "Zan. Zendegi. Azadi." *Woman. Life. Freedom.*

It echoed in her brain like a heartbeat. She picked up her scarf, tied it loosely, and walked out the door.

She didn't chant loudly. Didn't climb onto cars. She held a sign. Walked quietly. But her face was seen. Photographed. Shared.

Tears streaming now, no words, Maryan understood it was her choice, her choice to participate in the march against the Hijab, a simple protest that now had destroyed her family.

And now her family was gone.

Tears streamed down her cheeks, hot and constant.

Her mouth couldn't move. Her throat felt bruised.

Her body ached. Something was broken in her rib.

Maryan knew this was not just a consequence. It was a message.

They were teaching her. Punishing her. Erasing her.

But deep beneath the fear, something else stirred: rage.

She remembered her father's voice, calm and sure, quoting Ferdowsi:

"If you do not rise to defend your rights, you will be crushed beneath the boots of tyrants."

And her mother:

"Your body is not shame. Your voice is not shame. Speak even if your voice trembles."

And Marineh, screaming as they took her:

"I am not afraid of you!"

Maryan closed her eyes, her face covered in tears.

She would survive.

She would remember.

She would become the world.

Chapter 3:

The Slaughterhouse

Waking up to the stench of urine, vomit, animals, and human sweat was not the kind of birthday Maryan had intended to celebrate — not for herself, and certainly not for her friend, Anoush.

Anoush, who led the protest Maryan participated in, was one of the fiercest girl Maryan knew. Unafraid to knock the *muam'am (the white hat often worn by clerics),* off of a clerics head, she inspired all the young women in Tehran.

Maryan cried thinking about the torture Anoush was enduring.

But it was her pain, the acid fumes pain, that burned the inside of her nose before her eyes cried as they tried to flutter open.

Her body screamed in protest. Every muscle ached, her bones felt disconnected from the tendons meant to hold them, and she could no longer see out of her left eye. Swollen shut, crusted with blood, her eyelid was a sealed door to the outside world.

Inside, though — her skull throbbed, and a faint metallic taste lingered in the back of her mouth. Internally, she knew the bleeding was far from over.

She tried to move, but her body didn't listen. Her arms were dead weights, her legs useless stumps. She couldn't even lift her head, not fully.

And then she heard it. The trickle.

At first, she thought it was water. A leak, maybe, from the rusted barn roof above. But then she smelled hot, sharp, unrelenting. Urine. Someone — maybe another prisoner, maybe a guard — was urinating right next to her head. So, close she could feel the heat radiating off the soaked ground beneath her cheek. Her mouth hung slightly open. She gagged but nothing came out.

Tears spilled from her working eye. Not because of the smell, but because of what she had become. What had happened to her.

She had been someone once. Not a prisoner. Not a victim.

She had been Maryan Darya. Eighteen years old, studying at the University in Tehran. The firstborn of two daughters to a father who beamed with pride every time she passed an exam, who saved newspaper clippings about "women in medicine" and read them aloud like bedtime stories. The girl who could diagnose a textbook illness.

Now?

Now she was a body on the ground. Barely human. Breathing, somehow, in a makeshift prison built for livestock.

It was at that moment — surrounded by decay, filth, and the rotting promise of what her life could have been — that Maryan finally broke. Anger, hatred, sadness, pain, and fear gripped her in a violent fist, and she sobbed. Not the kind of soft crying she remembered from childhood.

These were animal sounds, loud and wet, gulping, desperate, and entirely involuntary.

That was when she heard the voice.

"Wake up now, girl."

It was cracked, like old stone rubbed raw in the sun. Faintly musical. And impossibly close.

Maryan's good eye managed to turn. A shadow hunched over her — a woman, tiny and rail-thin, knees like roots bent underweight, skin so darkened by mud and age it blended with the shadows of the barn.

"Maman-joon?" Maryan whispered, through cracked lips. Was this death? Was her grandmother here to take her?

The woman chuckled — a sound so dry and fleeting it barely registered. "Child," she said. "I haven't been called that in years."

Before Maryan could speak again, the woman reached into a fold of her dirt-caked cloak and pulled out a grey cloth, soaked with something. She spat directly onto it, then began wiping Maryan's face.

The cloth smelled of rot and mold and old teeth, but the woman's touch was surprisingly gentle. Maryan flinched at first but then let herself be cleaned. The filth on her face, her neck, her forehead — wasn't just dirt, it was identity. A visual marker of the torture she had endured. With every wipe, something lifted. The smell didn't go away, but the shame dulled slightly.

As the old woman worked, Maryan's eye adjusted. The contours of the barn came into focus — or what was left of it. The building, long abandoned, had once been an animal hold. Rusted metal gates lined the wall. Piles of straw, long yellowed, mixed with human waste. A few fluorescent lights hung from bent wires, flickering weakly in the thick heat.

In the corners, other women stirred. Nine of them in total. All filthy. All battered in their own way. A few slept, two rocked back and forth, one sat muttering to herself in Armenian. The one nearest had an eye swollen shut just like Maryan's. They looked like ghosts of one another — strangers bound by a shared doom.

The old woman finished wiping and tucked the cloth away.

"You're lucky," she said. "You were out for three days. Most don't wake up."

Maryan coughed. Her voice was barely there. "Where am I?"

The woman nodded to the high, crumbling windows. "Slaughterhouse on the old highway, near Qarchak. After the last strike, Qarchak Prison lost a whole wing. They moved us here. livestock stalls are easier to keep secure."

That word struck Maryan. "Slaughterhouse?"

The old woman smiled, but it wasn't kind. "We are not the first animals kept here, child."

The realization settled over her like wet wool.

She remembered bits and pieces — the explosion, the sirens, the rush of footsteps down cement hallways. Guards screaming. Then the sound of a drone overhead. The next thing she remembered was being dragged — not carried — dragged by her shoulders across pavement.

She had arrived three nights earlier, beaten beyond recognition, but alive.

Her heart clenched at the memory.

"Marineh....she whispered. "Where's Marineh?"

The old woman's face changed. The humor left her eyes. She didn't answer at first.

"Please," Maryan begged. "Is she alive?"

"I have not seen anyone new, but you child," the woman answered.

"A young woman came in the day before you, but is unspeaking," she continued.

Maryan tried to push herself up. Her arms buckled, but the old woman steadied her.

"Don't rush. You'll reopen the wounds."

Maryan crawled. Inch by inch. Across the slimy floor. Her knees scraped the stone. Her fingernails cracked. But she got there.

Yasna, her friend of many years, was lying on her side, eyes wide open, unmoving. Her cheek pressed to the ground.

Her hair — once long and perfumed — was matted with blood. One arm twitched, the other held tightly to her chest.

Yasna her friend at school and at the protest, green eyes like Maryan, she was one of the prettiest girls Maryan knew, but now, now she was dark, part of the slaughterhouse floor, a animal worse that the poorest peasants in Iran.

"Yasna?" Maryan whispered.

No response.

"Yasna, it's me. It's Maryan. Please…"

A soft moan, then silence.

Maryan reached out, brushing the girl's cheek.

Yasna flinched, recoiled — not recognition, but instinct. A mouse beneath the hawk's shadow.

Maryan broke again.

She slumped beside her friend, cradling her own head in her arms. Her body shook from the effort. From grief. From knowing she had survived — and Nare had not.

The old woman came and laid a small tin cup beside them.

"Water," she said. "Share it. There's only a bucket a day for the ten of us."

Maryan drank slowly, then placed the cup by Yasna's lips. After a moment, the girl sipped. Barely.

"She's in there," the old woman said, nodding. "But far."

Maryan turned. "What's your name?"

The woman sat cross-legged, knees cracking as she moved. "They called me Arezou, once. Before all this. I used to teach Farsi poetry at the girls' school in Rey."

Maryan nodded. "Thank you, Arezou."

Silence fell again. The barn buzzed with the sound of flies. The others barely moved.

Then a distant shout — a male voice. Then another. Footsteps.

The women all froze.

A metal gate groaned open.

Two guards entered, faces covered with black scarves, holding batons.

"Time for selections," one growled.

Arezou rose to her feet and stood before them.

"Not her," she said, nodding toward Maryan. "She can't walk."

They ignored her.

The younger guard pointed. "That one. The tall one. And the girl next to her."

"No!" Maryan cried. "Please! She's not well!"

They grabbed her by the shoulders, hauling her up. She screamed, twisting in their grip.

"Stop it!" Arezou cried, swinging a broken broomstick. The older guard slammed her to the ground with the back of his hand.

The world tilted.

Maryan's head struck the edge of a metal feeding trough. Her vision blurred.

But before blacking out, she heard it — Yasna's voice, soft and hoarse:

"Don't fight them… it's worse when you fight…"

Then silence.

Chapter 4

Darkness

Passed out or dreaming or having a nightmare, Maryan's mind unsure of reality, raced.

Trying to regain some semblance of order, she struggled putting anything together.

She remembered they took her blindfolded.

She was shoved inside a small office, cuffed at the wrists and ankles, her mouth taped, her eyes covered with a hood that smelled faintly of chemicals and dust. The guards didn't speak to her except to bark orders. "Left." "Sit." "Shut up."

She could hear a gate clatter shut behind her. The air was dry, metallic. She was placed on a chair, her hands still behind her. The hood came off, but the blindfold remained.

Then, a voice.

Calm. Male. Young.

"Maryan Darya."

She said nothing.

"You know why you're here."

Still, she didn't answer.

A pause. Then a slap — fast, not hard, but humiliating.

"I ask again," the voice said. "Do you know why you're here?"

She nodded, barely.

He stepped closer.

"You think your little paintings matter? You think hashtags make revolutions?"

Another pause.

"You Christians, Islam has no place for you." Trying to fight the hijab, the sign from Allah of a woman's purity."

Another slap.

Angrier this time, another slap.

"We will teach you that they do not."

It was the fifth or the tenth slap, she stopped remembering, when she went dark.

The slaughterhouse had no official name, no paper trail. It wasn't Evin Prison, with its notorious reputation and rotating teams of interrogators. This place was quieter. Dirtier. Private. Run by the Revolutionary Guard Intelligence branch and known only by those they brought in alive.

She was kept in a room, and beaten over and over again, until she was unconscious.

She had no idea of their questions, or what answers she gave. But she knew she gave them everything they wanted, every name, every place, every secret that girls in Tehran kept.

They used pain as a weapon.

She would go hours, only hearing a kick or a punch.

Then suddenly, a bang on the door. A scream. A man shouting down the hall. A woman sobbing. Then silence again.

Her first interrogation came after what she guessed was two days, but lasted only 8 hours. She had been deprived of sleep, food, and the sound of her own name.

The room had a single table. Two chairs. A man in olive uniform with a short beard sat with a pen and clipboard.

He smiled like a teacher.

"Maryan Darya," he said. "You are an artist?"

She didn't speak.

He opened a folder.

"These are yours." He slid photos across the table. Murals, paintings, flyers — her work, some from years ago, some from the protests just weeks prior.

"You are talented," he said. "Wasted on propaganda."

Still, she said nothing.

He leaned forward.

"You painted the burning hijab mural on Ferdowsi Square, yes?"

Her eyes flicked to the photo.

"No."

Another man entered. Heavyset, eyes like stone. He walked behind her.

"I'll ask again," the first man said, more firmly this time.

"I did not paint that one," she replied. "It was a student."

A fist came from behind. It struck the back of her head, quick and blunt. She cried out, more in shock than pain.

The man in front didn't blink.

"We have your signature on an internal flyer. We have footage of you near the mural site. Do not insult our intelligence."

Maryan breathed slowly, trying to steady herself.

"I am just an artist."

"Yes," the man said. "But art kills kings."

The torture began with beating, now just pure pain, as she was made to stand mostly naked for an hour in the center of the room, while the guards yelled at her.

They left her standing for hours — blindfolded, facing the wall, arms raised. The door behind her remained ajar. She could hear them talking, joking, drinking tea.

If she lowered her arms, a voice would snap: "Up!"

Eventually her muscles spasmed. Her legs trembled. Her body began to betray her. She urinated on herself once and they laughed.

"This is the girl who will bring down the Islamic Republic?" someone jeered.

Putting a hood on her, they forced food in her mouth, forcing her to eat rice from a spoon she couldn't see. She choked more than once.

After a week — or what she thought was a week — this continued, Beatings, questions, Her ribs were the first target. Quick kicks from steel-toed boots. Then her feet — bastinado, an old method. She screamed. They ignored it.

Her hands were strapped to a metal pipe once. A wet cloth was stuffed into her mouth, and she was left that way for what felt like an hour. When they removed it, she gasped like a drowning swimmer.

Each time they brought her out of the cell, they gave her a name she didn't recognize.

"Where is Laleh Mansouri?"

"I don't know."

"She's your contact. She gave you the stencil."

"I don't know her."

A slap. A shock. A punch to the gut.

"Where did you get the paint?"

"From the university storeroom."

"You lie."

Eventually, they dragged her into a separate room — larger, darker. A camera sat on a tripod.

"You will make a statement," said the officer. "You will say the protests were foreign-funded. That you were tricked. That you regret your actions."

Maryan, eyes half swollen shut, shook her head.

The man struck her again, this time across the mouth.

"You are not brave," he whispered. "You are a virus."

Blood spilled out of her, on the floor, while they laughed.

They stopped asking questions eventually.

Her body broken, inside she was dying she could feel it- slowly. Her mind, racing on nothing but pain.

She began to hallucinate. Her mother, whispering lullabies. Her father, standing in a wheat field. Marineh crying in a corner. She spoke to them. Out loud. The guards listened and laughed.

Once, they brought in another woman — older, wearing a torn chador. She sat next to Maryan in the hallway. They weren't allowed to speak. But their shoulders touched. And Maryan felt, for the first time in days, a shred of humanity.

The next day, the woman was gone.

They tried to make her clean the floor of the interrogation room. Her own blood still smeared one corner. They gave her no rag, but to use her tongue, but by now unable to stand or crawl, she just fell.

"Please kill me." She begged.

Laughter was their answer.

Days or weeks or months, in and out of consciousness, and dreaming of goats, lullabies, paint brushes and a be, she would wake up, only to be in the same spot, the same hell hole, that smelled of animals and death.

Then as quickly as the guards burst into her home her torture stopped.

But no more beatings, no more interrogation, no more, no more anything.

Days went by, the old women keeping her feed, and drinking water.

Slowly her body was healing, her mind was still in pieces.

After what had seemed like weeks or months she was allowed a bath — in cold water. A guard stood and watched her, smirking. She looked at the floor the entire time.

They gave her clean clothes.

A sign, she realized. Something was changing.

It took days before she could even trust it.

At first, she thought they were preparing her for execution. The sudden quietness, the absence of fists and boots—it seemed too deliberate, too unnatural. She whispered to herself that this was what came before the end. A lull, a pause, then the gunshot.

But the days stretched on.

The old woman appeared again, the one who had fed her scraps before, sometimes rice, sometimes broth so thin it was more water than food. Now the bowls came more regularly. Twice a day, sometimes three. Water, too, not just a dirty cup left once every few days, but a steady supply. She drank until her stomach cramped, her body shocked by the sudden mercy.

Her body, bruised and broken, began the long crawl back toward health. At first, she could hardly lift her arms to take food from the woman's hands. Her fingers trembled so badly that she spilled more than she managed to eat. But the woman would kneel, muttering under her breath, and patiently scoop the grains back into Maryan's palm, pressing her fingers shut as if to remind her:

Eat.

Swallow.

Live.

Her mind, though, was still in pieces.

The dreams did not leave her. Some nights, she woke screaming, her throat raw from sounds she hadn't realized she'd made. She dreamed of goats again—the ones from her childhood, small and stubborn, their bleating echoing in the courtyard of her grandparents' village home. In dreams, she tried to paint them, but her brushes were always broken, the bristles falling apart in her hand. She would smear black streaks across a canvas that kept dissolving into smoke, until the paint became blood and the goats began to bleat like children.

She clung to the old woman's presence like a fragile anchor. The woman never spoke much, only small gestures—a nod, a grunt, the soft rustle of fabric as she knelt beside her. Sometimes Maryan wondered if she was a prisoner too, or a servant forced to tend the broken ones. Her face was lined, her hands rough, but her eyes held a kind of steady watchfulness that Maryan had not seen in months.

After what might have been weeks—or months, she still could not tell—something new happened.

She was allowed another bath.

It was not warm, nor private. The water was cold, so cold that her skin prickled and her teeth chattered the moment it touched her. A guard stood watching the entire time, leaning against the wall, his arms folded. He smirked as though the sight of her frail, shivering body amused him. Maryan kept her eyes on the floor, refusing to give him the satisfaction of her shame. She scrubbed herself quickly, biting back the humiliation. Still, when she rubbed her arms and the dirt came away in streaks, when her hair finally smelled of something other than sweat and rot, she felt—if not clean, then at least human again.

They gave her clean clothes.

Rough fabric, plain, nothing of beauty—but *clean.*

But cleanliness was a change.

Change terrified her more than the beatings had. Pain had been a known quantity. It was brutal, predictable, and it kept her world small: survive this moment, breathe through the next. But change meant uncertainty. And uncertainty meant danger.

She knew enough to sense what was coming: a fate worse than death.

Death had not come, not yet. But strength was coming back.

First came strength in her hands—she found she could grip the bowl without spilling. Then came the return of her voice, croaky and hesitant, as she whispered to herself to stay sane. She recited the names of colors in Persian and English, rolling them on her tongue as though she were painting in her mind. *Sefid. White. Ghermez. Red. Sabz. Green.* The sounds reminded her of canvases, of tubes of oil paint she used to squeeze until they bulged.

Her legs took longer. When she first tried to stand, the floor tilted beneath her, her knees buckled, and she fell hard enough to bruise her hip. The guard outside had laughed when he heard the crash, muttering something crude under his breath. But Maryan pushed herself up again, teeth clenched, and tried once more. Each day she stood for longer—five seconds, ten, twenty. The old woman would watch silently, her arms crossed, as though judging whether the effort was worth it. One day, she gave the faintest of nods. That single gesture filled Maryan with more strength than any meal.

Still, the silence gnawed at her.

She was no longer interrogated, yet her mind continued the questioning on its own.

Why had they stopped?

What did they want from her now?

If they had spared her this long, surely it wasn't out of kindness. Every act of mercy, she knew, was a prelude to cruelty. She had seen this rhythm before, on the faces of other women dragged through cells—some given hope, then snatched back into despair when they realized the "reprieve" was just a prelude to a worse fate.

She prayed, though she did not know to whom anymore. Her childhood prayers had been whispered to God in secret corners, her teenage years to freedom itself, her adult years to art. Now she whispered only for endurance:

Let me keep my mind.

Let me keep myself.

The guards, once a constant storm of violence, became distant shadows. She still heard their boots, their laughter, but rarely at her door. Sometimes they passed by, pausing to look in, their eyes assessing her like a piece of livestock. She learned to keep her face blank, her gaze lowered.

It was during one of these inspections that she understood what was coming.

The man who entered that day was not one of the usual guards. He was younger, his uniform newer, his hair neatly trimmed. He looked her over, not with contempt, but with calculation. She had seen that look before, years ago, when neighbors in Tehran had inspected her family's possessions after raids, deciding what could be stolen, what could be claimed.

Now she realized: she herself was the possession being measured.

The thought hollowed her.

She tried, in the days that followed, to cling to fragments of herself. She traced invisible lines on the wall, sketching murals no one else could see. She hummed songs under her breath, lullabies her mother once sang. Sometimes she spoke aloud to her sister, as though she were sitting beside her in the cell, laughing at a shared joke. Other times she simply lay back and let memory carry her, imagining she was in her studio again, the smell of linseed oil filling her lungs.

Her health returned more quickly than her spirit. Her ribs mended, the swelling on her face subsided, her body regained some strength. But inside, she felt fragile, like glass repaired with cracks still showing.

The old woman, sensing perhaps that Maryan was no longer on the edge of death, began to withdraw. She still brought food and water, but less often stayed. Maryan almost begged her to remain one evening, her voice trembling on the edge of speech. But the woman shook her head and left quickly, as though she too feared what came next.

The night before it happened, Maryan dreamed of painting again.

In the dream, her canvas was enormous, stretching across the walls of the cell. She painted in furious strokes, colors bursting from her hands—reds, blues, greens, golds. But every time she tried to step back to see the whole, the guards would close in, tearing strips of color from the walls until only black remained. She woke with tears running down her face.

And then, the next morning, she was summoned.

Her clothes were taken again, replaced with another set—cleaner, sharper, almost ceremonial. Her hair was combed by the old woman, who for the first time touched her face with something like pity. Maryan wanted to ask her what was happening, but the woman's silence was absolute, as though she had been ordered not to speak.

When the guards came, their smirks told her enough.

The change was here.

And she understood—death would have been easier.

Chapter 5:

The Bargain

Maryan knew the voice outside the shared cell, a voice that made her tremble, a voice from when she was a child.

She knew it was him the moment she heard his voice in the hallway — smoother than the others, more careful with tone, arrogance, pride, weakness while pretending to be strong.

Then he stepped into her cell.

He wore a military uniform now, but his face was the same. Older, thicker around the eyes, but unmistakable.

"I told them to stop hurting you," he said.

Maryan said nothing.

Silence pressed against her like a second skin, hot and suffocating. Her body trembled on the cold concrete floor, though whether from fear or exhaustion she no longer knew. The thin fabric of her prison dress clung to her skin where sweat had dried and turned clammy. Dust floated in narrow shafts of light from a barred window high above, particles drifting lazily as though indifferent to the suffering below.

He sat across from her, legs planted wide apart, elbows resting loosely on his knees. He wasn't tense—not yet. His calmness unsettled her more than rage would have. His composure suggested he had rehearsed this moment, imagined it, savored it.

"You were stupid," he said, not unkindly. His voice was softer than the clamor of boots and keys and the clang of iron doors she had grown used to. "You should have stayed quiet. You were always too loud."

Maryan lowered her eyes to his boots. Black leather, gleaming. They didn't belong here among the filth of prison floors, among the damp stains and human decay. The polish was absurd, obscene even, a reminder that power came dressed differently than the rest of them.

"Do you remember me?" he asked.

The question struck her chest like a blow. Of course she remembered. She wished she didn't, but memory had a way of rising unbidden.

She remembered his lustful eyes, his jealousy of her family's modest but warm home, his casual hatred of Christians—her, her parents, their quiet faith. She remembered the boy

who hovered too close on the walk home from school, trailing behind just enough to seem accidental, yet always there. She remembered the sudden appearances at the corner grocer, the offered fruits, the awkward smiles.

And she remembered, most of all, the way his eyes had lingered.

Armin Tehrani.

-

Armin Tehrani was born into a house divided between smoke and prayer.

His father's cigarettes left yellow ghosts on the walls of their narrow Tehran apartment, a two-room box above a grocery that always smelled faintly of onions and kerosene. His mother countered that odor with jasmine oil dabbed behind her ears and verses whispered before dawn. She would stand on the balcony in her night shawl, face turned east, lips moving in private conversation with God, while her husband downstairs cursed the news on the radio and poured another glass of cheap aragh.

Aragh sagi is a type of Iranian moonshine. This distilled alcoholic beverage usually contains around 50% alcohol. Being made underground in Iran, it was Armin's father's favorite drink. A drink that he drank In silence, in a city which outlawed alcohol.

Armin learned early that silence could mean peace. When his parents argued, he would retreat to the stairwell and count each tread until the voices blurred. At school he was a quiet boy—polite, thin, often overlooked. Teachers liked him because he never caused trouble, and classmates tolerated him because he would take any side that asked. Watching became his instinct, and soon his gift.

The street outside their building was always alive with contradictions: women hurrying to market with scarves loosely tied, students whispering Western lyrics learned from contraband cassettes, old men debating theology beneath the portrait of the Shah. Armin watched them all. He liked to imagine he could see the invisible lines connecting one life to another—the merchant who cheated a widow, the widow's son who worked at the police station, the police chief who owed favors to the merchant. To a boy who rarely spoke, those lines were language enough.

When the first protests came, he was twelve.

He heard them before he saw them—a roar swelling at the end of the boulevard like a storm with human lungs. By the time he reached the corner, the crowd had filled the intersection: men with banners, women with uncovered hair, boys his age shouting words he did not yet understand. His father stood beside him for a moment, expression unreadable. "They think change is simple," he muttered. "They'll learn."

That night the family's power flickered out, and by candlelight his mother whispered that the revolution was God's correction. His father rolled his eyes and asked for another drink. Between them, Armin sat motionless, feeling the pull of two tides.

Over the following months he carried messages for neighbors, fetched bread during shortages, learned which radio stations to trust. He watched soldiers march past his school and heard gunfire echo from distant squares.

Sometimes he would run to the roof just to see the smoke rising—proof that the city's heart still beat, even if it bled.

When the Shah fled, people danced in the streets. Armin's mother cried from joy; his father locked himself inside with a bottle. At thirteen, Armin didn't celebrate or mourn. He just watched.

Nazam Military High School accepted him at fourteen. His mother had begged, bribed, and prayed for that letter. "You will learn discipline," she said. "A man must have structure, or he dissolves." His father only shrugged: "If they make him pray five times a day, maybe one will stick."

At Nazam, discipline was oxygen. The dawn call to prayer cut through dreams like a blade. Armin folded blankets with geometric precision, polished boots until they mirrored his face, memorized regulations as if they were scripture. For the first time, he felt certainty—not happiness, exactly, but the relief of knowing where he stood in the world.

The instructors spoke of duty, purity, sacrifice. They told stories of martyrs who had died smiling, of traitors who wept before the firing squad. Armin absorbed every tale, not because he believed but because belief gave shape to the formless hunger inside him: the need to matter.

On rare free afternoons he wandered to the neighborhood where he had grown up. The city looked different now— posters of martyrs instead of movie stars, mosques louder, laughter quieter. Once, near the market, he saw a girl sketching in a notebook under a mulberry tree. Maryan Darya. The name fluttered through him like wind through curtains. She had been his neighbor years ago—the girl he'd given a poem disguised as homework, the one who never replied.

He almost called her name but stopped. She looked older, self-possessed, a smudge of charcoal on her fingers. He watched from a distance until the call to prayer scattered the square.

Back at school, he wrote her name in the margin of his physics notes and crossed it out. When his mother died later that year, he did not cry. He stood at her funeral in his stiff uniform, receiving condolences like salutes. The mullah said she had raised a son of discipline. Armin bowed his head and vowed to make that true.

Emotion, he decided, was the enemy of purpose. And purpose was the only proof he existed.

By seventeen, Iran was at war. The city spoke in sirens and funerals. Armin volunteered for the Revolutionary Guard not out of zeal but directionless gravity—everyone he knew either joined or vanished. The uniform promised clarity; it offered a single answer to every question: obey.

Training stripped him down and rebuilt him in lines and commands. He learned to fire, to interrogate, to salute without hesitation. They praised his composure—"Tehrani does not flinch." Inside, though, he often felt hollow, a machine awaiting instruction.

During air raids he would stand on rooftops, watching tracers stitch the sky. The explosions reminded him of the cheers during the revolution—bright, consuming, proof that something larger than any one life was at work. He convinced himself that serving that something was enough.

Yet at night, when the dormitory fell silent, he dreamed of Maryan. Not of the woman she might be but of the girl with the smudge of charcoal, eyes alive with things he could not name. In his dreams she turned toward him, reached out, and dissolved into smoke.

He woke before dawn, recited verses, and told himself dreams were indulgence. Still, he kept the scrap of paper with his childish poem folded inside his wallet. The words had faded; the habit of needing them had not.

Years blurred into assignments. He guarded prisoners, escorted convoys, wrote reports so carefully phrased they could mean anything. The regime rewarded ambiguity—it kept men useful. Armin rose quietly through ranks, unnoticed except for his efficiency. He thought of his mother's voice saying discipline is faith. He had become faithful indeed.

The name felt strange on her tongue even unspoken, as if it belonged to another life. Yet here he was, standing transformed. No longer the lanky boy from the neighborhood, no longer the boy with dirt on his knees, but a man—flanked by two others, each dressed in uniforms that carried an air of untouchable authority. Dark green, pressed crisp, with gold emblems that seemed to flicker in the dim light. The insignia of the Islamic Revolutionary Guard Corps glared at her like fire against ash.

Armin Tehrani, the boy born to a liberal Muslim family in Tehran, whose mother's fervor had carried him into the arms of ideology. She could see traces of his youth still in the lines of his face: the curve of his jaw, the slope of his nose. But his eyes—his eyes were sharper now, trained, burning with both discipline and something more personal. Something directed at her.

From the union of zeal and apathy, Armin had been born. And now, before Maryan's eyes, she saw how both currents had shaped him. He was polished, uniformed, postured straight, but beneath it he remained—just existing. Not handsome, not ugly, merely present. The only remarkable thing about him was the intensity in his gaze, a passion tethered somewhere between her and the revolution he had sworn to serve.

That desire unnerved her more than the guards' rifles ever had.

She remembered overhearing his mother's words once at a neighborhood gathering, her voice shrill with self-righteousness. "Christians are a disease," the woman had said. "If they do not convert, they should be removed. Iran will never be pure with them among us."

Maryan had shrunk deeper into her seat, clutching her mother's hand, but the words had settled into her memory like thorns.

Now here he was. The boy who had written her a love poem. The boy whose mother had wanted her erased. The boy who had transformed his awkward longing into polished authority.

And he looked at her with the conviction of someone who believed he was saving her.

In his eyes, she was not a prisoner. She was a soul to be rescued from corruption, from Christianity, from her own stubborn resistance. His compassion—if it could be called that—was twisted, obscene. It required her full submission, her erasure, her absorption into his faith, his revolution, his vision of purity.

Armin believed, she realized with a cold clarity, that he was not condemning her but redeeming her.

The irony nearly made her laugh, but the sound caught in her throat and stayed there, bitter as bile.

This zealot, this polished soldier, this boy-turned-man, now stood in front of her as both captor and savior. He believed himself both. And perhaps that made him more dangerous than any guard who had beaten her.

Pointing to her, his men quickly picked her up and brought her to a private room, this time not for torture or pleasure but for her future.

As she was carried out of the room Armin smiled.

Maryan was sat in a chair, not the cold metal kind, but a padded chair, clean, no blood, nor vomit, just a normal chair. The normalcy of the chair shook her.

Her father once designed a chair, as a child she thought it was magnificent, but this chair with its padding felt like she was sitting on a throne.

Looking up Armin smiled at her.

Armin began.

"Upon reviewing the files about terrorists, I saw your name in the folder. A name I had not seen in years, but a name I enjoyed thinking of. Upon seeing it, I made calls to my mother, who confirmed your family was arrested and your tiny coup destroyed."

Maryan sat in silence.

Armin continued, "I know this must be a shock to you, seeing the little boy who wrote you poems, in front of you, but it is true, I have always cared about you and am here as your protector."

Maryan unable to breathe.

"I am here to make you a deal, a way to save your family." He goated. " A way to survive death."

"My proposition is simple, you will marry me, become an honorable Muslim wife, and bear me children."

"If you agree to this, I will get you out and bring your family back home."

Tears now streaming down her face, all her dreams gone, all gone. Maryan said nothing.

"This ends this week, if you agree."

Maryan shook to the core. He mind spinning, racing …. She was in a full panic, but head down, panicked inside, she starting to cry.

Armin taken back by the tears, looked at her, then not knowing what to do, checked his watch.

"I will give you one day to agree to it." , Armin stated and he quickly grabbed a package, dropping it on the chair, he was just seated in.

Then as quickly as he came, he walked out and closed the door behind him.

Maryan, staying silent, finally opened her eyes.

Confused, lost and scared, did she just hear what she thought she heard.

Did he really want this wretched girl to be his wife?

Wiping the tears from her eyes, she opened her eyes.

This was not a prison cell, but a small room with a bed, a sink, and a shower. A shower, could it be, a real-life shower.

Unable to believe, she got up, and hobbled over to the wall, and moved the lever. Water hit her head, cold at first but soon warm, not hot but warm.

The warm water was freedom, no matter how long it lasted, it was freedom, freedom from the world she was trapped in. Freedom she once had.

But now she had a choice, life in one cage or life in another cage.

Armin was the cage, the cage of an Islamic wife, not the freedom her mother had as a Christian, or the freedom that used to exist in Iran.

Iran where women were women once had more freedom than the West, sadly that changed when the mullahs took over.

The same mullahs that imprisoned her, the same mullahs making Islamic law that will trap her in a fate going forward.

Now under the first shower she had in who knows how long.

With bruises and cuts still viable, she only cared about this shower, this brief moment of freedom. Just freedom.

After drying off, she looked at the package, that was on Armin's chair.

It was just a box, a box wrapped in brown paper.

She carefully picked it up, and began to unwrap it.

It was carefully wrapped with a brown sting.

It was not wrapped by a woman, Maryan could tell. It was wrapped by a man, carefully but still wrapped by a man.

After peeling the outer layer, she was able to see the box.

The box, contained nothing of significance on the outside, but upon opening, she noticed it contained clothing, underwear, bra, hairbrush, toothbrush, toothpaste and other items.

Had Armin, done this himself, she wondered.

Looking at the dress, it was a very traditional boring dress, that the older Islamic women had been wearing latterly. Not black, but boring.

At least it's not black, like the black robe bitches, she thought.

It was obvious that Armin bought this, with the help of the more conservate Islamic women, but he left some style in it for her.

The dress, though not hideous, was nothing she would normally wear or look at.

But here it was staring at her, requiring her to put it on, and being her new life, as a prisoner in an Islamic marriage.

It was all too much for her, and after the freedom of a shower, she laid down on the bed.

___

Startled by noise, she was unsure how long she sleep.

But with footsteps approaching, it was morning. The door opening was confirmation it was.

Armin with his over polished boots, opened the door.

"I hope you have made a wise decision." He said coldly.

Armin with those stupid polished boots. Armin with his hair, that contained too much mousse. Armin her warden for the next 70 years.

That Armin stood there staring.

Stating waiting for an answer.

She had no choice, she needed to survive, survive anyway possible.

Sitting up in the wire frame bed, she simply said "I will marry you."

Armin, with more surprise than she expected, cracked a smile, which he noticed. This made him quickly dissolve it into a stern look.

"Good, I will have the men help you to the car." – He bluntly stated.

Two men, really young boys, with limited beards, stood her up, and moved her through the slaughterhouse.

Having never seen the size of this place, it was coming into focus just how many rooms and pens they had for prisoners.

She had not seen any male prisoners, this looked like a place for women. Women the regime threw away.

Women raped repeatedly so they could not get into heaven.

Women beaten for wanting freedom.

Women who live under Islam.

She had to close her eyes, as it was all too much.

Upon reaching the car, she was placed carefully into the backseat, a driver sat up front, Armin was already in the car on the phone.

She said nothing as she was placed in the car.

Leaning against the car pillar in the back seat, she was lost without hope, without freedom, without love.

What seemed like hours, she soon pulled into a familiar neighborhood. The prisoner of a conquering hero.

To her though he was the villain, the villain destroying everything around her.

Maryan spoke.

"Why?" Her voice was flat. "Why me?"

Armin hesitated. "Because I've always cared about you."

Maryan laughed, but there was no joy in it. "You cared about the girl from the alley. The one who smelled like jasmine and studied anatomy under her father's lantern. That girl is gone."

"No, she's not," he said quickly. "You're still her. Just... just bruised."

She turned away, breathing hard.

"I'm trying to save your life!" – Shouted Armin, which surprised even the driver.

"By owning it?", Maryan retorted.

He looked wounded. "No. I'm trying to give you a future. You're wasting away in a barn with no trial date. They're cycling girls out in batches for 're-education' camps or worse. You know what happens when they say that. You're not stupid."

She crossed her arms.

She studied him.

And for the first time, felt something strange. Not pity. Not anger. But contempt mixed with familiarity. Armin hadn't become evil. He had become a man of the system. Still longing for her, still chasing his childhood fantasy — but now with the power of an regime behind him.

"You never really saw me," she said softly. "Even back then. I was just something you wanted."

He looked away.

She paused then pulling her knees closer, pushed herself into the pillar as far as possible, resigned to her fate.

Chapter 6

Iblis

Her parents' house was still in pieces.

She could see it as they turned the corner.

Windows and doors broken. A sign on the outside wall, she had no clue what it said, but she imagined.

The car rumbled down the street with the same solemnity as a hearse.

Outside the cracked passenger window, Maryan watched familiar houses drift by like ghosts. Every corner, every streetlamp, every crooked sidewalk stone screamed childhood to her, and yet everything felt foreign. What had once been her sanctuary now looked like a battlefield. She hadn't seen this neighborhood in months.

Since the raid.

Since the scream.

Since her body had been thrown like garbage into the van.

Then, their house came alongside.

It looked like it had been torn apart by wolves.

Doors were splintered from their hinges.

Windows jagged and gaping

She could see the furniture broken like bones.

She could see blood on the floor—brown now, crusted in the corners like rust. She did not know whose it was.

On the stoop stood two figures bent and slow. Her parents. Her mother and father sweeping shards of glass from the doorway with bare, bruised hands.

She hadn't seen them in what she believed was months.

As the car rolled to a halt, Maryan's breath locked in her chest.

Amin turned to her. "Stay in the car."

She didn't respond. She lowered her gaze instead, signaling her obedience. It was the safest answer.

He stepped out, straightening his uniform and placing the dark green cap upon his head as if crowning himself king. The boy she remembered—lanky, awkward, skin oily with adolescence—was gone. In his place stood a man barely grown into his role, the buttons of his uniform still too stiff, the fabric still foreign against his skin. But he wore it like armor. Like power. And in this house, for now, it made him God.

Maryan knew it. Her father knew it. And worst of all, Amin knew it.

One protest. Just one. That's all it took to undo everything. One women's march, chanting for hijab freedom, for dignity, for something like hope.

She had been warned. Everyone had. But that day, the anger inside her had boiled over. She thought, for just one hour, that a woman could walk proud and speak loud.

Now she knew better.

From the window, she saw her father—once tall with squared shoulders, now hunched and shuffling like a servant—look up at Amin. His head lowered quickly again, a deep bow of defeat. Her mother stood beside him, eyes red, face hollow. She didn't blink. Didn't flinch. Just stared.

Amin approached them quickly. She couldn't hear the words, but she'd memorized the script already.

"As agreed," Amin was saying. "Your daughter is free. In one week's time, we will be married and move into my parents' home. Afterward, I will assist you in obtaining work. I will speak with connections about returning Marineh. That's my offer."

Sahar, her father, once the great architect with a poet's soul, looked at the ground. He had no strength left to argue.

"Yes," he said.

A simple word. But it echoed through Maryan's body like a death sentence.

It wasn't a marriage. It was a ransom. Amin had taken her life and offered back a sliver of it, wrapped in promises and conditions. She could taste the humiliation on her tongue.

Amin had always hated their family. They were Christians who prospered. That alone made them enemies.

When word had spread through the neighborhood that Maryan was arrested, his parents were the first to call for action. His mother—veiled and pious and always judging—told anyone who would listen that the Christians had poisoned their daughters with Western ideals.

Armin's father, a man of no consequence, always sneaking a drink, with a cigarette in the hand. A foreman on some construction site. Unremarkable. But even he seized the moment, muttering in cafés that "maybe now, they'll see we suffer because of them."

Maryan knew all of this. She had grown up among them.

Amin's hatred wasn't political. It was personal. It was generational. And now, he had the upper hand.

It was his mother who had pushed him into the military academy, his mother who scolded his father's drinking, who filled Amin's heart with shame and pride and discipline. She told him he would rise through faith. That the Quran was his ladder. And she wasn't wrong.

He had studied. He had risen. And now he had *her.*

From the window, Maryan watched as Amin glanced at his watch. Then, like a stage director calling for the final act, he opened her car door.

"I have made sure, your fathers' effects, have been returned, and all state acquired property has been returned, including any money" Armin said coldly.

"Now Go," he said.

Maryan stepped out, trembling. The dry wind tangled in her hair, her old shoes crunching glass as she moved. She didn't look at Amin again.

He spoke one final command before retreating to the car: "My mother will be staying with you when she returns from my grandparents' village. Make sure a room is ready."

The door slammed. The car reversed, the tires spitting gravel and dust as it sped down the street.

Maryan stood alone now.

She just stood there unmoving, her parents stuck in the same pose.

Then she ran. Tears already falling. She couldn't help it.

Her father met her halfway, arms open, and for the first time in months or years, she felt safe.

Safe, her father always made her feel safe.

Safe for one moment.

He pulled her into his chest with such strength she feared her ribs might snap.

"Maryan-joon…" he whispered. "My girl…"

Behind him, her mother appeared.

Her mother, once a gentle woman with a quick wit was nearly unrecognizable. Cheeks hollowed, skin pale. There was a gash along one cheekbone that hadn't healed properly. Her headscarf shook with every step, clinging to graying hair.

"They said you…. you were gone," she sobbed. "They told us nothing. Nothing."

Maryan tried to speak, but her throat closed. Only tears came.

Her mother embraced them both, and they cried together. The wind rustled the torn curtains behind the smashed window. A neighborhood dog barked distantly. But inside, there was only silence. The silence of grief too large to name.

Hours later the silence became unbearable.

Silence wasn't peace. It was residue, the way smoke lingered after fire.

The living room was a museum of damage. Not just broken things, but a catalog of destruction that spoke of intention. Every photo frame shattered. Every bookcase overturned. The floor was smeared with blood and dust in patterns Maryan could not decipher, abstract stains that made her dizzy to look at. She could not tell what belonged to her family and what had been left by the last prisoners who had lived here, because that was what they had made of their home: a holding cell, a crime scene, a warning.

The television was gone. So were the radios, the silver bowls her mother polished each spring, her father's collection of prayer books in Armenian script. But nothing had been looted in desperation. This was not the work of hungry thieves. This was confiscation, the state's peculiar form of theft. They had called themselves "investigators" as they stripped the shelves bare.

Her mother brewed tea on a small propane burner since the gas lines to the kitchen had been shut off. The smell of burning metal mixed with the bitter scent of black tea, filling the wreckage with something almost domestic, almost normal, but not enough. They drank in silence, sipping from chipped cups, the act of lifting porcelain to their lips a fragile rebellion against despair.

"How long…" her mother began, then stopped. Words fractured in her throat.

Maryan knew what she meant. She had practiced the answer in her head during the car ride home, when she still thought she might never see this house again. " Armin said, three months in Tehran," she said evenly. "then two in Shiraz."

Her mother's eyes tightened. "They moved you?"

"I have no understanding of the move, or the timing, and I can not tell if Armin was lying or telling the truth." Maryan said.

Her father sat in the corner on a stool that had lost one leg, its seat tilting like a wounded man. He held a cracked rosary in one hand, the beads worn smooth with decades of prayer. He mouthed something she couldn't hear at first.

Then, when she tilted her head, she realized: a prayer in Armenian, ancient syllables sliding past his lips.

Her father and mother, unspeaking of their captivity or assaults.

Maryan knew the trauma her parents had, were not of their captivity but of losing their children.

She refused her minds desire to ask.

Finally her father spoke aloud. His voice cracked. "We thought you were dead. They told us they lost your file. That's what they said. Lost."

Maryan nodded once. She could still hear the guard's laughter when he told her the same thing. Lost files meant lost people, disappeared forever into unmarked graves. It had almost been her fate.

"I didn't think I'd make it out," she admitted, her voice so low she hardly believed she'd spoken.

Silence again. But this silence was different, softer. Not residue, but recognition.

Then her mother said, so quietly Maryan almost missed it, "You cannot marry him."

The words landed between them like a stone thrown into still water, sending ripples of grief through the room.

Every was silent, thinking of the pending slavery she would face in the marriage.

"I have to," Maryan said. Her own voice startled her with its flatness. "He promised to get Marineh back. He promised to protect you."

Her mother looked away, her eyes fixed on the broken glass embedded in the rug. Shame hung heavy in the air, mingling with steam from the tea.

Her father didn't speak. His rosary beads clicked softly, his lips moving again in wordless prayer.

Maryan couldn't sleep.

The room was half-intact, if that word could still mean anything. A mattress on the floor, springs poking through one corner. Broken drawers spilled their contents across the floor, childhood things scattered like evidence of another life. A melted Barbie shoe, blackened by fire. Her old painting palette, still speckled with dried streaks of crimson and cobalt. A school poetry journal, its pages warped and edges eaten by mold. All of it dusted with ash, as though her past had been burned and only remnants survived.

Her mother had given her a nightgown pulled from the back of a storage trunk. It smelled faintly of cedar and lavender soap. It smelled like her. It smelled like the past. Maryan pressed her face into the fabric when no one was looking, ashamed of the tears that came unbidden.

She lay awake and stared at the ceiling. A crack split the plaster above her head, jagged like lightning frozen mid-strike. The room still smelled of smoke, though the fire had been months ago.

Downstairs, her parents whispered. Not fighting—there was no energy left for that. Just unraveling quietly, like fabric fraying thread by thread.

Maryan listened, straining to catch pieces of their murmurs. Words surfaced now and then: *God's will. Protection. Marriage. Amin.* Each one stung worse than the last.

Her thoughts refused to quiet. They spun like a carousel she could not step off. The future loomed: one week.

In seven days, she would stand beside Amin, her wrists bound not by iron but by vows. In seven days, she would be both prisoner and bride.

She imagined the neighbors gathering, those who had cheered her arrest, now stuffing their mouths with sugared almonds, applauding as she kissed the boots of her captor in the name of holy matrimony. She saw their smug faces, their thinly veiled relief that it was her and not them.

In seven days, she would become his.

His property, as the Quran was often quoted. She had heard the verses twisted in court, in prison, in casual conversation between guards. A wife must obey her husband. A wife may be beaten if she disobeys.

Well it was not straight to beating, first the wife who disobeyed, would be chastised, then denied the marriage bed (Maryan always thought this was weird, who wants to sleep with someone who just chastised you), then finally beating, then more beating.

Beaten was something Maryan already knew. Beaten was muscle memory, her body anticipating the arc of fists and batons before they landed. She had survived it, absorbed it, numbed herself to it. But could she survive seventy years of it? Could she endure not just pain, but the obliteration of her will?

Life now seemed worthless. Death seemed cleaner, easier, preferable. Yet death had been withheld from her. She had begged for it once, in the corner of her cell after a week of silence and darkness. But death had refused her. Instead, life had returned in this grotesque shape: a wedding dress, a promise, a cage disguised as protection.

Her eyes drifted back to the crack in the ceiling. It looked like a fissure in the world, as if at any moment the plaster might split apart and swallow her whole.

She thought of escape, not practically but as a dream. A vision of flight across borders, of trains heading west, of freedom she had once glimpsed in foreign films. But every time she let the dream unfold, Amin's face appeared, blotting it out, reminding her that his hand was on her future now.

And yet, somewhere deep beneath the fear, a stubborn ember still glowed. She had carried it through prison beatings, through nights when rats gnawed at her food, through days when guards laughed as they dragged women away. That ember refused to die, no matter how much she told herself she was ready for death.

She closed her eyes and clung to it, the way her father clung to his cracked rosary.

Chapter 7

The Father's Canvas

The following morning, her father, Sahar, rose early.

He was not a wealthy man, but he had a reputation — a respected artist well known in Tehran's quiet art circles.

In addition to his architecture work, his artwork, although limited was often bought by buyers in Europe and Dubai, often via "friendly" galleries that skirted the censors.

Although art was often banned, criticized and destroyed by followers of strict Islam, by and large Iran allowed art to flourish underground, and above ground in certain areas.

As Sahar was part of the famous architectural team, he often used his credentials to build large works of art, room sized painting, statues and even furniture design. He was loved by the art circles in Iran, and his critics were far and few in between.

Oddly one of the loudest critics of his art, in the old neighborhood had been Armin's mother, who used her criticism to show how pious she was.

That morning, he called his old friend, Farshad Yeganeh, who worked at a gallery in Isfahan with connections to shipping firms that specialized in "cultural preservation logistics."

Over encrypted Signal messages, he asked one simple question:

"How soon is your next container leaving for Germany?"

Farshad's answer came a few minutes later.

"Three days. Frankfurt. Fine art manifest. Tight inspections."

"Is there space?"

"Maybe. But not for art."

Davoud only responded with a single emoji: 🎨

Farshad's reply: 🧳

They understood each other.

This painting, this canvas would carry the most important creation he ever made.

Maryan was distraught when she heard her father's plan. Sitting with her mother in the broken room, her mother explained it was the only way.

Maryan shouted, "But what about Marineh, they will kill her, or worse."

"No, she is too young, they are putting her through Islamic education now, she will be released, and when she is, your fathers' friends will help her escape."

"But what about you, they will kill you." cried Maryan.

"Enough. If they do, they do, you are our future, you and your sister.

If we get out, we get out, until then our friends will get your sister out, and I will get you out." Said Sahar coldly.

Maryan knew to hold her words, as it was decided, unless she wanted to die in Iran either in prison or with Armin, neither seemed better, she needed to follow the plan.

The next day Maryan played the part well. She had no choice. If she faltered, if she betrayed even a flicker of resistance, the illusion would shatter—and with it, whatever fragile hope still lingered for her family's survival.

She rose early, the ache in her ribs a dull reminder of what had been endured and what still hovered like a storm just beyond the horizon. Her mother urged her to eat, pressing a piece of flatbread into her hand, but Maryan barely chewed. Her mouth was too dry, her stomach tight with fear. Still, she forced the bread down, knowing her mother's eyes were on her, begging her without words: *Stay alive. Comply. Buy us time.*

The morning sunlight was deceptive, too cheerful, streaming into their broken home as if it had forgotten the raids, the shattered windows, the stains that could not be scrubbed away. Her mother fussed over her hair, tucking stray strands beneath her scarf, as though the small gesture could shield them both from what was coming.

They walked together, two blocks down the narrow street to the seamstress. The neighborhood was quieter than Maryan remembered. Curtains twitched as they passed, women's eyes peering through thin veils of lace, measuring her with curiosity, pity, or perhaps jealousy.

Rumors had spread quickly: the girl taken by the Guards, the one returned, now to be married to one of their own. A bargain sealed with gold and silence.

The seamstress, a stooped woman with sharp eyes and calloused fingers, greeted them with a professional detachment. She did not ask questions; she did not need to. Instead, she lifted bolts of fabric from shelves, laying them out one by one—satins, silks, and laces in shades of cream and ivory. Maryan stood stiffly as her mother and the seamstress discussed cuts and seams, their voices low but brisk, as though the matter were routine.

Maryan barely heard them. She stared at the fabric, each fold of silk like a shroud.

The gown she was fitted for clung to her like a betrayal. The seamstress wrapped her in muslin first, pinning it to measure her frame. Maryan stood motionless, her arms limp at her sides, staring at the floorboards worn smooth by years of women before her. How many had stood here? How many had dreamed of marriage as liberation, as joy, as the beginning of a future? For her, it was a cage lined with silk.

And then—the hijab.

The stupid, idiotic, man-made hijab.

But the hijab was the prop, the prop in the new play she was in, so she played the role.

Following Islamic custom, the seamstress selected a piece of pure silk, shimmering faintly in the sunlight that filtered through the narrow shop window. She draped it over Maryan's head, smoothing it down over her shoulders with a reverence that felt mocking. Maryan's

With her mother dreams of seeing her daughter marry the love of her life were gone.

To keep from dying inside her mother pretended the silk belonged in an Armenian weeding.

 An Armenian weeding, the most beautiful symbol of love in the world. The wedding journey begins with Khosk-Kap, the formal engagement. Traditionally, the groom's family visits the bride's family to officially ask for her hand. Symbolic offerings—such as fruits, sweets, and flowers—are presented, and once the families agree, the couple exchanges rings. This gathering emphasizes the importance of family approval and blessing in Armenian culture

An approval Armin stole, at the barrel of Islam.

Maryan would never have a crown, never dance the Kochari, never be crowned, she would never be in love.

But Nare knew, everyone's life was depending on deception, so she would cry alone tonight.

Maryan on the other hand could not get the hijab out of her mind.

The hijab. The *stupid* hijab. The hijab that had been the beginning of her end. The one she had loosened in the streets during the protests, the one that had marked her as a threat, as a woman who dared to resist. For this piece of cloth she had been beaten, interrogated, broken. For this cloth, her mother had nearly lost her child, her father his soul.

She bit the inside of her cheek until she tasted blood, forcing her fury down.

Desperate but smart, Maryan held her tongue. She would not give them the satisfaction of seeing her break now. She would wear their costume, smile their smiles, bow her head when expected. Every act of compliance would be a mask, a mask that gave her one more day, one more breath, one more chance.

The seamstress clucked her tongue, muttering about seams and hems, and Maryan's mother nodded dutifully, reaching into her purse for the first payment. Maryan kept her eyes on the ground until they were allowed to leave.

When they returned home, the house felt even smaller. The walls pressed in, heavy with silence. Her father sat at the table, his hands clasped tightly, his knuckles white. He looked up as they entered, his eyes searching Maryan's face for something—anger, despair, resolve. She gave him nothing. He gave her the faintest of nods, an almost imperceptible signal that he understood her silence, her restraint.

Her mother, on the other hand, left to cry.

That afternoon, a messenger arrived. He was young, barely more than a boy, but he carried himself with the swagger of one who knew his position gave him power. In his hands was a parcel, neatly wrapped in brown paper, tied with twine. He handed it over with a smirk, bowing slightly as if bestowing an honor.

Inside were the gold coins.

Five in total, heavy and gleaming, stamped with the insignia of the state. The *Mahr.*

The Mahr, or the Gift, was tradition—law, even. A mandatory offering given to the bride before *Nikah*, the Islamic marriage contract. It was meant as a token of respect, a recognition of her value, something that remained hers even if the marriage ended. In theory, it was security. A safeguard for the wife.

But Maryan knew the truth.

The gift was nothing more than a golden shackle.

Yes, the coins were hers by law, even in divorce. Yes, she could claim them if she chose to leave him. But that choice would never be allowed. Women like her did not walk away from men like Armin. Not alive.

She turned the coins over in her hands, feeling their weight. They were cold, impersonal, yet searing against her skin. Gold that glittered like a promise but felt more like a curse.

Her mother whispered a prayer of thanks, her voice trembling. Her father remained silent, his jaw clenched so tightly Maryan feared his teeth would break.

Along with the coins came a note. A short message, written in careful, deliberate script.

My mother will visit in two days.

Chapter 8

The Preparation

Maryan read the words twice,

Armin's mother was coming.

Armin was coming.

There was no backing out now, she needed to be moved out of the country immediately.

Walking to her father's shed, she saw the canvas.

The "canvas" was not merely a painting—it was the plan, the vessel of escape, the work that would carry her beyond these walls.

She looked up. Her father's eyes met hers, and for the first time since returning home, she saw fire there. Quiet, controlled, but burning nonetheless.

The next hours blurred into a fever of preparation.

Her mother busied herself with household chores, scrubbing the floor as though cleanliness could mask the decay, polishing the brass samovar until it gleamed like new. She muttered constantly, prayers and curses tangled together. Her hands shook, but she kept moving, unable to stop.

Her father stayed in his workshop, a cramped room at the back of the house where canvases leaned against the walls in uneven stacks. He had not painted—not since the raids, not since the Guards had taken Maryan. But now he moved with purpose, pulling down a large, stretched canvas, examining it under the light.

Maryan called out to him, her heart pounding.

"Baba?" she whispered.

He turned to her, his face etched with exhaustion, with grief, but also with determination. He placed a finger to his lips, silencing her. Then he beckoned her closer.

On the surface of the canvas, faint outlines of a landscape were visible—trees, a river, the beginnings of a mountain range. But as he tilted it in the light, Maryan saw more. Hidden beneath the brushstrokes were markings, barely visible unless one knew where to look. Symbols, directions, coded notations.

Symbols of Maryan's work. Names of women who suffered at the hand of the regime. Symbols of Christ, symbols of Armenian pride.

Each symbol a direct protest again the regime that destroyed beauty.

Whispering he explained that his contacts, men who still dared to resist in quiet, unseen ways, had devised the plan.

The painting would be shipped, as so many works of art were, out of the country. Crates crossed borders with less scrutiny than people. And within one such crate, hidden beneath wood and canvas, Maryan would be concealed.

It was dangerous. It was desperate. But it was possible.

Maryan pressed her hand against the rough fabric of the canvas, her breath shuddering.

Her fathers painting, would be her shield. He had shielded her, all her life, a true father, one willing to die for their child. His act of protest on canvas, would allow her to escape.

"I understand," she whispered.

Her father closed his eyes briefly, as though in prayer, then opened them again. "You must play the part," he said softly, his voice breaking. "Until the last moment. Every smile, every bow, every stitch of that cursed dress. Do you hear me?"

"I hear you," she said.

That night the planning was completed. Her father told her everything in whispers, usually under the hum of the kitchen exhaust fan, or near the old stereo playing classic Iranian ballads.

"There will be three containers. One has old carpets. One has plaster sculpture molds. The last is a special commission — a large canvas, with large wooden container, with false bottom bound for Frankfurt's Museum of Modern Islamic Art."

She nodded.

"That canvas will be your protector, as I am today." Sahar stated.

Maryan's breath caught.

"How long will I be in it?"

"Two days in Tehran. Then flying to Cologne. You'll be packed with food, a water bladder, and diapers. Not much space to move."

She trembled.

"And after that?"

"A freight truck from a church charity in Cologne will pick you up,

"What about you? What if they find out?"

Her father smiled — a smile that broke her heart.

"They won't care about me, Maryan. I'm old.

She grabbed his hand. "Baba—"

"No." He leaned in. "You are my masterpiece. And I will not let them hang you on their wall."

On the night of the shipment, the air in the Darya household was thick with anticipation, as if the walls themselves were holding their breath. The underground art world of Tehran, a network of painters, sculptors, and collectors who moved in silence and shadows, had entrusted them with a mission: a piece of art had to be shipped out of the country, smuggled through crates and cargo, before the authorities discovered it and destroyed it.

The canvas leaned against the wall in the corner of the living room, shrouded in old linen to disguise its importance.

Her father's allies had been carefully preparing the crate that would carry her out under the cover of legitimate exports.

He had friends in the art world still, men and women who remembered him from before the raids. They came together quietly whispering advice and designing logistics.

But on this night, as the final preparations were being made, headlights cut across the thin curtains. Tires pressed against gravel. A door slammed shut.

Maryan's heart leapt into her throat.

A black sedan, familiar in its menace, idled just outside. The neighborhood fell quiet, as if even the stray dogs knew what kind of danger prowled in that vehicle.

Armin's car.

Her prison had arrived.

The air in the room shifted. Her father's back stiffened; her mother's hand froze on the teapot she was carrying.

Maryan's knees buckled, and before she could stop herself, tears welled in her eyes. It wasn't just fear—it was despair, hot and merciless. For days she had been clinging to the fragile hope of escape, and now, at the exact moment of departure, the predator appeared at the door.

"Did the plan fail?" she asked silently with her eyes, her lips trembling but no sound emerging.

Her father, ever stoic, ever protective, turned to her. He didn't speak. Instead, he gave her a look—one that held both steel and tenderness. Then the smallest smile tugged at his lips, a smile that said *Stay quiet. Trust me. We are not finished yet.*

Maryan pressed her hand to her mouth, swallowing her sob.

The knock on the door came, firm but not hurried. Armin did not need to pound; his presence was enough to command obedience.

Her father smoothed his hair back, straightened his shoulders, and opened the door.

"Welcome, Armin," he said with deliberate calm, as though greeting a guest, not an intruder.

Armin stepped into the house like he already owned it. His boots clicked against the cracked tile of the entryway. His uniform, crisp and spotless, contrasted violently with the disheveled state of the Darya home, where broken furniture still lingered from the raid months earlier.

"I have come to ensure you have received the wedding gift," he said, his voice measured, his words chosen carefully. "And that you have everything in order."

Maryan wiped her tears quickly, forcing herself to stand straighter. The trembling in her chest did not stop, but she raised her chin. "Yes, Armin," she said, her voice fragile but steady. "That was beyond generous. You will make a wonderful husband."

The words cut her tongue like shards of glass.

Armin's smile spread, slow and satisfied, the smile of a hunter who knows the prey has nowhere left to run.

He walked into the living room with the ease of someone who had been there many times, though this time the atmosphere was different.

Her mother rushed to the kitchen to fetch tea, her hands shaking as she placed sugar cubes on a small porcelain plate.

In Armenia, Persia, and across the region, tea was hospitality; to deny it would be an insult, but tonight, it was also a performance.

Armin sat heavily on the family's worn sofa, its cushions sagging under his weight. His eyes scanned the room, pausing on the photographs still hanging on the cracked wall. His gaze landed on one in particular—Maryan as a child, in her school uniform, a stethoscope draped around her neck.

He lifted his teacup and gestured toward it. "You always wanted to be a doctor," he said.

Maryan's throat tightened. She nodded, her voice barely above a whisper. "Yes."

"You still can," he said.

She smiled faintly, a mask she forced onto her face. "Maybe."

For a moment, a shadow of sincerity crossed Armin's face. His shoulders softened, and the hardness in his eyes wavered. "I'm not your enemy, Maryan."

The words hung in the air, implausible, offensive even. But they carried a sliver of truth: he wanted her not dead, but bound to him.

She said nothing. Silence was her shield.

"You could grow to care for me," he continued.

She let out a slow breath. "I could grow to forgive you."

It was the closest she came to lying.

Armin reached across the small space and touched her hand. His grip was strong, his palm warm. Maryan resisted the urge to pull away. Instead, she let him hold her hand for a moment, her heart racing as if every beat were counting down to an explosion.

Abruptly, Armin stood. The tenderness evaporated like smoke.

"I wish to see my mother's room," he said, his tone commanding again.

Maryan's mother nearly dropped the tray of sugar cubes. She set it down quickly and nodded. "Of course."

The house was small, but they had worked tirelessly all week to rearrange it. Broken furniture had been moved into the parents' bedroom, stacked like corpses against the wall, while the best surviving pieces were placed in the room designated for Armin's mother. They had hung clean linens, patched curtains, even polished the cracked mirror. It was all theater, meant to convince him of their compliance.

Maryan's father led the way, his eyes lowered. Armin inspected the room slowly, touching the dresser, opening the small wardrobe, checking the corners. He was not just looking for comfort for his mother; he was looking for signs of deception.

Finally, he nodded. A smile crept onto his lips.

"With my mother moving in tomorrow," he said, "I will have her belongings delivered in the morning. Ensure all is ready."

Maryan's parents lowered their heads. "Yes," they answered in unison.

Armin's chest swelled. Satisfaction radiated from him like heat. He believed he had won—not just Maryan's hand, but dominance over the entire household.

As he turned to leave, he suddenly reached out and grabbed Maryan's hand again. This time his grip was firmer, possessive, as if to remind her—and her parents—that she belonged to him now. He held it for a long minute, staring into her eyes.

Maryan forced herself not to flinch.

Then, as quickly as he had come, he released her and strode toward the door.

The sound of the engine starting outside rattled her bones. The car rolled away, its tail lights fading into the night.

As the silence returned, Maryan's body broke. Tears spilled freely, unstoppable, burning her cheeks. She fled to her room, unable to face her parents, unable to bear the crushing weight of failure.

The art still leaned against the wall, waiting to be shipped. Hope still flickered, fragile and dangerous. But at that moment, all she could feel was the cage closing in.

Chapter 9

The Shipment

Around 4 AM, Maryan pulled herself up from the bed, knowing that this was the last time she would see her parents.

Her father and mother, who did not sleep, but weep all night, handed her a small satchel: protein bars, dried fruit, identity documents and two pictures — one of the family, one of her sister — finally he handed her a tiny bible her father had kept from his student days.

He kissed her forehead three time.

Three times, like a bride walking around the alter, symbolizing the Trinity. She knew what it meant, so did her mother.

Her mother burst into tears, realizing that the priest would never walk her daughter and son in law around the alter, there would be no future weeding, and this was the last moment her daughter would see her.

The tears were all consuming.

Outside the house a van pulled up, and a large tarp was draped between the van and the door. To the outside observer, it appeared they were getting ready for the wedding, and ensuring the house was prepared.

Maryan, then wiping tears, climbed into the gallery van and laid flat, in the empty box, as the false bottom was aligned over her.

Her father carrying the art from the shed, carefully laid the false bottom over her, while reciting the rosary, cried and smiled.

Finally her protector laid over her, his last piece of art he would ever paint. The canvas that would protect her, as he was unable to do.

She said nothing but cried as the false-bottom compartment was sealed.

As darkness enveloped her, she whispered a prayer.

"Protect those who love you;
because of you they are truly happy.
You bless those who obey you, Lord;
your love protects them like a shield. Amen"

At the Amen, the truck rolled forward.

As she laid down under the false bottom of the crate, wooden slats closed out the world. Darkness took over her, but the darkness contained hope.

She remembered the hammering of the nails, thinking of how Jesus felt, listening to his captives.

Those nails represented pain and suffering, mine represented freedom, she thought.

The air inside the space was dry, woody, almost sweet with the faintest odor of oil paint and cut lumber. The art supplies above her — real and forged — added a veneer of legitimacy to the shipment. Brushes. Canvases. Empty turpentine cans. She was packed like contraband beneath them all, a woman reduced to cargo, like woman in Iran had become.

The space allowed just enough room for her to shift her body into a curled position on her side. She had to keep her knees tight against her chest or angled to the side. Lying on her back was possible, but only for short spells. Her breath reverberated back to her from the narrow walls, hot and stale. Her heartbeat sounded louder than it ever had. She felt every inch of her own body — every twitch, itch, cramp, every drop of sweat collecting along her spine.

She had prepared as best she could. Two adult diapers, delivered by her father's allies in the art world, worn in succession over each other to minimize leaks. Two spares in a vacuum-sealed bag under her hip. A water bladder full of water, which she capped tightly and rationed with the discipline of someone who knew that one wrong sip could spell the end. She also had multiple protein bars, flattened to save space, four sleeping pills, if it came to that and finally photos and documentation folded and stuffed in her shoe and bra.

Despite the desperation of the planning, now seemed worse. Now she had to give her fate to God. All she could do is wait.

The first hour was the hardest. Every sound outside the crate startled her — footsteps, forklifts, voices in Farsi.

Some joking. Some shouting. Some mechanical. It was hard to tell where she was in the warehouse — near a wall or the center, high on a shelf or low to the ground. But she could tell there were others working close by, unaware they were walking past a living, breathing fugitive stuffed beneath the floor of a shipping crate.

Two hours in, her body started to complain. The floor pressed into her hip and shoulder. She shifted. Slowly. Very slowly. The wood above her creaked. She froze. Listened. No one noticed. She breathed again.

By the fourth hour, her thigh began to tremble involuntarily from tension. She bit the inside of her cheek to stay calm.

Time passed strangely. There was no way to mark the hours beyond her own guesses. Light filtered through thin cracks in the wood, but not enough to chart the day. She tried to sleep, and sometimes succeeded — a kind of half-sleep filled with confusion and fragmented memories. Once, in that haze, she thought she saw her mother walking through the rose garden with a basket of white sheets. Another time, she imagined her brother Amir on a skateboard, calling to her through an alley in Tehran. It wasn't real, of course. But her mind filled in the silence with memory.

On what she guessed was the first night, she wept — not for her situation, not even for her future, but because she smelled turpentine. Just the faintest trace, rising through the slats of the crate, maybe from a can above her or a residue soaked into the wood. It caught her completely off guard.

In an instant she was back in her father's studio. She was eight years old. He was mixing pigment, showing her how to thin the paint for longer brush strokes. He had dipped her hand in ochre and laughed when she smeared it across his cheek. The light had streamed in through the high windows. They had played classical music on a radio and danced between canvases.

In the present, lying flat in a crate destined for a different country, she pressed her fingers to her nose and cried silently, careful not to make a sound. Only once. Only then.

The warehouse outside eventually grew quiet. Night passed, she assumed. Morning came. Then more noise — more movement. At some point a dog barked. Another crate was dropped, nearby. The impact made her jump. Her head thudded lightly against the top plank. She stifled a gasp.

Her legs went numb. Then tingled. Then ached again.

Time stretched. She tried to track the hours with breathing patterns. Ten breaths. Then rest. Then ten more. She tried singing to herself — but only silently, mouthing the lyrics to old Persian lullabies her mother used to hum. She recited poetry. Forough Farrokhzad. Rumi. Even American lines she had memorized in school. Anything to remind herself she was still human, still more than this box.

She changed the first diaper near the end of what felt like the first day. It was awkward and degrading, but she did it quickly, with practiced shame. She didn't let herself cry again.

She took two sips of water. Just two.

And then more waiting.

Her second day in the crate was worse. Her body began to rebel. Her back spasmed when she moved too quickly. Her thighs cramped. A sharp itch developed under her bra line, unreachable and maddening. She pressed her fingers against the side wall just to feel something different. She talked to herself — not aloud, but in long, rambling inner monologues about everything from childhood memories to political theories to what she might do if she survived.

She thought about Armin. His hands. His eyes. His ambition. His cruelty masked in charm. She thought about her wedding dress folded, now on her bed, in her house — left behind.

She thought about the moment he offered her freedom, and how she said yes without hesitation. How strange it was to say yes to a man, in order to escape both him and a country.

She remembered her father's face the last time they embraced. The slight tremble in his chin. The whispered promise: *You will not die here.*

Then finally — the shift.

It was subtle at first, but unmistakable. The crate tilted, then jolted. A low rumble. The sound of machinery. Cranes, maybe. Men shouting. The clank of metal. Vibrations passed through her body like waves through a drum.

She was being moved.

Her whole body tensed. This was it — the last part of the plan. The crate was being loaded. Her heart pounded so loudly she thought it might echo. Another jolt. Then a dull thud.

Silence. Then a deep hum.

Engines.

The plane.

She pressed her forehead against the crate wall, barely breathing.

More movement. She imagined the cargo hold — cold and cavernous, with metal walls and straps and boxes stacked like toy blocks. She had seen photographs. Her father had shown her where the crate would go. She imagined the walls around her frozen with condensation.

The engine roared, and she knew they were ascending.

And then — stillness.

Darkness.

Cold.

But her father made sure to mark the shipment as sensitive, to ensure above 45 degree temperature at all times. Luckily, the temperature stayed about 50.

Despite her having a small blanket, this time was dangerous, and she worried about her temperature dropping. If her temperature dropped to much, her life would be in danger.

Time no longer made any sense. The hum of the engine dulled her senses, like a lullaby designed to numb. Her body was exhausted beyond imagination. She didn't fight the sleep when it came. She floated in and out — pain became abstract, her thoughts unraveling like thread.

She dreamed of rivers.

Of painting a mural on a stone wall near Lake Harriet, surrounded by schoolchildren asking questions.

She dreamed of swimming in the North Sea, even though she had never seen it, only imagined it from books. The water was grey and wild and alive.

She dreamed of a woman holding her hand and whispering in German.

She measured time by prayers. She slept in spurts. Dreamed of Armin breaking the crate with a crowbar. Of being dragged out midflight. Of drowning in her own cold sweat.

She dreamed of fire — the museum in Tehran, the smuggled painting, the chaos. She smelled smoke. She shouted for help, but the crate swallowed her voice.

When she woke, her mouth was dry beyond language. Her tongue cracked. Her joints throbbed.

One more sip of water.

One more change.

And then — nothing again.

Somewhere above her, outside the crate, life went on. People walked. Machines rolled. Things moved. Governments made decisions. Protests rose and fell. She existed in a space between realities — neither here nor there, neither alive nor dead, only becoming.

Eventually, the plane began to descend. She could feel it — a pressure in her ears, a low dip in gravity. A new rumble. Another shift.

And then — landing.

The impact shook her bones. Then silence. Then movement.

Unloading. Repositioning. Waiting again.

She tried not to breathe too fast. Her last diaper was soiled. Her water was gone. Her body screamed in protest.

Hours passed. Maybe more.

And then — the final journey. Forklifts. A truck. Vibrations beneath her again. The screech of tires. Wind. Language she didn't understand — *German? Dutch?* A radio. A phone ringing.

The crate stopped.

The driver noticing cracks int the case, called his supervisor over.

This was not a planed stop, the church was to pick up the box, but now, now...

A voice.

A pause.

The sound of nails being pried loose.

And then — light.

Bright. Blinding. Holy light.

The slats opened, and the face of an old man stared back at her, weathered and wide-eyed.

Jumping back – he yelled.

Summoning the courage, he peered back into the crate, he spoke to her in a whisper, almost afraid:

"Willkommen. Sie sind frei."

Maryan didn't speak. She couldn't.

She wept again — not silently this time.

The man, paused unsure what to do, or where to look.

Maryan squinted, shielding her face with a trembling hand as the old man — a dock worker in a grey wool sweater and reflective vest — helped her out of the crate. Her knees buckled when she tried to stand. He caught her under the arm and shouted something she didn't understand, his voice hoarse with disbelief.

And then she climbed out of the box that had become her coffin and her cradle, into the unknown.

Others came quickly. Two more men in uniforms. One with a clipboard. Another with a walkie-talkie. A third with thick gloves motioned for her to sit on an overturned plastic crate. She collapsed onto it, half from fatigue and half from sheer shock. The warehouse buzzed around her — machines, forklifts, the occasional seagull crying outside the high windows.

They didn't touch her roughly, not yet. But their expressions were taut with a mixture of concern and suspicion. Someone offered her water. She drank greedily, then wiped her mouth with the back of her hand.

They spoke rapidly in a language she couldn't follow. German, she guessed. Or Dutch. Maybe even Flemish. It didn't matter. Their words were barbed with urgency.

One of the younger men — thin, pale, maybe in his early thirties — asked gently, in halting English, "Do you speak English?"

She nodded. "Yes," she rasped.

He crouched in front of her. "Where are you from?"

She opened her mouth. The word wouldn't come. Her throat tightened. Her entire body still buzzed from the trauma of confinement.

"Iran," she whispered.

They all turned toward her, their faces shifting. The younger man looked back at his colleagues and said something quickly. One of them pulled out a phone.

"Police," the older one said to her, tapping his chest. "We call. You wait."

Maryan nodded. What else could she do?

They led her into a small port office nearby, a room lined with metal desks, stacks of shipping manifests, and two cracked leather chairs. There was a faint smell of coffee and old printer toner. A flickering fluorescent light above her gave the room a queasy hue. Someone wrapped a gray fleece blanket around her shoulders. She didn't resist.

She sat still, like a statue, while they made calls.

An older man — the shift supervisor, judging by how the others deferred to him — watched her with narrowed eyes as he dialed a number on a dusty landline. She could only understand fragments of what he said, but the words "Flüchtling," "Versteckt," and "Iranerin" repeated often.

Refugee. Hidden. Iranian woman.

Fifteen minutes passed.

The police arrived in a small van — two officers, both in navy uniforms. One of them, a woman with gray-blond hair pulled into a tight bun, spoke clearly and directly to her.

"You will come with us now, please. For questions."

The woman police officer noticing the stench originating from Maryan, smiled, turned to her partner and signaled to wait.

The woman then walked Maryan to the bathroom.

Water, toilets. Something Maryan was desperately needing.

Maryan quickly disposed of the diaper and washed herself in the sink.

Drinking some water, she smiled at the woman police officer standing next to her.

She was escorted — not handcuffed, not yet — to the van. The backseat was lined with plastic. She was too tired to feel humiliation anymore.

They drove through the port's maze of containers and cranes, out to a road lined with trucks and chain-link fences. The gray sky overhead seemed to sag.

After twenty minutes, they reached a small administrative building. Not a jail. A processing center. Fluorescent lights again. A waiting room with vending machines and plastic chairs. Cameras in every corner.

They took her fingerprints. Photographed her. Searched her belongings — which were few: a tiny ID card hidden in her bra, a folded family photo, and a paper tucked into her sock with an address in Hamburg scribbled in pencil — a contact her father had arranged through an artist friend.

The officers spoke little. Maryan tried to make eye contact, but they seemed trained not to meet her gaze. She was moved to a second room — an interrogation room, clearly. No mirrors, but one camera in the corner. Two chairs. A table. A stack of papers.

She waited there for almost an hour.

She tried to rest her head on the table, but couldn't find peace. Her back ached. Her bladder was swollen with anxiety. Her stomach growled. She hadn't eaten since the protein bar in the crate.

At last, the door opened. A new figure entered — a woman in plain clothes, with dark glasses and a thick file tucked under her arm. She was followed by a translator, a kind-eyed man in his forties, with a clipped beard and a maroon tie.

The woman nodded. "Maryan Darya?"

Maryan sat up straight. "Yes."

"I am from the immigration services. This is Mr. Kamal. He will help us speak clearly."

She switched to German. Kamal translated.

The woman sat and opened the file.

"You were found in the false bottom of a crate from Tehran. Is that correct?"

Maryan nodded.

"Do you understand the legal consequences of entering the country in this manner?"

"I understand," she said softly. "I had no other choice."

The woman's eyes flicked up.

"No other choice?"

"No."

There was a pause.

"Why did you come here?"

Maryan swallowed. Her lips were dry again.

"Because I would be killed if I stayed."

"Why?"

Maryan looked at Kamal, then back at the official.

She didn't know how much to tell — or how to begin.

After a moment, she said, "Because I was part of the protests. Because I spoke out. Because I am a woman."

Another pause.

"Protests?"

Maryan took a deep breath. Her voice trembled but grew stronger as she went on.

"It started with Anoush Abelyan. You've heard the name, yes?"

The official nodded slowly. "Yes."

"She was arrested for wearing her leading the protests in Tehran. They said she died of a heart attack. But we saw the photos. Her skull was fractured."

Maryan's hands clenched the blanket around her.

"It was a small protest. Just us fighting back, us students. We chanted *'Zan, Zendegi, Azadi.'* 'Woman, Life, Freedom.'"

Her voice cracked on the last word. Kamal translated with care.

"I posted videos," she said. "I painted murals on the university wall. I created art — digital, subversive. They knew. The Ministry. The Basij. They came for me in the middle of the night."

The woman wrote notes. Her pen scratched softly across the page.

"I was arrested. I was detained in a slaughterhouse outside Tehran. No trial. No charges. Just questions and threats. One man told me ..I could go free if I married him...... I knew him from before. He was... connected."

Maryan's throat burned. She pushed on.

"I said yes, to escape. But before the wedding, I returned to my family. My father — he is an artist, too. He used his connections. We arranged the crate. The shipping manifest. Everything. It was the only way."

The room fell silent. Only the sound of the pen.

The woman looked at Kamal, then at Maryan again.

"Do you have proof of your involvement? Any documentation?"

Maryan reached into the inner fold of her bra and pulled out a folded paper — an old photo a long-ago student art protest, smuggled from Tehran, with her signature in the corner.

A photo of a mural, the same mural behind them bore the same motif she'd painted during the protests: a unveiled woman with her fist in the air wrapped around a hijab.

The official took both documents. Examined them closely.

"You'll need a medical exam," she said. "You are dehydrated. Likely in shock."

Maryan nodded, her eyes half-closed now.

"You'll be transferred to a temporary shelter. Then a hearing. An asylum request."

"Please," Maryan whispered. "Don't send me back."

The woman didn't respond immediately. Then she said, almost gently, "We won't. Not yet."

Kamal translated the last part softly.

Maryan blinked back tears.

"And if I am allowed to stay?"

"We begin the integration process."

"What does that mean?"

"You'll be interviewed. Given an identity number. A lawyer. Shelter. Language classes. If your asylum claim is accepted, you may eventually work. Live. Apply for residency. But it will take time."

Maryan nodded slowly. "I will wait."

Kamal smiled gently. "You have already waited long."

The official stood and closed the file.

"You are safe for now, Maryan Darya"

Safe.

The word sounded unreal, it sounded comical.

Maryan smiled.

"Safe." She said in English.

In the hours that followed, Maryan was moved again — this time to a medical tent set up just outside the port authority. A nurse took her blood pressure. Another checked her pulse, her reflexes, her hydration. They asked questions in English. She answered with nods and short phrases. Her body was battered, but intact. Her spirit — bruised but unbroken.

Later, she was taken by van to a refugee shelter in the city. She slept for nearly a full day, under warm blankets in a cot surrounded by other women and children.

But even in her dreams, she could still smell the turpentine.

Chater 10

Farfignugen

Farfignugen—or *to drive* in German—was a Volkswagen ad that the American kids on TikTok had revived from the 1990s. Before the protests that landed her in jail, Maryan and her friends used to mimic the American kids, mimicking their parents saying *Farfignugen.*

It was a funny word, and it made her laugh thinking of it, as the translator asked if she spoke German, she thought about saying it, but she just nodded no.

The brief laughter made her feel mad. Mad at herself for being happy, even momentarily, as she knew her parents were being tortured—maybe even killed. Her face visibly changed, a flicker of guilt replacing her smile. It was noticed by the German official, who paused for a moment, then looked down at her paperwork as if giving her space to collect herself.

The air in the immigration office smelled faintly of disinfectant and strong coffee. The walls were a soft shade of gray-blue, clearly painted with the intention of soothing nerves, though their effectiveness was debatable. A small potted plant leaned toward the fluorescent lights overhead, its leaves dry at the tips.

The translator—a woman with a kind face, maybe in her early forties—repeated the question, more gently this time.

"Deutsch? Sprechen Sie Deutsch?"

Maryan shook her head. "No. I speak Farsi. English... a little."

The woman nodded. "Okay. No problem. We will use English then. Welcome to Germany. You are safe now."

Safe now.

Two words that felt like a cruel joke. Safe? She wasn't safe. Not really. Not while her parents were still in Iran. Not while she had no idea what had become of her younger sister, barely thirteen, when the Revolutionary Guard raided their house. Not while she still felt the phantom ache of handcuffs cutting into her wrists in that filthy detention center.

But she nodded anyway. Because it was what you were supposed to do.

The German official stamped something in a manila folder and handed it to the translator, who turned to Maryan.

"This is your refugee ID for now. You will be taken to a temporary housing facility. You may request to be moved later. There are counselors and support workers. You'll have an appointment with an asylum officer soon. Do you have any questions?"

Maryan opened her mouth. Closed it.

She had a thousand questions. Where am I exactly? Is my father's friend here? Did the shipping container make it intact? What if they find me? What if they come looking?

Instead, she asked, "Will I be able to talk to my family?"

The translator's expression softened. "We don't know where your family is. But there are people here who can help you try. There are human rights workers. Journalists. Advocates. You are not alone."

Alone.

The word struck her harder than she expected. She was surrounded by people: officials, refugees, translators, guards. And yet she had never felt more isolated. Like a ghost moving through a world that didn't see her fully. Not really.

She nodded again.

They led her through a series of long hallways—sterile, white, bureaucratic—and finally out to a loading dock where a white shuttle van waited. It was raining. A fine, cold mist that reminded her of the movies she used to watch—German or maybe Swedish ones—where everything looked washed out and cold and clean. So unlike Tehran, with its dust and chaos and sun that scorched even in the spring.

The driver didn't say anything. Just pointed to the back seat. She climbed in beside a mother and her two children, clearly new arrivals as well. The mother clutched a paper bag of belongings, and her eyes looked just as vacant and frightened as Maryan felt.

The van pulled away.

She didn't know where it was taking her, and she didn't
ask.

The temporary housing facility was on the outskirts of a
small city called Bremen. At least that's what the sign said
when the van passed it. Maryan didn't know what Bremen
was famous for, only that it sounded familiar—maybe from
a fairytale. The Brothers Grimm?

Her room was a narrow cell with two beds, a steel-framed
desk, and a radiator that clicked and hissed like it was alive.
She had a roommate: a Syrian girl named Nour who had
been in Germany for three weeks. Nour spoke English,
enough to bridge the gulf between their languages, and
she offered Maryan a protein bar as a kind of welcome.

"You're from Iran?" Nour asked that night, while they lay in
their twin beds with the overhead light off.

"Yes," Maryan whispered.

"I'm from Aleppo," Nour said. "My brother is still missing.
He was arrested two years ago. No one knows where."

Maryan turned her head toward the wall. "I'm sorry."

"Me too," Nour said. "Do you want to talk about it?"

Maryan shook her head, forgetting Nour couldn't see her
in the dark. "Not yet."

"That's okay."

Silence filled the room, but it was a gentle silence. A companionable one. For the first time since arriving in Europe, Maryan didn't feel entirely adrift.

The days passed in a slow blur.

There were orientation sessions, paperwork, language classes, and visits from case workers. Maryan began to understand the rhythm of the place: when breakfast was served, when the shower lines were shortest, when the community room was empty enough for her to sit alone and write in her journal.

She'd brought almost nothing with her.

One afternoon, while waiting for her asylum interview, she began to sketch again. Faces mostly. Women from the protest. Her cellmate. Her mother. Herself, though the version she drew looked far stronger than the girl who sat trembling with a pencil.

"Your art is very powerful," said a social worker who passed by. He had long hair tied back in a bun and wore thick glasses that made his eyes look enormous. "You should apply to the arts relief grant. It's for refugee artists. We help them connect to galleries. Sometimes it leads to residency."

Maryan didn't know what to say. A part of her recoiled at the idea. Art was her father's thing. Her thing, too, once— but now it felt like something from another life. How could she draw when her hands still remembered the sting of slap after slap? When her body still ached from days in that filthy holding cell?

And yet, she took the flyer he handed her.

She hid it in her notebook.

The asylum interview was held in a government building with marble floors and cold metal chairs. A female officer sat across from her with a translator beside her.

They asked questions. Maryan answered.

They asked her to recount what led her to flee Iran.

She did.

They asked about her political activity, about the protests.

She told them. About the chanting. The arrests. The friends who disappeared.

They asked her if she had been harmed.

Maryan's voice faltered. She nodded. "Yes."

"Would you like to describe what happened?" the officer asked.

"No," she said, then after a pause: "I mean, I can. But I don't want to."

"That's okay," the woman said. "We believe you. You don't have to relive it."

Maryan broke then.

Tears fell silently at first, then faster. She wiped her eyes with her sleeves. The translator offered her a tissue. The officer paused the interview.

In that moment, Maryan realized something strange. She wasn't being interrogated. She wasn't being tricked or coerced. These people didn't want to break her. They weren't the Revolutionary Guard. They were just... trying to understand. To document. To help.

It didn't make her feel better. Not exactly. But it did crack something open.

Weeks later, Maryan was relocated to a different facility. This one was in Hamburg, in a renovated dormitory building with wide windows and slightly less depressing furniture.

Her roommate was a Ukrainian woman in her thirties who barely spoke but sometimes played violin in the courtyard. The music was haunting and sad and made Maryan think of her mother's hands—so gentle, always kneading dough or fixing a collar or brushing a strand of hair behind her ear.

Maryan began going to language classes. She hated German. It was hard and spiky and so different from the soft curves of Farsi. But she tried. She practiced phrases under her breath. *Ich heiße Maryan. Ich komme aus dem Iran. Ich spreche ein bisschen Englisch.*

Sometimes she cried in the shower. No one judged her for it.

Sometimes she laughed with Nour over text.

Sometimes she stayed up until dawn, staring out the window, hoping for a message.

None came.

Chapter 11

Words and Letters

Then one morning, she received a letter.

Not an email. Not a phone call. A real letter, in a thin blue envelope with smudged ink. The kind people don't send anymore unless they have no other choice—or unless the message they carry is meant to be held, felt, and buried in a drawer beside other things too sacred to delete.

It had no return address, no stamps from Tehran or anywhere recognizable. The postmark was a blur. Only the faded scribbles of her name in Persian and a line of German text written neatly underneath: *Frau Maryan Darya*. The handwriting looked unfamiliar at first glance, like a stranger had attempted to remember her.

She didn't open it right away. She sat with it in her lap in the cramped studio apartment above the bakery, just staring at it. The windows were open to let out the yeast and sugar smell that crept up the walls every morning. She could hear the whir of the trams several blocks away, and beyond that, the muffled rhythm of the city humming along.

Her fingertips trembled. It had been months since she'd heard anything—months of wondering, fearing the worst, imagining a dozen different fates for her father and none of them good. Months of waiting for word, any word, until hope had grown brittle and useless, like the crust on week-old bread.

Still, she didn't open it. Not yet.

She made tea. She burned the edge of her finger when the kettle hissed and jumped. She wrapped the finger in a dish towel and sat at the little wooden table in the kitchen nook, knees pressed up against the drawers. She placed the envelope on the table like an offering. It looked almost shy there, a pale blue whisper against the dark pine grain.

Finally, she tore the top gently.

Inside was a single sheet of paper, folded twice. The language was German. But the voice—oh, the voice was unmistakably Persian. More importantly, it was unmistakably *his*.

He was alive, her father was alive.

It was coded, of course. Written through a contact who had access to embassy channels, or someone in the underground courier network she'd heard whispers about. But she could tell it was him. She could tell by the turns of phrase. The reference to the way they used to add cinnamon to their rice dishes, even though her grandmother hated it. The memory of the tiny scar on her knee from climbing the fig tree behind their house. The mention of her mother's pigeons.

Her mother was not alive.

That part came at the end. Simply written. Not dramatic. Not sorrowful in tone, and maybe that was what made it hurt most.

"Your mother's heart could not bear the weight."

Maryan folded the letter four times and held it to her chest.

She didn't cry.

Not right away.

She sat for several long minutes, maybe longer. Time became strange and flexible, like soft glass just before it hardens. She stared at the wall—at nothing. The kettle was still warm. Her tea sat untouched.

Her first thought was irrational and childlike: *Why is my mother dead?*

Of course she knew, but her mind was gone.

Did someone come to the house and kill her? Did Amin kill her?

Was she alone?
Her mind scrambled like that for a while, weaving together timelines, blaming herself, blaming the government, blaming the air, blaming the silence.

Then, needing air she couldn't find in her apartment, Maryan walked out.

Not crying, not yet, joy for her father, sadness for her mother, worry for her sister. Too many emotions, emotions she hid walking outside.

The city park near the center wasn't far—fifteen minutes at a quiet pace. She passed the same streets she always did: the little bookstore with posters of American crime novels in the window, the Turkish grocer who always offered her a smile and a ripe pomegranate, the public art mural that children had helped paint—bright and chaotic.

The weather was damp, the kind of misty gray morning Germany did so well. She could feel the cold working its way through her sleeves. But she welcomed it. She wanted it to cut through her. Wanted it to stop her from curling inward.

She sat beneath a tree near the duck pond. A birch, with bark like shedding paper. The grass around her was wet and stuck to her jeans, but she didn't care.

And then the grief came.

It came in waves.
It came in fists.
It came in the German rain, washing over her face as if the whole country was mourning with her.

She didn't sob right away. It began with a strange, shuddering exhale. Then another. Her arms wrapped around herself like a brace. Her head tipped forward. She whispered something—maybe her mother's name, maybe just a sound.

And when the tears came, they were not delicate. They were not poetic. They were wild and angry and silent all at once. Her body shook, not just from cold now, but from something far more ancient, deeper than language or ideology. It was grief that had lived too long under the surface, buried beneath fear and obligation and the constant struggle to survive.

A pair of children ran past her at one point, laughing. One looked back briefly, confused maybe by the sight of a woman on her knees in the rain. But they didn't stop.

She stayed outside for hours.

Sometime later, when the rain was only a drizzle and her jeans were soaked through, Maryan lay back in the grass and looked up through the leaves. They trembled in the breeze, like pages turning.

She remembered a morning years ago in Tehran, when she and her mother had gone to the bazaar to find fabric. They weren't looking for anything in particular—just something soft and pretty to make curtains for the kitchen. Her mother had been laughing at something a vendor said, and Maryan remembered thinking how young she looked in that moment. Younger than usual. Lighter.

Her mother used to hum when she cooked. Used to pretend she didn't care when the pigeons flew into the house, even though she always grumbled as she chased them out with a broom. She had once spent three days making an embroidered table runner that they used only once because someone spilled ash on it during a dinner party.

And now—she was gone.

No last phone call. No hand to hold. No grave she could visit.

Gone.

Maryan pressed the heels of her hands into her eyes until her vision pulsed red. Then she rolled onto her side and let the rain continue to fall.

Eventually, her body tired of crying. She sat up slowly, like someone recovering from illness. A snail crawled near her foot. A dog barked in the distance. A woman jogged by wearing a neon windbreaker and earbuds.

It all felt absurd.

The world was still moving. How?

She reached into her coat pocket and took out the letter again. The paper was beginning to warp from moisture. She read it once more, tracing each line like it was scripture.

Her father was alive.

Somewhere, in hiding or in captivity or maybe just lying low in the old neighborhood. The letter didn't say where he was or how he managed to get this message to her. But it was his voice. And he was alive.

She thought about writing back. But to where? To whom? The letter had no signature. No direction. Only the hope that it would reach her.

She would carry that hope now.

Her mother's death didn't erase that hope. But it changed the shape of it. It made it heavier.

She didn't remember walking back.

She found herself at her apartment door, key in hand. Her feet ached. She peeled off her wet socks and left her soaked coat on the floor.

The kettle was still on the stove. The tea was cold.

She sat on the floor and tried to remember the sound of her mother's voice.

Later that night, She took the letter and slipped it into the back of her sketchbook, between pages of charcoal smears and watercolor ruins. Her fingers were stained from painting earlier in the week—a portrait of a girl without a face, standing in front of a burning museum.

She pulled the blanket around her shoulders and watched the streetlights flicker on outside the window. The city didn't know her grief. It didn't care. And yet, she was grateful for its indifference. For the way it just kept going.

She didn't sleep that night. But she didn't feel awake, either.

She floated somewhere between.

The next morning, Maryan walked back to the park. The ground was still soft from yesterday's rain, and the birds had returned, pecking at crumbs near the benches.

She brought a small bag of seed and scattered it near the tree where she had wept.

It felt like a ritual. Like laying a stone on a grave she couldn't visit.

A part of her wanted to scream. To tear out the roots of that birch tree. To demand from the sky some explanation.

But instead, she sat.

And watched the pigeons gather, as her mother's mourners.

Chapter 12

The Grant

In the following months, Maryan changed.

Not all at once. Not in some cinematic arc. There were no loud declarations, no montage of victories. Just the slow, almost imperceptible shifting of weight inside her, as if a tectonic plate had started to slide beneath the surface. Something hardened. Something else unfurled.

It began with her hands.

For weeks after the letter—the one that said her mother had died and her father was still alive—her hands wouldn't stay still. They fidgeted, clutched, picked at old paint on her windowsill, toyed with invisible threads in the hem of her coat. Sometimes she would wake at dawn to find her fingers already curled, as if drawing lines in the air while she slept.

She painted again. At first, tentatively—small strokes, hidden notebooks. Then larger. Angrier. Her strokes grew urgent. Her colors darker, heavier, until the entire apartment smelled like turpentine and rainwater.

She wasn't sure what she was painting. Only that it had to come out.

The pieces were ugly and dark at first, but slowly her art became refined, penetrating to the viewers.

It was the Syrian poet who told her about the grant.

His name was Rami. He was 27, spoke five languages, and had a face that looked like it had been carved from wind and fire. They met at a refugee center where a community organizer had hosted an "arts evening"—which was really just tea, cheap cookies, and a borrowed projector that didn't work.

But Rami read a poem that stopped the room.

A poem about Syria, the life of Christian's years ago.

About the beaches, about the nightlife about all the things lost under Islamic rules.

Syria like Iran before the revolution, was wonderful. Women had equality and full job force participation.

Maryan listening, understood that throughout the middle east women, once fully part of all life, had been pushed to the side by religion leaders who cared only about power and their interpretation of Islam.

She was so moved by his interpretation and poem, she began to cry, not loudly but enough that tears poured down her face.

Then clapping, then standing. The poet from Syria, had shocked the room.

Afterward, they talked. Not about their pasts, not yet. But about colors, words, and exile. During the conversation he mentioned the *Künstlerförderprogramm*, the Berlin artist grant for displaced creatives.

"You should apply," he said, his voice casual but his eyes sharp. "Your hands know something."

Maryan laughed, shaking her head. "I don't even have a proper portfolio."

"You have pain," he said. "That's all they're looking for. Pain that shapes something."

Maryan at first rejected it outright, but the more he spoke about her, the more she felt worthy.

Worthy enough to at least apply.

She was about to tell him, but the poet was dragged away, away to an audience that understood the work.

The application was in German. Rami helped translate. She included photographs of her canvases—some painted here in Berlin, others rescued from Tehran through blurry phone images her father had hidden in an encrypted drive long ago.

She mailed it in late June, just before the deadline, then promptly tried to forget it.

She did not want to be rejected, her life, was full of rejection, something she could not bear to think of.

In July an envelope arrived.

She had been accepted.

She read the letter twice, then a third time with her hands shaking. She wasn't sure what to do. She wanted to scream. She wanted to run. Instead, she sat on the kitchen floor and let the news settle in her chest like a heartbeat.

The program offered her a small stipend and access to a shared artist studio on the edge of Kreuzberg. It was housed in a converted factory building—concrete floors, massive windows, exposed pipes that hissed in the morning.

Her new co-residents were as scarred and brilliant as Berlin itself.

There was Camila, a Venezuelan sculptor who worked in broken mirrors and plaster casts of hands. She had a laugh like a cracked church bell and wore the same paint-smeared denim jacket every day. Her Spanish was fast and furious, but her eyes were kind.

There was Joseph, a Congolese photographer whose portraits of refugees had been featured in magazines across Europe. He never took pictures of people without asking. "Dignity is not assumed," he would say. "It is invited."

And there was Rami, of course, who wrote poems directly on the studio walls in erasable marker, pausing only to ask, "Is this too much?"

Maryan took the far corner—closest to the windows. She taped up old sketches, unpacked her brushes, and set her paints in rows like soldiers preparing for battle.

She began again.

Each day followed a rhythm.

She arrived before noon, often with a paper bag of bread and soft cheese from the Turkish market nearby. They worked mostly in silence, broken only by the occasional blast of Arabic music or someone reading a line of verse aloud.

Maryan painted like she was remembering a dream. Fast, then slow. Layered. Sometimes violent.

She painted faceless women with hands pressed against broken glass.

She painted cities dripping with blood and smoke, but always—always—there was a light source somewhere. A matchstick. A flicker.

One canvas she returned to again and again: a street in Tehran lit only by fire, and in the foreground, a pair of boots—one standing, one overturned.

She never gave it a title.

Camila once watched her work in silence for ten minutes, then muttered, "You don't paint people. You paint what's left of them."

Chapter 13

The Invitation

It came in late spring, the kind of spring that couldn't decide whether it wanted to be rain or sun. The light was thin, metallic, the kind that revealed more than it softened.

A curator from a Berlin gallery—small but respected—had seen Joseph's photography in an online feature about refugee collectives. He had emailed, then called, then asked to tour the studio.

He arrived dressed entirely in black, from collar to cuff. His shoes were polished, his hair neat, his expression unreadable. His accent was Danish, clipped and precise, his German flawless, his English elegant. His eye was sharp. He walked slowly, speaking little, but when he looked at a work, it was not a casual glance. It was an autopsy.

Maryan noticed everything: the rhythm of his gait, the pause of his breath, the way he leaned in as if listening to the canvases. He gave off an aura she recognized instantly—money. Not the vulgar wealth of flashy cars or jewelry, but old money, educated money, money that moved quietly but decisively.

Her stomach twisted. Money meant power. Money meant a door, perhaps, but also a gatekeeper.

When he paused in front of her canvases, she stopped breathing.

He stood there for a long time, silent, his hands clasped behind his back. She felt exposed, as though her prison years, her bruises, her hiding, her secrets—all of it—were suddenly visible on those stretched linen surfaces.

Finally, he lifted his chin slightly and pointed. First to one, then another, then a third.

"These," he said. His voice was almost too soft. "These belong on a wall."

Maryan blinked. It was as if he had spoken in code.

"You… you want to show my work?" she asked cautiously, her accent betraying both Farsi and fear.

"Yes," he replied simply. "In June. We are doing a feature on refugee artists. But don't worry—" and here his eyes softened, briefly—"this is not charity. This is skill."

Her head spun.

A show. A show to show *my* art.

She repeated the words in her mind like a prayer. *My art.*

But the thought was followed immediately by doubt.

How could it be? I am not my father. He is the artist. He is the one with talent. I am just a shadow of him. I am just a survivor with charcoal-stained hands.

She didn't know whether to cry, laugh out loud, or collapse to the floor. Instead, she simply whispered:

"Yes."

The curator smiled faintly, mumbled something about sending more information, and walked away as quietly as he had arrived.

Maryan stood frozen, then slowly sank to the floor, staring at nothing. Her whole body trembled. For the first time in years, possibility felt heavier than fear.

The Berlin gallery was indeed small, but it radiated quiet wealth. It was located in Mitte, a district that still carried traces of its divided past but had been remade into a pristine hub of boutiques, cafés, and art spaces. The gallery's walls were whitewashed to perfection, the floors polished to a sheen, the halogen lights ruthless in their brightness.

Opening night smelled like white wine, perfume, and rain dripping off coats. The guests—patrons, collectors, critics—were shiny, rich, and urban. They moved as though their presence itself was a form of currency.

Maryan arrived early. She wore a simple black dress, plain to the point of invisibility, but Camila insisted on adding a thin gold line beneath each of her eyes.

"To show your fire," Camila said, brushing her cheek affectionately.

Her three selected paintings had been hung on the central wall, given prominence despite the gallery's size.

- **Untitled (Tehran Nights)** — boots, fire, silence rendered in violent strokes of red and black.

- **Without Permission** — a faceless figure dissolving into gauze-like layers of charcoal.

- **Separation** — a diptych: one panel of a woman screaming, the other of a pigeon in flight.

The labels listed only her name: *Maryan Darya.*

No bio. No country. No refugee backstory.

She had asked for that deliberately. She didn't want pity. She didn't want the narrative of "Iranian woman, survivor, refugee." She wanted the work to stand.

At first, people trickled in. Some stopped, some didn't. Some tilted their heads, squinted, crossed their arms. The murmurs were in German, French, English. She caught words like "raw," "urgent," "beautiful in its violence."

A man stood crying in front of *Tehran Nights* for nearly ten minutes. He wiped his eyes, looked at her, and simply nodded before walking away.

An older German woman touched her arm and whispered, "Danke." Thank you.

Maryan nodded back, her throat too tight for words.

Later, a student approached her, notebook in hand. "Can you explain the meaning of the diptych?"

Maryan shook her head gently. "It's not for me to explain. It's for you to feel."

The girl smiled. "I felt it."

Maryan's chest tightened. The art was speaking. Speaking for her, louder and more eloquently than she ever could. It was both liberation and terror.

As the night went on, she realized something she hadn't expected.

She felt seen.

That was new. That was dangerous.

For so long, invisibility had been her armor. In Tehran, hiding was survival. In prison, silence was protection. In Berlin, keeping her head down on the U-Bahn, not meeting eyes, not drawing attention—those had been habits carved into her bones.

But here, under halogen light, people saw her. Not Maryan the refugee. Not Maryan the prisoner. Not Maryan the daughter of a disgraced artist. They saw Maryan the painter.

It frightened her more than invisibility ever had. Because being seen meant being vulnerable. Being seen meant she could be broken again.

When the night ended, she returned to the studio shaken, exhilarated, and exhausted.

The next morning, Rami burst into the studio with coffee in one hand and excitement in the other.

"They want to feature your work in KünstlerHaus Bethanien," he said breathlessly. "It's a much bigger venue. A major platform."

Maryan stared at him as though he had just told her she had wings.

"You're joking."

"No," he grinned. "They loved your Tehran canvas. They want it. And they want more. They said you paint not just pain, but memory."

Her knees went weak. She sat down heavily.

"More?" she whispered.

"Yes. Can you give them more?"

She looked down at her stained fingers, then out the window where the Berlin sky was split between clouds and sunlight.

"I have more," she said slowly. "I'm just not sure how much."

Rami's grin widened. "Then give them exactly that."

The next day, she stretched a new canvas, larger than any before. It loomed against the studio wall like a door she was afraid to open.

She didn't begin with color. She began with silence.

She sat in front of the blank surface for two days. Staring. Listening. Waiting.

Then she drew a single line.

Then another.

Then the flood began.

She painted not just Tehran, but the container ship. The suffocating dark of the false bottom. The port office with its flickering lights and interrogations. The loneliness of Europe—the quiet parks, the gray concrete, the faces that turned away.

She painted the alley behind her childhood home, where she had hidden with friends. She painted the face of the maintenance man in Minneapolis, the one who had smiled at her when no one else dared.

She painted the sound of protest. The silence of grief. The bitter taste of fear. The fragile warmth of hope.

Her brush moved as if guided by something larger than herself.

And as she worked, the room grew warmer.

As she worked, she changed—again.

Not all at once. But enough.

Chapter 14
Künstlerhaus Bethanien

Künstlerhaus Bethanien wasn't the Louvre.

But it didn't need to be.

The name alone carried weight in Berlin's art world, a former hospital turned into a crucible for contemporary visionaries. It was known for installations that disturbed, performances that unsettled, and paintings that refused to be forgotten. Maryan had passed it many times before, always looking through the tall windows as if peeking into a dream too large to hold.

Now, her work was inside.

Not in the grand foyer or the glowing main hall but tucked in a far corner gallery—Gallery Room 4C, behind a heavy black curtain and an aging placard. There was no fanfare. No press release dedicated solely to her. Her name didn't appear on the banners out front.

But that didn't matter.

Because people were finding her.

The opening night was crowded from the start, even by Bethanien standards. Thirty artists shared the space across multiple rooms. Wine flowed freely, glasses clinked, and German, Spanish, Arabic, Farsi, and English rose in a murmur that pulsed like a living organism.

Maryan had arrived early, dressed in a plain dark blouse and wide-legged trousers, her hair in a low braid. She wasn't there to perform. She was there to witness. Camila had tried to convince her to wear color, "Something fierce, mujer," but Maryan didn't want to distract from the work.

Her corner wasn't supposed to be a focal point.

But somehow, it had become one.

People walking into the gallery strolled past neon sculpture, past video loops of kinetic dancers, past the massive painted wings on the hallway wall—and made a quiet, instinctive pilgrimage toward her corner. Forty, fifty people at a time. It wasn't a crush, but it was enough that Maryan, trying to stay unnoticed, kept getting nudged further back, until she found herself outside the doorway, peeking in.

It was surreal.

From a distance, she watched a young man whisper something to his friend and point toward her triptych.

Another couple stood directly in front of her Tehran canvas—**Untitled (Tehran Nights)**—talking in hushed tones as if they were inside a cathedral. The man's hand brushed the woman's wrist gently, as if seeking reassurance. Their heads tilted. They didn't move for a long time.

Someone inside asked, "Is she here?"

Maryan backed up instinctively. Then she inhaled, held it, and stepped forward.

A woman in her sixties with silver hair and gold-rimmed glasses stood inches from *Separation*—the diptych of the screaming woman and the flying pigeon. Her eyes were wet.

"I used to teach political prisoners," she said, noticing Maryan approaching. "In Chile. Many of them couldn't speak of what they saw. But when I see your work... it speaks *for* them."

Maryan blinked. "Thank you. I didn't think anyone would..."

"Understand?" the woman said, softly. "You'd be surprised. Oppression is different everywhere. But grief? Grief knows no borders."

Maryan smiled, and they stood in silence together for a moment. A shared ache stretching across decades and continents.

The curator who'd selected her work—a tall Danish man named Lars with a long navy coat and scuffed boots— found her mid-evening near the hallway water cooler.

"You've started a migration pattern," he said, smiling. "We may need to rehang the show if this keeps up."

Maryan laughed nervously. "It's only because I'm in the back."

"No," Lars said. "It's because you're cutting through something most of us only pretend to understand. You're not making politics. You're making memory."

She didn't know what to say to that.

He handed her a fresh glass of sparkling water. "People think they come to see war art and trauma art. What they don't expect is to see themselves in it. But that's what you've done."

At one point, Rami found her by the window, where she was sipping ginger wine and trying to breathe. The crowds had not lessened. If anything, more people had begun to spill into her corner. A journalist from a Berlin arts zine had scribbled her name down. Someone else had asked if she'd consider a residency in Sweden. A small girl had asked if the pigeons in her paintings were real.

"You're famous," Rami teased.

"No," Maryan said, brushing a hand through her braid. "Just briefly visible."

"But visibility is power."

"Sometimes," she said. "And sometimes it's danger."

Rami nodded, the levity fading. He understood. They all did.

As she stood there, listening to a violinist warm up in the adjoining gallery, she remembered being a girl of nine, painting flowers on the courtyard tiles with her mother. The sun had been bright. They had used cheap watercolors and laughed when the paint evaporated faster than they could work.

That day, her mother had said, *"We make things, so we don't disappear."*

Maryan clutched that memory like a lifeline.

She had not disappeared.

Not tonight.

Maryan was beyond tired. It was the kind of tired that lived in her bones, that no amount of sleep or coffee could dissolve. In the days after the Berlin opening, she found herself drifting between elation and emptiness. Her body ached from standing too long, her head from the bright lights and constant chatter, but more than anything, she felt drained from being looked at—really looked at—for the first time in years.

Her art had sparked something in people. She had seen it with her own eyes: the way strangers lingered before her canvases, the way their brows furrowed or their lips trembled, the way their eyes sometimes shone with unspilled tears. Rich patrons in pressed suits, students with secondhand coats, even fellow refugees who had slipped in quietly, curious to see one of their own on the wall—all of them had stopped and listened to what her brushstrokes had to say.

It was as though the paintings spoke words she could never allow herself to say out loud. Rage, grief, longing, defiance—things that had once been dangerous to utter in Tehran were now hanging openly in a gallery under halogen lights, and people were not turning away. They were listening.

For the longest time, Maryan felt that silence could break without punishment.

Then it happened, she woke to Rami pounding on her door, a folded newspaper clutched in his hand.

"Maryan!" he shouted from the hallway. "You're in the paper!"

Still groggy, she pulled on a sweater and opened the door. Rami shoved the newspaper toward her, his grin wide.

It was the *Berliner Zeitung*, near the back of the arts section. Not a feature, not even a column—just a small article, two paragraphs tucked between a review of a modern dance premiere and an announcement about a theater renovation.

But there it was. Her name. In print.

It described her as "a new young artist from Iran who had escaped the terrors of her homeland and found a voice through painting." It mentioned her three works by title, praised the emotional rawness, and suggested that her presence added "urgency and depth" to the Berlin art scene.

Maryan read it once, then again, her eyes tracing her own name as though it belonged to someone else.

Her throat tightened. Two paragraphs. That was all. Two small paragraphs in a sea of newsprint. But to her, it was enough to make the ground shift beneath her feet.

She remembered her father's art studio back in Tehran, write words and tape them to the wall.

"Every word matters," he used to say. "Every word is a witness."

She thought of him now, far away. She imagined his voice reading the article aloud. She imagined his pride, his quiet smile.

For the first time in years, she felt something close to hope.

Word spread quickly among her circle of friends. That evening, Camila showed up with a bottle of cheap champagne, followed by Rami with another. Then two more friends arrived, carrying paper cups, music from a speaker, and bags of pastries. It was not a party anyone had planned, but soon the small studio was alive with laughter and chatter.

Someone stuck the clipping from the newspaper to the wall with masking tape, right above the sink. "The first of many!" Camila declared, raising her glass.

Maryan smiled, though her chest felt tight. She was not used to being the center of joy.

They poured the champagne into plastic cups, and the bubbles fizzed over the edges. The room smelled of sugar, yeast, and citrus. Music played—Brazilian beats from Camila's phone, mixed later with Persian ballads Rami insisted on adding to the playlist.

They danced in the cramped space, knocking into chairs and canvases, laughing when they spilled drinks. Someone lit a candle stuck into a croissant like a makeshift cake, and they all sang loudly, off-key, not knowing what song they were supposed to be singing.

Maryan leaned against the wall, watching. She saw the way her friends looked at her—not with pity, but with pride. Not with suspicion, but with recognition.

Her art had given them something to celebrate. And through their joy, she began to feel it too.

Yet beneath the laughter, a quiet unease stirred in her.

She remembered other nights of noise—Tehran streets filled with chants, the pounding of boots, the flash of fire. She remembered the prison, where sound was pain, where laughter was stolen from mouths before it could form.

To be surrounded by joy now felt both intoxicating and terrifying.

Her friends toasted her name again and again. Each time she smiled, nodded, sipped, but inside she whispered to herself: *Don't trust it. Don't trust happiness. It can vanish in a second.*

Still, when Camila hugged her tightly and whispered, "This is just the beginning," Maryan let herself believe. Just a little.

In the quiet after everyone had gone, when the bottles were empty and the crumbs swept into the trash, Maryan sat alone on the floor. The newspaper clipping stared back at her from the wall.

She thought of all the places her art had already traveled—through the cracked walls of her prison cell, through the suffocating dark of the shipping crate, across borders and oceans, and finally here, to a whitewashed gallery in Berlin.

She thought of all the people who had seen it, who had felt it, who had recognized something in it that even she hadn't always recognized in herself.

She thought of her father. Of the stethoscope photo Armin had once mocked. Of her mother's trembling hands pouring tea. Of all the voices silenced in Iran, voices that would never reach this room.

And she realized something new.

Belief was not a sudden thing. It was not a firework. It was not a switch flipping on.

Belief was a slow thaw. It was the smallest shift in the chest, the quietest opening of a locked door.

Maryan began to believe—not in safety, not in permanence, not even in success. But in herself. In her ability to carry memory into color, to turn silence into shape, to speak without words and still be heard.

She wrapped a blanket around her shoulders and lay down on the floor beside her canvases. The studio smelled faintly of paint and champagne.

Her eyes closed, and for the first time in a long time, sleep came without dreams of chains.

Chapter 15

Snow and Canvas

She never thought she'd leave Europe. Let alone fly over the Atlantic, to a place she had only seen in Hollywood movies and protest footage. But there it was—in her inbox, translated into English, with a time difference that made the timestamp feel like a message from the future.

Subject: Invitation to Exhibit at the Minneapolis Institute of Art

The email was formal, gracious. The curatorial team had discovered her work through a Berlin arts foundation partnership. They were hosting a season-long exhibit titled **"Flight and Form: The Refugee as Artist"**—a survey of global voices shaped by exile, protest, and survival. They wanted her to participate. No, more than that. They wanted to feature her.

Maryan read the message three times. Her throat tightened. Her first thought wasn't pride—it was panic.

They'll never let me in. I'm Iranian.

She had no passport. Only a refugee ID. She hadn't even been approved for permanent residency in Germany yet. Her legal status was fragile like everything else in her life. Suspended in process.

But the museum had done their homework. They knew. And they had already arranged sponsorship through the State Department's cultural outreach wing. It was political—everything was—but also real.

Maryan emailed back. Her fingers trembled over the keyboard.

Yes. Thank you. I accept.

The flight from Berlin to Minneapolis was brutal. Twenty hours, two layovers, and a delayed landing that left her half-delirious and overstimulated.

But it was the snow that woke her up.

She had seen snow before, in Tehran and once in the mountains near Shiraz. But this was different—wider, colder, endless. Minneapolis in January was a frozen cathedral. Icy trees arched above highways. The streets sparkled under streetlamps like scenes from postcards or dreams. She pressed her face to the window of the museum-arranged car and stared.

The driver was an older man with a thick Minnesotan accent and a knit Vikings hat pulled over his ears.

"First time in America?" he asked.

She nodded.

"Well, welcome. Hope you brought a coat."

She had. A gift from her artist friends in Hamburg—a long black wool coat with deep pockets and a soft lining that made her feel like a movie character. She clutched it now like armor.

The museum put her in a boutique apartment near the Walker Art Center. Her room overlooked Loring Park, and she could see couples skating on a frozen pond below, their scarves trailing behind them in bursts of color.

It was beautiful.

It was terrifying.

Maryan stood by the window that first night and whispered her mother's name. *Nare,*

This was a world her mother never saw. Would never see. Maryan ached with the unfairness of it, the cruelty that she was here—free, honored—while her mother's body was likely buried in an unmarked grave in the outskirts of Tehran.

She went to bed without eating.

The next morning, she met the curatorial team.

They were kind. Eager. Almost reverent.

"Your pieces speak to things we can't even articulate," said one of the lead curators, a Black woman named Chelsea with bright green glasses and an unmistakable air of command softened by warmth. "Pain. Transformation. Memory."

Maryan didn't know how to respond. She wasn't used to being praised so openly, and certainly not in English. Her German wasn't even fluent yet. Her English, even shakier.

But she had learned one thing as a refugee: say less. Let others project what they want.

So, she nodded and said softly, "Thank you. I am grateful."

They walked her through the gallery. Her work had been given an entire wing. Tall white walls. Spotlights positioned like starlight. The largest painting—*The Place Where the Women Went*—stretched across twelve feet. Layers of reds and blacks and ochres spiraled into a central blur that looked like a storm, or a bruise.

Beneath it, in sharp type:
Maryan Darya. Mixed Media on Canvas. 2025.

The curator looked at her. "Do you want to say something at the opening?"

Maryan hesitated. Public speaking wasn't her strength— not in English, not even in Farsi anymore. She had spent too long being silenced to find comfort in standing before a microphone. And yet, something inside her wanted to speak.

"I'll try," she said.

The opening night was full of contradictions.

Hundreds of guests filled the Minneapolis Institute of Art's soaring halls. Gallery-goers with wine glasses and statement scarves. Students taking notes. Reporters.

Professors. Donors. Immigrants. Survivors. Activists. And—unexpectedly—a few Iranians.

Maryan recognized the accents immediately. One older man spoke with the particular Tehranian lilt her father used to have when he was nervous.

"I had to come," he said when he met her. "We heard about you from BBC Persian. You give us hope."

Hope.

She had no idea what to do with that word anymore. It felt like a delicate thing. Breakable. But she bowed slightly and thanked him.

When it was time for her to speak, Chelsea introduced her.

"This is a woman who has carried war in her body. Who crossed borders not just with her feet, but with her art. Please welcome Maryan Darya."

There was applause. Warm. Encouraging. Maryan stepped up to the podium. Her knees felt like water.

She looked out over the crowd.

They were all watching her. Not as a refugee. Not as a headline. But as a creator.

She took a breath.

"I used to think art was something soft," she began, her accent thick but her voice clear. "Something we do for beauty. But I learned it can be a weapon. A shield. A map."

She paused. She saw someone in the front row crying.

"When I was in prison, I drew in my head. I imagined colors when all I saw was gray. I imagined shapes when all I felt was pain. That's how I survived. That's what these pieces are. Memory, and resistance."

Silence.

Then applause again. This time louder. Not polite. Deep.

The next few days were a whirlwind.

Maryan felt as though she had been dropped into someone else's life—one filled with questions, microphones, and lights. Not overwhelming, not yet, but strange. She had been invisible for so long that visibility itself felt like a costume she wasn't sure fit her.

She gave interviews—small ones at first. A college radio station, where two earnest undergraduates with oversized headphones asked her what color she thought grief was. She hesitated, then said, "Gray, but layered, like smoke." They leaned forward, eyes wide, as if she had just given them the answer to an exam question.

Then NPR Minnesota. A studio with clean lines and serious voices, where the host introduced her with words like *courage* and *resilience.* Maryan sat stiffly, her hands folded in her lap, afraid she might fumble the English, but the questions were kind. They asked not about politics, not about scars, but about paint. About the way memory took shape on canvas. She relaxed. She even laughed once—soft, surprised at the sound of it leaving her own throat.

Then there was the podcast. Two gay Iranian-Americans, brothers, living in Minneapolis. They arrived at her apartment lobby with a box of donuts—pink-frosted, sprinkled, some with fillings she couldn't identify—and smiles that disarmed her instantly.

"We heard you might be homesick," one said. "So we brought sugar. It helps."

They set up their recording gear in the apartment lobby, wires trailing across the table, and began with questions in Farsi before switching into English for their audience. They asked her about Tehran, about Berlin, about the way her art held silence as much as sound. They teased each other, interrupted each other, and made her laugh in a way that felt like family.

When the microphones were off, one of them leaned across the table.

"Have you seen Lake Superior yet?"

She blinked. "No."

"You should. It's like standing at the edge of the world. Come with us on Monday—the museum's closed."

Maryan hesitated. She had not traveled outside cities since arriving in Europe. She was used to tight streets, to urban shadows. But something in their eyes—something playful, something safe—made her nod.

"Yes," she said. "I'd like that."

On Monday morning, they picked her up in a battered Subaru that smelled of coffee and winter air. Snow clung to the edges of the windshield.

"Buckle up," one brother said, grinning. "It's three hours north. You'll see a lot of nothing. But it's beautiful nothing."

Maryan pressed her forehead to the glass, watching. In Tehran, winter was gray and biting, but not like this. Here, the land itself seemed asleep under snow.

They stopped at a gas station where everything smelled of fried food and diesel. Maryan wandered the aisles, staring at shelves of beef jerky, candy bars, rows of gum. A universe of choices for travelers. She picked a pack of spearmint gum, her fingers trembling slightly as she handed over coins. Small rituals of belonging.

Back on the highway, the brothers told her stories—about growing up in Minnesota, about their parents leaving Shiraz in the 1980s, about how they still mixed Farsi and English at home.

"You'll hear it when we fight," one joked. "Farsi curses land harder."

Maryan laughed, surprising herself again. She hadn't realized how much she missed the sound of her language in casual, joking tones. In Berlin, Farsi often came to her only in whispers, in hushed memories. Here, in this noisy car, it was alive.

By early afternoon, they crested a hill, and suddenly the horizon opened.

The lake stretched before them, vast and frozen, its surface a pale silver under the winter sun. It looked like an ocean—a borderless expanse, cruel and majestic.

Maryan stepped out into the wind, her coat whipping around her. The air was sharp, burning her cheeks, but she barely noticed. She had seen snow before—in Tehran, in the mountains near Shiraz—but never this. This was water made into stone, motion trapped mid-breath.

"It reminds me of the Caspian," she whispered.

Her companions nodded, understanding.

She thought of standing ankle-deep with her mother years ago, waves tugging at their skirts, her mother's laughter mingling with the salt air. Collecting shells before the morality police appeared, shouting about modesty. Her mother's hand closing over hers, both of them pretending not to be afraid.

Now, here she was, half a world away, the cold biting just as fiercely, the shells replaced by snowflakes melting on her gloves. She bent down, scooped a handful of frozen sand, and let it spill through her fingers.

The brothers took pictures, their breath steaming in the air. One insisted she pose with the lake behind her. She smiled—not the practiced half-smile of openings and interviews, but real, wide, her teeth bared to the cold.

The camera clicked. The wind roared. And for a moment, she felt both small and infinite.

They drove back at dusk, headlights cutting through the blue-gray twilight. Maryan sat quietly in the backseat, her heart still full of the lake's vastness. She felt as if some part of her had been rinsed clean by the cold.

In her apartment that night, she looked at the photos they had sent her—her own face smiling against the immensity of water and ice. She hardly recognized herself.

She whispered to the empty room, "Maman, I wish you could see me."

And for the first time since leaving Tehran, the thought didn't bring only grief. It brought a thin thread of peace, fragile but real.

As she climbed into bed, her laptop sputtered sounds.

Tempted not to open it, she slowly did.

Urgently she pressed the wrong keys, almost losing the connection, when she saw it was her father's friend.

He shared no details, no reasons, only a simple message.

"Your sister is alive, she is out, in Turkey, we expect more news in a week or two, but she is safe."

Alive.

This was beyond belief, was she in bed dreaming.

No, her sister was alive.

Maryan covered her mouth and sobbed.

Chapter16

Protesting Freedom

Tina could not believe it, two years in, now in her third year of college.

It seemed like only yesterday she left Minneapolis for Madison.

In those two years she found a home, a real home.

Tina Sanders grew up between two worlds—one made of pine and water, the other of asphalt and noise.
Her mother used to say Ely, Minnesota, home of the boundary waters, was paradise. She said it so often, with such a practiced mix of pride and melancholy, that Tina could never tell if she believed it or was trying to convince herself.

Their house in Minneapolis carried the ghosts of that northern paradise like fading perfume. The walls were lined with old photographs—her mother, sunburned and smiling, reeling in a walleye twice the size of her arm; Tina, six years old, in an oversized life jacket, holding up a wet paddle as though it were a trophy; her father, blurry and distant, in only a handful of frames, always half-turned away from the camera, half-belonging to somewhere else.

Between those photos hung Jim Brandenburg prints—wolves in snow, loons mirrored in black water, birches painted in morning light. Her mother said Brandenburg was the only artist who truly understood the north. "You can smell the air in his pictures," she'd whisper. "That's what Ely feels like."

Tina would stand in the hallway sometimes, fingertips grazing the frames, trying to smell that air.

But Minneapolis had its own weather—bus exhaust, rain on pavement, Thai food from the restaurant down the block. It wasn't wild, but it was alive. Her mother said they'd moved for "a more exciting life."

Tina wasn't sure who "we" meant.

Her father, Dave Sanders, still lived in Ely, or somewhere near it. He was an outfitter—ran canoe trips through the Boundary Waters, guided tourists with shiny paddles and waterproof cameras through a land that belonged more to silence than to people. When Tina was little, she thought "outfitter" meant explorer, a kind of modern-day pioneer who slept under the stars and ate only fish he caught himself. Her mother never corrected her, though sometimes she'd roll her eyes when the phone rang from a number with an Ely area code and say, "Well, your mountain man finally remembered civilization."

Dave sent postcards instead of presents. The handwriting always looked rushed, like the words were sliding downhill. *Hope you're doing great, kiddo. Lake was glass this morning. You'd love it. – Dad.*

Once, when Tina was nine, he took her up for a week. It was June, the air thick with mosquitoes and pine sap. They slept in a canvas tent near the water, and at night he'd tell stories about the voyageurs—men who carried canoes across miles of wilderness with song and sweat. He spoke

like he was talking about saints.
That week was the closest she'd ever come to understanding him.

He never yelled, never lied, never promised much of anything. He was just gone more than he was there.

Though popular in high school, being 5-8, blonde with blue eyes and a track star helped, she never fit in, oh she had friends, but not the kind you are intimate with, more city friends.

She did have a love in high school, Thomas Quinn.

Him and his brother Quincy Quinn, were just called QT or cutie, but the girls at Southwest, where the two brothers went to school.

She truly did love him, but they wanted different things, he wanted a life she did not want, so like most things in Tina's life, she let go of him to find herself and she did.

She found her self at the University of Madison in Wisconsin.

Her first week at Madson was a blur.

To this day, everyone called her the goat. Not because she was the greatest of all time, but because of a literal goat.

See the first week of college actually the third day, she found herself.

She had just wanted a cold brew, maybe a blueberry muffin from the co-op café she'd started going to because someone on her dorm floor said Starbucks was "late-stage capitalism in a cup." But the quad was a different world today—drums beating, flags waving, bodies moving in rhythm and rebellion.

A flyer had slapped against her shin like divine intervention:

"FREE PALESTINE: Emergency Protest. Noon. Library Steps."

Tina read it three times. The words made her heart thump a little harder. She'd read *half* of a Vox article on Gaza the night before, then fell asleep watching a TikTok explainer by a guy in a balaclava who made politics look... kind of hot. Something was happening, and she wanted to be a part of it.

Ten minutes later, Tina was there—blonde ponytail high, Doc Martens tight, wearing her "Girls Just Wanna Have Fundamental Human Rights" T-shirt. She was trying to look serious, but not *too* serious. She was starting to become liberal but still smiled too much in tense situations.

The protest was already in full swing. Someone was screaming through a megaphone, their words bouncing off the clock tower. A group of students chanted back, their eyes blazing with urgency. Tina stood at the edge, clutching her oat milk latte like a talisman.

"Hold this," a girl with septum rings and a Che Guevara tote shoved a sign into Tina's hand. It read: "ZIONISM = COLONIALISM" in red paint. Tina blinked.

"Is it okay that I'm holding this?" she asked nervously.

The girl had already vanished into the crowd like a protest ninja.

Soon, the protest morphed into what Tina could only describe as *a movement that forgot what it was moving toward.* Someone had climbed the lion statue and started screaming in Arabic. Someone else was passing out vegan cupcakes that said "RESIST" in purple frosting. A guy in a banana costume—Tina still wasn't sure why—was yelling about the military-industrial complex.

And then, the goat appeared.

Not metaphorically. A real goat. On a leash. Wearing a keffiyeh.

"Who *brought a goat?*" Tina whispered to no one.

The goat bleated defiantly, standing atop a bench like it had revolutionary intent. The crowd roared. Tina found herself cheering too, though she wasn't sure if it was for the goat or for the chant now rising like a tide:

"From the river to the sea—Palestine will be free!"

Tina mouthed the words cautiously, wondering if she was being brave or reckless. Her Political Science professor had *not* covered this in "Intro to Global Conflict." A guy with dreadlocks handed her a sharpie and told her to write a slogan on the campus sidewalk. She froze.

She ended up writing: "Stop Being Mean :("

At some point, the police and campus security showed up, but they were wearing bright vests and holding zip ties like they wanted someone to *do* something. Then someone did.

Soon a boy wearing full black, hurled a bag of flour into the air like it was tear gas. A gust of wind carried it straight into Tina's face. She coughed, blindly stumbled toward a bench, tripped over the goat's leash, and fell into a pile of cardboard signs.

That's when someone shoved a megaphone into her hands.

"Speak!" a girl yelled, shoving sunglasses onto Tina's face. "Say something!"

Tina blinked. She was on the library steps now. The goat was beside her like a war general. The crowd hushed. The megaphone squawked in her trembling hands.

"I just think," Tina began, "we should listen to each other more. And also maybe—uh—read more books. About things."

Silence.

Then an eruption of cheers.

She wasn't sure if they were clapping ironically, but someone threw a sunflower crown on her head, and another person took a selfie with her. For thirty seconds, Tina felt like the face of the revolution.

An hour later, she was back in her dorm, goat hoof prints on her jeans and her inbox full of new Instagram followers.

She opened her laptop, Googled "history of Palestine conflict," and promised herself she'd actually read the whole article this time.

She had just started reading when her roommate, Melissa, walked in, earbuds in, mouth stuffed with pita chips.

"Whoa," Melissa said, pulling the earbuds out. "You look like you got jumped by a food co-op."

Tina pointed to the goat prints. "There was a goat."

Melissa dropped her backpack. "Please tell me it was wearing a tiny protest sign."

"No. Just a keffiyeh. And rage."

Melissa laughed, then sat on her bed. "You gonna go full activist now? Change your major to Global Justice Studies?"

Tina shrugged. "I don't know. Maybe. It felt important. Like, I don't even know everything, but I want to. I want to figure out what's true."

Melissa nodded, surprisingly thoughtful. "Good. Just... don't get swept up. Stay curious. Not just loud."

Tina stared at the search bar. "Working on it."

And work on it she did.

After two solid years of protests, and fighting for human rights, she finally felt like she had found herself.

It only took, changing her major twice, dying her hair pink (then black, then back again), and memorized the names of more political prisoners in Gaza and Chiapas than she had ever learned in U.S. history class.

During this time she'd made friends—real ones. Friends who showed up to rallies in minus-ten weather and slept on the floors of administrative buildings demanding fossil fuel divestment. Friends who passed around books like *The Wretched of the Earth* and *Pedagogy of the Oppressed* like sacred texts.

There was Jada from Milwaukee, who brought her to her first BLM meeting.

There was Lior—yes, an Israeli, but a "good one"—who argued passionately for a one-state solution and had taught her the history of the Nakba with tears in his eyes.

And of course, there was Zahra, half-Iranian, who had introduced her to Friends of Palestine.

Madison wasn't just school. It was a revolution.

And Tina knew she was meant for more than papers and exams.

She wanted to change the world.

Now she had the chance.

The group chat lit up at 6:04 a.m.

Zahra: *They hit Tehran. Bombing last night. Israeli jets. Civilian casualties.*

Jada: *What the actual fuck.*

Lior: *Can confirm. Multiple injuries. One of my cousins is in the region. Not a weapons lab. A bakery.*

Zahra: *We have to respond.*

Tina's heart pounded as she scrolled through the attached article. The headline blurred, but the image stuck: rubble, smoke, and a bloodied doll lying face-down in the dust.

She didn't need to think. She knew what needed to be done.

Tina: *Protest. Public. Big. Make it messy. Make it count.*

Zahra: *Minneapolis. Maryan Darya exhibit. She's Iranian. We show up there.*

Tina: *Perfect. Artists want truth, right? Let's give it to them.*

---

24 hours later Tina stood at the center of a crowd gathering outside the Minneapolis Institute of Art, her scarf tight around her face, a bullhorn in her hand.

"THEY WANT TO BOMB OUR STORIES—BUT WE WRITE LOUDER!"

The crowd roared.

Her voice echoed off the marble columns. She could see security huddled near the museum entrance, walkie-talkies clutched like rosaries. Some museum patrons turned away. Others stopped to listen. Some filmed her on their phones. She didn't care.

Signs waved behind her:

"Stop Bombing Iran"

"Palestine, Iran, Yemen—One Struggle, One Fight!"

"U.S.–Israel: War Crimes Have No Borders"

But the best one was hers.

"Maryan Darya—Speak Out."

Tina hadn't meant it as an attack. She loved Maryan's paintings. She had seen them online—a haunting fusion of expressionism and protest art. She thought, *surely this woman understands*. Surely an Iranian artist—someone who had been in prison—wouldn't stay silent now.

But when they asked inside, museum staff said Maryan wasn't taking questions. "She's not political," one of the docents had said.

Tina seethed at that.

Everyone was political.

Silence was political.

Maryan needed to speak or was she part of the problem.

The protest tripled in size by late afternoon. Local Palestinian activists joined. So did students from the University of Minnesota. A drum circle formed near the entrance. Someone handed Tina a megaphone made from a traffic cone. The air smelled like chai, incense, and snow-damp wool.

She saw someone in a keffiyeh holding a candle. She saw another wearing a "Silence = Death" patch.

It felt like the edge of something.

Zahra grabbed her arm. "Museum just released a statement. Vague as hell. 'Sorrow over loss of life.' That's it."

Tina gritted her teeth. "We push harder."

She took the bullhorn again. "We will not be quiet for their comfort! We are not here for vague condolences. We want truth. We want solidarity. And we want it from the artists they celebrate on these walls!"

Cheers again. Foot stomps. Someone banged a paint bucket like a war drum.

It happened on the tenth day of her exhibition.

Maryan was in the museum's east wing, sketching quietly in the gallery space where her paintings hung. The air was calm, museum-calm: muted voices, distant footsteps, the soft hum of the climate control system keeping the canvases safe. The smell of fresh paint still lingered faintly in the air—hers, drying on a new canvas in the corner. A piece she hadn't planned to create in America, but one that insisted on existing the moment she touched her brush down.

Then came the first sound—chanting.

At first, she thought it was a school group, the excited shuffling voices of middle schoolers echoing near the entry. But the rhythm was too sharp. Too urgent. Too angry.

Then she heard the words.

"No more war! No more lies! U.S.–Israel, hands off lives!"

"Stop bombing Iran!"

Maryan stiffened. Her pencil slid off the edge of the page. She stood, brush still in her hand. Her breath came faster.

A museum staffer rushed in, headset pressed to his ear, face flushed with nervous energy. He looked barely older than a college intern.

"There's a protest," he said breathlessly. "In the lobby. Security is handling it. Peaceful so far."

Maryan blinked. "Protesting what?"

The man hesitated. "There was a bombing. In Tehran. Israeli airstrike, allegedly targeting weapons development sites. But... civilian casualties. Over fifty dead. Maybe more."

Maryan's chest constricted. Her lungs suddenly couldn't find the air. She gripped the edge of the display wall to steady herself. The word *Tehran* cracked through her like ice.

"Is there a list?" she asked. Her voice didn't sound like her own.

"Not yet," he said gently. "But media outlets are already trying to confirm. The museum's comms team is drafting a response."

She closed her eyes. Her fingers curled around the edge of the plywood display until they throbbed.

Tehran. Again. Her home. Her city. Her mother's grave.

She felt it all at once: the smell of jasmine near Evin prison, her father's friend with joyous news, the sound of helicopters. Bombs now, not in Kurdistan. Not in Gaza. But on the rooftops of her childhood.

It wasn't just the weather that shifted. It was energy.

The museum had decided not to stop the small protest in the lobby.

Tina led the group that entered—fifteen or twenty of them—into the lobby. Some took off their boots and left them by the door. Some kept their signs. Others knelt, silently, forming a circle.

Guards watched closely but didn't interfere.

They were inside now. Inside the machine. Inside the temple of culture.

And then the impossible happened.

Maryan appeared.

She walked into the lobby, alone, wearing a long coat and no makeup. Her eyes were sunken. Her hands trembled slightly as she looked at the group.

Tina stepped forward, heart thudding in her chest.

"You have power," Tina shouted. "You can speak. People listen to you. Your silence is evil, you are behaving entitled, and evil."

Tina's voice getting angry, "You are being entitled, you are being on the side of the invaders with your silence."

Loud cheers from the background voices.

"You have no choice but to speak, or we will ensure no one gets in to see anything until you do" – Tina growled.

"Answer me!" – Tina shouted.

Guard's began to move and surround Maryan.

Maryan silent, shook her head, and simply said "I will speak tomorrow." and slowly walked away.

Tina not satisfied but seeing the air come out of sails of her fellow comrades, simply lowered her head and walked out the door.

Chapter 17

The Call

Tina sat up, rubbing her eyes, and stretched her arms wide until her shoulder blades popped. Her poster paint-stained fingers left faint streaks on the pale gray sheets. Her stomach growled, but she didn't move. The adrenaline of the protest had faded, and all that remained was a strange hollowness.

Then her phone buzzed on the desk, lighting up the dim room with its screen.

FaceTime Request: Thomas Quinn.

She stared at it. Her heart thudded once, hard. It was 11:06 p.m. What the hell?

She hadn't spoken to Thomas since before the semester started. There had been a few likes on Instagram, a quick emoji reply to a story of her campus bookstore haul. But this? A FaceTime call? Now?

She could ignore it. She could pretend to be asleep.

But the curiosity itched at her like the elastic of the flower crown. And part of her—maybe the same part that still wore his hoodie when no one was around—wanted to hear his voice.

She tapped "Accept."

The screen shifted. There he was—Thomas, in full glowing resolution. His dark hair tousled, a backwards cap half-on, and a half-empty bottle of Miller Lite on the table behind him. He looked like he was in his parents' basement, the grainy Minnesota Vikings flag flapping slightly from the ceiling fan draft.

"TINA!" he shouted like she was on the other side of a stadium.

She winced. "Jesus, Thomas, lower the volume."

He grinned. That same grin. Cocky, crooked. "Was that YOU I saw on Facebook?"

She blinked. "What are you talking about?"

He turned his phone screen around. It was a screenshot of her at the Art museum. Thomas added the words above the picture "Liberal Arts Student Goes Full Radical. Parents Weep."

Tina groaned, flopping back onto her pillow.

"Are you okay?" he asked. "Do you... like, do you even know what you were chanting?"

"I mean, kinda," she said. "It was a Free Palestine protest and a protest to help Iran. There were like, a hundred people there."

"You know that's complicated, right? That whole situation's, like, a thousand years old."

She sat up straighter, adjusting the crown. "Yeah, I do know it's complicated. That's why I'm learning about it. Because it's not just ancient history—people are dying now."

Thomas leaned back in his recliner. The worn pleather squeaked. "By shouting into a megaphone?"

She narrowed her eyes. "Yes"

"He laughed. "What's next? Gonna burn the flag and rename your dorm 'Che Hall'?"

"It's not funny, Thomas," she said. "This isn't a joke to me."

"I'm not trying to make fun of you. I'm just... surprised. You go to college and suddenly you're a revolutionary in Doc Martens."

She corrected him instinctively. "They're vegan leather."

He smirked. "Of course they are."

She took a deep breath, pushing back against the rising tension. "I didn't go to that protest because I want to tear things down. I went because I care. Because the world is broken and I don't want to be ignorant anymore."

He looked at her for a moment, eyes softer than before. "Alright. So... explain it to me. Seriously. Give me the Tina Breakdown."

She hesitated. "You want me to explain why I was protesting?"

"Yeah. Educate me, Professor. Just... no weird made-up words. I mean the art center, is part of my bosses' clients, so yea, explain it to me."

She chuckled despite herself. "Fine. Basic version? The Palestinian territories—especially Gaza—have been under military occupation for decades. People can't move freely, homes are demolished, infrastructure's bombed constantly. Two million people live in Gaza with restricted access to water, medicine, even electricity. It's like an open-air prison."

"And Hamas?" he asked, raising a brow.

"I don't support terrorism," she said firmly. "No one I marched with did. We were chanting for a ceasefire, for dignity, for an end to the occupation. Wanting justice doesn't make you anti-Israel."

"But that 'river to the sea' chant—come on. You know what that means."

"At the time, I didn't," she said, cheeks flushing. "It felt powerful. Everyone was shouting it. Later I learned how loaded it is. Some say it means the end of Israel. Others say it's about freedom across all borders. I'm still figuring that out."

"At least you're honest," Thomas said. "I'll give you that."

There was a silence. Not awkward. Just... weighty.

"Do you remember in tenth grade," she said, "when you got mad at that football player for kneeling during the anthem?"

"Yup. Still think that was disrespectful."

"But then when people protested in the streets, you said it was too disruptive. And when we wrote letters to the school board, you said it was a waste of time."

He frowned.

"So what's the right way to protest?" she asked gently.

He took a sip from his beer. "Fair question. I guess I just don't like when it feels like people are blaming America for everything."

"I'm not blaming everything on America. But we have done some messed-up stuff. Sometimes being patriotic means being critical."

He sighed. "You sound like your mom."

She laughed. "She did give me *The Shock Doctrine* for Christmas."

He groaned. "That book gave me a headache."

"Yeah, well, it made me want to scream into a pillow. Then go scream into a megaphone."

He smiled.

"I don't want to fight," she said softly. "I just want people to listen. And care. Even when it's messy."

They sat quietly. The hum of a football game played faintly in the background of his end. On hers, the radiator pinged like a ticking bomb.

"Can I ask you something?" she said.

"Shoot."

"Why do you always assume protest means destruction? Maybe it means... healing."

He looked away. "Maybe. Or maybe I'm just scared that if we tear down everything, there won't be anything left."

"Maybe we just want to rebuild better."

He glanced back. "You're still hot as hell, you know."

She smiled. "Thomas."

"I'm just saying. I can disagree with you and still remember how you looked at prom."

"That was a lifetime ago."

"Not to me."

She didn't say anything. Her phone buzzed with a new message. *Free Palestine Chat Group: Meeting tomorrow at 9. Bring art ideas for posters.*

"If you're ever back in Minneapolis... to not protest" Thomas began.

"I'll look you up," she said. "Deal."

"Later, T."

She hung up. The screen went black.

Tina exhaled deeply and leaned back on her pillow.. Her fingers still smelled of acrylic paint. Her heartbeat with contradiction and longing and something like hope.

The world was on fire. But maybe, just maybe, she was starting to see the map.

And somewhere on it... maybe Thomas was, too.

Meanwhile, in Minneapolis...

Thomas didn't sleep.

He'd ended the call with a joke, like always. Flirted just enough to leave the door open. But now he was staring at the same Facebook post he'd shown her—the one of Tina on the library steps, eyes wild with purpose, one fist in the air, the goat chewing a protest banner behind her.

She looked so... alive. Charged. Different from the girl who used to sneak into Vikings games with him using borrowed IDs and fake passes from his brother's college friend.

There was something about her now. Something bigger.

It made him proud.

And afraid.

He knew guys at work who would laugh if they saw her like that. Say something crude. Call her a "woke snowflake" or worse. And Thomas had never been the kind of guy to argue. He liked to blend in, to go along. It was easier. Safer.

But Tina... she never played it safe. Not anymore.

He knew he still had feelings for her, not like the old, but something new. Something that was not love, or infatuation, it was something he could not understand.

"She broke up with me." He thought.

But still, should he ask her out on a date, call her, go see her.

Thomas felt he needed to wait, wait until she texted him or called him, otherwise it would seem desperate, something he was not.

Sure there were lots of girls, and girls for the night, but nothing at all what he wanted. He wanted that connection, that special feeling you get when you know the person.

Checking one last time.

He opened his texts. Scrolled to her name. Hovered.

No new message. Not yet.

Maybe later.

Maybe next time.

For now, he shut off his phone, leaned back, and closed his eyes.

But sleep didn't come.

All he could see was her face. Her voice. The fire in her eyes. The map she was drawing in her mind—and the small, persistent question rising in his chest:

Where did he belong on that map?

Tina, for her part, felt that spark after talking with Thomas. But it was different, she was different.

She needed to grow up, needed to become a leader, a true leader at college.

As part of the leadership, a lot rode on her shoulders, including meetings and every social media postings.

She did not have time for a relationship, no matter how much she wanted it.

She had lots of guys at the rallies ask her out, lots of hook ups, lots of men chasing her, and more than a few women, but still Thomas represented her first love.

But she thought, also her past.

Her past when she did not understand the world.

She now understood the world and her responsibility to it.

She needed to protest, she needed to show America that the American police, were not the good guys, they needed to be removed, just like Israel from Palestine.

So for now Thomas would need to wait, she needed to be free to change the world.

Chapter 18

Boran The Queen of Iran

The auditorium, barely able to hold 250 people, was overflowing the next day, along the side the local press with cameras.

Tina arrived early, wearing a red scarf and sitting with her comrades Zahra and Lior near the front. She wasn't sure what to expect. She hoped for a call to arms. A denouncement. Something to go viral, something to drive her as a student leader across the United States, the next Greta.

The rest of the hall was a mix of protestors, supporters and staff. Some wore protest gear—keffiyehs, black coats, taped-over mouths. Others wore art-world scarves and silver jewelry.

Maryan stepped up to the podium. Her hair was pulled back. Her coat draped over her like armor. Her face was pale but still.

This time, there were no flashbulbs. No champagne. No press kits.

Just people.

"The women of Iran are powerful, despite their present situation. Most of you do not know Iranian history, and that there were four queens of Iran, leading an empire more powerful than Europe at the time."

"Women lead Iran, when Western women, were stuck at home. "

"Today, due to the revolution, Islam has become a terrorizing force upon the women of Iran."

"What you take for granted such as protesting, wearing clothing you want to wear, going to church and education are things you take for granted."

"I attended a simple protest, to not to be forced to wear clothing."

"For that I was arrested, beaten, assaulted, starved and denied water."

"The leadership of Iran is evil, they have used Islam to control and destroy women. Like they do in Afghanistan, Syria, Gaza and other locations. "

"I am saddened by the bombing of innocents."

"I am not a politician,", her voice clear and unflinching. "But I come from a country where art has always been political. Where women write poems under their breath. Where music is banned in places. Where colors mean danger."

She took a breath. Her hands trembled, but she didn't stop.

"I was in prison for drawing art, for standing up for women, for the simple act of saying no."

"The art I draw now, represents truth." Maryan continued.

"Art is a medium in which all of us can share the truth of Iran. I never wanted to be an artist, I wanted to be a doctor, but a protest changed the course of my life."

Tina now bouncing in her chair, as there is no condemnation of American yet, what was she waiting for.

Tina gave Maryan a dark stare, but Maryan continued.

"When I was in prison, I saw what bombs do. Whether dropped by America, Israel, or Iran. Bombs do not liberate. They bury. They erase. They kill children."

The crowd held its breath.

"I do not speak for Iran. I cannot. Iran speaks through its grief, every day. Through the mothers who bury their sons, and the students who vanish. Through the women who chant in courtyards before they are dragged away."

She scanned the room. People leaned forward.

"But I will not be silent just because I am afraid. I am afraid. But I will still speak."

A man in the third row stood. "Will you condemn Israel?"

Maryan paused. She saw the trap. She saw the truth. She stepped forward.

"I will condemn any government that kills civilians. That bombs homes. That treats children like targets. I condemn violence. From wherever it comes."

There was silence. Then someone clapped. Then more.

A protestor in the second row shouted, "Say their names!"

Maryan's hands trembled. She pulled out the paper.

"These are some of the names confirmed dead from yesterday's bombing," she said, and began to read.

One by one. Thirty-two names. Some full. Some only initials. Ages listed when known. The youngest was four.

By the time she finished, there wasn't a dry eye in the room.

Tina then stood up, and shouted, "Why will you not condemn the Israeli genocide on your people."

Maryan, in shock at the arrogance, stayed silent.

Tina continued, "The Iran leadership is peaceful, they have not dropped bombs except in self-defense, and you say nothing."

Maryan had enough, "That peaceful regime kills women, for speaking out, they destroy art, they rape those who speak into silence. My art speaks for those that suffer, if you want to see what the regime does just look at suffering, the poems, the art, the songs of its victims."

Maryan continued, "This regime must be toppled, by who I do not care, if Israel topples it, I do not care. Iran belongs to the women, to the children, to the artists, to the song writers, to the poets, not to a bunch of religious zealots, who think women are property."

Angry and shocked, Tina continued.

"No Iran is peaceful, yes women deserve freedom, but America needs to be put in its place. American leaders need to go to jail, to be removed and their wealth with it. America needs to end as it is."

Maryan in shock just stared.

Tina continued, "it is on you to speak, as the dead can not."

Finally Maryan had enough.

"You want to see me speak, then let me show you this. "stated Maryan.

"I want to walk all of you through the art of Iran."

The lights then dimmed. The crowd grew silent.

The silence happened so fast, Tina had no choice but to sit.

Maryan brought up a slide show, with the most expressive art Minneapolis had seen in generations.

Walking the once noisy crowd through each piece, you could hear crying throughout the auditorium.

After an hour Maryan was completed. She wished the crowd goodbye and walked off the stage.

Tina and the protestors slowly walked out.

That night Maryan sat in her apartment with the curtains drawn tight, watching news footage of the bombing again and again. A reporter's voice narrated over clips of rubble. A child was pulled from the debris. Someone screamed off-camera. Her sister sent a voice note—he was safe in Istanbul, but a cousin was dead.

"It doesn't end," Maryan thought. "It just changes shape."

Maryan cried for the first time in weeks. Deep, heaving sobs that came from some buried chamber inside her.

Then, at 3:41 a.m., she sat at the she had an idea for a new piece.

In the day that followed, the museum received both hate mail and donations. Some accused Maryan of antisemitism. Others of cowardice. Others still called her brave, naïve, radical, moderate, dangerous, inspiring. The words blurred together. She stopped reading most of them.

But one message stood out.

It came from a young Iranian girl in Canada.

"I didn't know it was okay to feel angry and still make something beautiful," it read. "Your paintings made me cry. Your voice made me believe. Thank you."

Maryan printed the email.

She taped it above her desk in the temporary studio they'd given her.

Then she picked up a new brush.

And painted again.

This time, not from memory.

From fire.

____

Chapter 19

Sparks

The protest became a memory, folded into museum press releases and activist Instagram reels. Hashtags that once surged through timelines like a tidal wave now sat buried beneath newer outrages, newer causes, newer spectacles. For a few weeks she had been a name, a headline, an image printed on glossy newsprint: the refugee artist who stood against violence, who called out Tehran's cruelty, who read aloud the names of the dead.

But the tide of attention ebbed, as tides always do. People moved on.

Some critics, mostly older voices in conservative exile circles, still referred to her dismissively—"that refugee painter who stands against Iran's people." As though her mourning for the bombed-out neighborhoods of Tehran and Shiraz, her grief for the silenced voices of girls beaten in the streets, were some betrayal of homeland pride. Their comments appeared under online reviews, small and venomous, but fewer each week. The world forgot, or perhaps the world simply shifted its gaze elsewhere.

Maryan didn't.

Every morning, before she walked to the museum, she lit a candle in her room. A small ritual, stubborn and private. Flame, wax, smoke—the elements tied her to memory. She whispered her mother's name, her sister's name, her father's. She whispered to the unknown grave that might or might not exist in some quiet Iranian cemetery. She whispered to the sea, to Berlin where her past clung, to Tehran where her youth had been ripped apart.

Then she dressed, wrapped her scarf, packed her paints. She checked her phone obsessively for news: about protests, about prisoner releases, about her sister's visa case that had now been "under review" for seven endless months. A simple approval could reunite them. A simple denial could sever them forever.

Still, she painted.

She painted until her fingers ached, palms raw from turpentine and pigment. She stained her nails black and blue with charcoal, rubbed her skin red from scrubbing oils off each night. Her canvases grew heavier, their textures layered like wounds that refused to heal. Silhouettes appeared then disappeared, swallowed under brush strokes, only to reemerge as ghosts when the light struck at an angle. Faces half-hidden, bodies blurred, figures that seemed to walk into the canvas only to be dragged back inside.

The gallery staff, sympathetic if somewhat wary of her intensity, let her use the loading dock behind the west wing. It was a cold space, concrete underfoot, drafty in winter, but cavernous enough for her massive canvases. The echo of her brush against linen sounded like footsteps in an empty hall. Trucks rumbled in and out, workers shouting, crates being wheeled past—but she stayed at her corner, headphones in, lost in the kind of labor that numbed her grief into color and form.

That morning she was crouched on the floor, experimenting with soaked linen streaked with charcoal. A song played on her Bluetooth speaker, a haunting Farsi folk tune her mother used to hum while washing rice or chopping herbs. The melody curved through memory like smoke.

Then the sound of wheels. A ladder scraping. Boots.

She looked up, startled.

A young man, maybe twenty-three, entered the dock. He was broad-shouldered, wiry in the way of someone who worked with his hands, wearing a faded flannel under a neon maintenance vest. His hair was damp from the cold, his jaw clean-shaven but shadowed with the beginnings of stubble. He maneuvered a ladder toward the far ceiling.

"Sorry," he said quickly, glancing at her with an embarrassed half-smile. "Light issue. Won't be in your way."

Maryan nodded, but her eyes betrayed her. She let them linger too long before turning back to her canvas. Handsome—her mind whispered it without permission. Athletic. Young. She reminded herself she was done with men, or men were done with her. It didn't matter. She had no place for that part of life anymore. But the reminder did nothing to still the odd flutter in her chest.

She dipped her brush in charcoal water, bent low, and kept painting. Pretended his presence was nothing. Pretended her hands weren't trembling slightly.

But he didn't leave as quickly as most workers did. Usually they came and went—rolling crates, hammering nails, fixing something overhead—without even glancing her way. This one lingered, fiddling with a light panel that probably didn't need so much attention. She felt his eyes on her more than once. Not crude, not hungry. Curious. Unsure.

Finally, he spoke. His voice cracked through her music.

"Do you always play this kind of music when you paint?"

Maryan blinked, startled. "What?"

He gestured toward the speaker. The folk song still trembled softly in the background, the singer's voice like water poured over stone.

"It's beautiful," he said, cheeks faintly red as though afraid of intruding. "I don't understand a word, but... it feels like it means something."

Maryan studied him more carefully. His expression wasn't mocking, wasn't patronizing. He looked earnest, almost reverent, as if he were afraid of insulting whatever sacred thing the song carried.

"It's about loss," she said at last. Her voice caught in her throat. "And staying."

He nodded slowly, like he was trying to absorb it. "I like that. Sounds like something worth knowing."

Something shifted in her chest, unexpected. She wanted to ask his name, but the words froze on her tongue. Instead she bent back to her canvas, smearing black across soaked fabric.

She didn't turn the music off. That was as much of an invitation as she could give.

He worked silently for another few minutes, adjusting wires, tightening bolts. Once, she caught him sneaking another glance her way. His eyes darted back immediately, as though ashamed of being caught. She felt heat climb her cheeks.

Then, just as suddenly as he had arrived, he gathered his ladder and left.

The dock fell quiet again, the song playing into echo.

Maryan sat back on her heels, charcoal dust smudged across her wrists, and realized her heart was racing. Over nothing. Over a stranger in a flannel shirt. Over a moment so small it should have dissolved instantly.

Instead, she felt alive in a way she hadn't in years. Not triumphant. Not free. Just alive, as though a corner of her had been stirred awake.

She pressed her palm against the canvas, streaking it with her print. The mark looked almost like a signature, or a wound.

Her grief was still there, a constant weight. Her anger still pulsed. Her fear still lingered every time she checked her phone for news. But in the silence after his departure, she realized she had felt something else, too—something that carried the faint shape of possibility.

She picked up her brush again. Downbeat, but burning with fire, she returned to the work.

He came back two days later.

Maryan was bent over her canvas, hair falling loose from her bun, sleeves rolled to her elbows. The dock was cold that morning, damp with late-winter air, but her skin was hot from the labor of smearing charcoal and turpentine across soaked linen. She had been at it for hours, so lost in her strokes she barely registered the clang of the metal door opening.

Then his voice:

"Gotta replace a ballast this time," he said cheerfully, wheeling in the ladder.

Maryan froze, brush suspended midair. Then, slowly, she smirked without looking at him.

"Again?" she asked, the word edged with playful skepticism.

He laughed, a sound that rang genuine and boyish in the drafty space. "Okay. No. You caught me. Truth is, I saw the painting through the door and wondered what happened next."

Maryan turned her head sharply, caught off guard. His honesty disarmed her. No attempt at macho swagger. No clever rehearsed line. Just that.

She looked at the canvas—an unfinished mass of shadow and texture that sprawled across the concrete floor—and then back at him. "It's not finished."

"I didn't think so," he said easily, tilting his head as if the piece were something to be respected even in its half-formed state. "The ones that hit you hardest never are."

Maryan raised an eyebrow. A line that poetic, she expected, would come from a curator, or an artist, not from a man holding a roll of electrical tape in his back pocket. "You know art?"

He shrugged, casual, but his eyes didn't leave hers. "Electrician since I was nineteen. But my high school— used to take field trips here twice a year. So I learned a little bit. Enough to keep from embarrassing myself when people talk about it."

Maryan let herself chuckle. The sound startled her. "It is," she said, nodding at the canvas. "It's about claiming space."

His smile widened. "Exactly."

The word hung in the air between them, like a spark that refused to fizzle out.

There was a pause. Both of them nervous, both suddenly aware of how quiet the loading dock had become. The hum of the overhead lights, the faint strains of her music, even the distant clatter of crates seemed far away.

He shifted, leaning on the ladder as if it were a prop he didn't quite know what to do with. Then, in a voice softer than before, he asked:

"Would you want to get coffee sometime? Or... I mean, if that's weird, just ignore me. I'm bad at this."

Maryan blinked. Coffee. The word landed like a pebble dropped into still water, sending ripples through her chest. For years, invitations from men had carried weight, danger, obligation. Coffee could mean a proposition, a trap, a risk. But his tone was different. Careful. Hesitant. Almost apologetic.

She studied him closely now. His posture wasn't overbearing. He wasn't leaning in, wasn't crowding her. His eyes held no pity, no condescension. Only curiosity. Only warmth.

And maybe—just maybe—a flicker of nervousness that mirrored her own.

She surprised herself when she said it. The word came out before she could stop it, soft but steady:

"Okay. Coffee."

He blinked, then grinned, like he hadn't actually expected her to agree. His grin was lopsided, shy and delighted all at once.

"Yeah?" he asked.

Maryan, almost amused by her own decision, folded her arms. "Don't make me change my mind."

He laughed again, rubbing the back of his neck. "Right. Noted. I'll, uh, try not to screw it up."

Maryan tilted her head, curious now, emboldened by his awkwardness. "Do you always ask women out in loading docks?"

"Only the ones covered in charcoal," he shot back.

She felt her lips twitch. A laugh escaped her, quieter this time. She hadn't flirted—really flirted—in years, and the muscles of it felt stiff, like speaking a half-forgotten language. Yet the words came, almost against her will.

"Dangerous habit," she said. "Might give you black lungs just standing near me."

He gestured to his maintenance vest. "Hey, I work with wires all day. Sparks, smoke, shocks—kind of used to it. I'll take my chances."

Their eyes met again, and the silence that followed wasn't heavy, wasn't strained. It was alive, humming, the way silence sometimes gets when two people realize they're standing closer to each other than they thought.

Maryan broke it first, retreating slightly, as though she'd let herself wander too far. She bent down, picked up her brush, and said, "Coffee, then. But just coffee."

"Of course," he said quickly, nodding like it was a sacred vow. Then he paused, biting back a smile. "Although, if I'm really charming, maybe I'll get a cookie too."

She rolled her eyes, but the corner of her mouth betrayed her. "You're very sure of yourself for someone bad at this."

"Not sure," he corrected. "Hopeful."

The word landed softly, and for the first time in a long time, Maryan didn't feel the urge to correct it.

***

That night in her room, she caught herself pacing, replaying the moment. She almost laughed at how absurd it was: she, who had faced interrogations, beatings, prison cells, and protests—nervous about a coffee.

But it wasn't absurd, she realized. It was human. And perhaps, for the first time since she'd arrived in the West, she allowed herself to remember what it felt like to want something simple. Something unguarded.

Chapter 20

Whittier

Their first date was at a café in the Whittier neighborhood, the kind of place that seemed caught between eras. Exposed brick walls carried a century of soot and polish, hung with trailing ivy and spider plants that curled lazily from clay pots. Wide windows let in the thin winter light, filtered through streaks of frost, and the scent of coffee beans roasted just a little too long clung to every corner.

Whittier itself was always changing, like a restless sleeper who could never settle. The neighborhood had been called many things—bohemian, immigrant, trendy, broken, reborn. People came and went, businesses opened and closed, murals appeared and were painted over. Minneapolis, Maryan thought, was like that in miniature: in constant flux, never finished, forever cycling between decay and revival.

A lot like her.

She arrived first, early, because she didn't trust herself not to retreat at the last moment. She chose a corner table where she could see the door, her scarf looped twice around her neck—not for modesty, but for comfort. It gave her hands something to fidget with, a tether to hold onto. The scarf was wool, soft against her chin, and the color reminded her of midnight in Berlin when the sky was clear.

She traced the rim of her cup—black coffee, bitter as memory—when he walked in.

He carried himself with the easy confidence of someone who had grown up in a place and claimed it without trying.

His jacket was utilitarian, his boots dusted with snow, and in his hand was a silver thermos, dented from years of use. He spotted her quickly, and his grin cracked open like sunlight.

"Hey," he said, lifting the thermos as though it were a trophy. "Brought you something."

He set it in front of her like an offering.

Maryan blinked. "What is it?"

"Tea," he said. "My grandma's recipe. Strong, sweet. Keeps the cold out better than coffee."

Her eyebrow arched. "Better than coffee?"

"Way better," he insisted, mock-serious. "And anyway—" he leaned conspiratorially closer, lowering his voice—"it's too cold for iced anything."

She laughed, the sound surprising even her. "This city," she said, shaking her head, "is colder than Berlin."

"Colder than Mars," he countered, deadpan.

Maryan found herself smiling, actually smiling, and she poured a little of his tea into the café cup. Steam rose, fragrant with cloves and something citrus. It warmed her hands immediately.

They began to talk.

At first, the conversation trailed safely along surface lines: food, weather, the absurdity of Minnesotan winters. She told him about Berlin pastries she missed, the dense black bread that could cut your gums if you weren't careful. He told her about State Fair cheese curds and the best food trucks.

Then it shifted.

Thomas told her about growing up in South Minneapolis, about block parties where neighbors grilled ribs in backyards, about bike rides near the falls, about baseball. Always baseball. His voice lit up when he described it: the crack of the bat, the smell of dirt and leather, the rhythm of the game that was both meditative and electric.

Thomas, the younger brother of two, just under twelve months (their parents never explained how that happened), was more of a natural heartthrob than his brother. Brown hair, brown eyes, 6′, 180, mostly muscle, with a wit that would charm most moms of the girls he dated.

The type of guys that every girl wants to follow on social media, but social media was not his scene. He preferred to be out, living, not taking pictures. Out being alive, not faking it for followers.

He grew up in a house which sat near Lake Harriet, far enough away to be middle class, but close enough to walk when needed. The neighborhood was a breezy, walkable neighborhood where runners, strollers, and golden doodles made their daily loops.

Thomas grew up wanting to work with his hands and find love.

He did have a love in high school, but she went on to other things, a fact Thomas struggled to get over.

Today though it was different.

Today was about having fun.

"You've never seen a game?" he asked, incredulous.

Maryan shook her head. "Never."

His eyes widened, playful indignation filling them. "That's a crime against humanity. We'll fix it. When the season starts, I'm taking you."

Her lips curved. "You assume I'll still be here."

"Then I guess," he said, shrugging with mock gravity, "we better start with the home opener. Just in case."

She tucked the suggestion away, unwilling to admit how much the promise—any promise—stirred something fragile inside her.

When her turn came, Maryan spoke of Tehran, but carefully. Her words moved like a tightrope walker, balancing between truth and silence. She mentioned the streets filled with protestors, the banners, the chants. She spoke of prison briefly, only enough to signal the shadow without dragging him into the full darkness. And she spoke of her mother, her voice faltering as she did.

She expected the conversation to buckle under the weight of it, for his eyes to shift with pity or discomfort. Most people changed the subject, fumbling to escape.

But Thomas didn't flinch.

He didn't rush to fill the silence, didn't apologize for something he hadn't done. He only tilted his head, his brow furrowed in quiet thought.

Then he asked the simplest, strangest question.

"What color was her favorite?"

Maryan blinked. "What?"

"Your mom," he said softly. "What was her favorite color?"

For a moment, she couldn't speak. All the stories she'd held back, all the horrors she'd swallowed—he hadn't asked about them. He'd asked about color. Something ordinary. Something human.

"Cobalt blue," she said finally, her throat tight.

He nodded slowly. "Then I'll remember that."

And somehow, in that moment, she believed him.

The afternoon stretched. One cup of tea became two, then three. The café shifted around them—students typing on laptops, couples drifting in and out, a barista humming along to the music overhead. Snow began to fall outside, thick flakes blurring the street.

Their conversation spiraled outward. They swapped stories of loneliness, each hesitant but willing. She told him about the way exile felt like a constant ache, how her Berlin studio smelled of turpentine but never of home. He told her about nights he spent alone fixing things in silence, about how even surrounded by people, loneliness could settle like dust.

And then, just as easily, they laughed. About the ridiculousness of Instagram dogs in sweaters. About his failed attempt to learn French in high school ("I only remember how to say, *the library is big*"). About her first attempt at American diner food, when she confused gravy for soup.

The flirtation was clumsy, unpracticed, but real. When she teased him about the way he stirred his coffee too aggressively—"you're beating it like it owes you money"—he grinned and said, "Better than staring at it until it stares back."

When she told him his thermos looked like it had survived a war, he shot back, "It has. Three Minnesota winters and a car accident. Stronger than me."

Playful. Tentative. Alive.

The entire time, Maryan's mind moved in two directions at once. One half remained guarded, reminding her of danger, of how quickly warmth could turn cold. The other half, traitorous and eager, wanted to lean into the light he offered.

She thought about how easy it would be to dismiss him, to fold this encounter into the long list of near-connections she had already abandoned. But then she'd catch him listening—really listening—and her defenses faltered.

When she spoke, he didn't stare at her scarf, or her accent, or the smudges of charcoal still clinging to her cuticles. He stared at *her*.

And she found herself wondering if it was possible, after all she had survived, to let someone hold even a corner of her story.

Eventually the café grew crowded, and the spell of their corner table broke. The barista wiped down the counter with pointed glances, and Maryan realized hours had passed.

They bundled up, stepping into the evening. Snow lay thick across the sidewalks, and the streetlights turned the flakes into gold dust.

Thomas walked beside her, hands deep in his coat pockets. Their steps crunched in unison. At the corner, where they would part ways, he hesitated.

"I had a good time," he said simply.

Maryan tugged at her scarf. "Me too."

There was another pause, filled with the electric possibility of what might come next. He didn't reach for her hand, didn't push. Instead, he gave her that lopsided grin again and said, "So, second date? Or do I have to bribe you with more tea?"

She smirked. "Depends how strong the tea is."

He laughed, shaking his head. "Dangerous answer. You might get hooked."

And before she could stop herself, she said, "Maybe I already am."

The words slipped out, lighter than air, but when she saw the flicker of surprise and joy cross his face, she didn't regret them.

That night, alone in her room, Maryan set the thermos he had given her on the desk. She poured the last of the tea into a cup and stared at its deep amber color. Not cobalt blue, not her mother's shade—but still something worth remembering.

She sipped, and for the first time in years, she let herself imagine a tomorrow that might be softer.

Chapter 21

Bella

The phone buzzed just after five.

Maryan hesitated, staring at the glow on the nightstand as if it were some test she wasn't ready to take. Calls always unnerved her. A voice asked for something right away. No time to revise or dodge. Just immediate response.

The name flashing across the screen made her pulse jump. Thomas Quinn.

She hovered over the phone, her scarf tight around her shoulders, until the buzzing stopped. Then it started again.

This time, she answered.

"Hello?" Her voice was cautious, softer than she meant.

"Hey." His voice carried warmth, unstudied. "Sorry if this is bad timing. I was just wondering... would you maybe want to go out tonight?"

"Tonight?" She turned, scanning the small room as though looking for an excuse among the scattered brushes and half-finished sketches.

"Yeah. Dinner," he said, laughing nervously. "Unless that's too soon. Or too weird."

Maryan hesitated, gripping the edge of her scarf. Too soon, too weird — yes. But also, something in her chest stirred at the thought of being anywhere but this room, of hearing laughter and forks against plates instead of silence.

"What do you have in mind?" she asked finally.

"There's a place in Bloomington. Ciao Bella. My mom calls it *fancy but not snobby.* Good pasta and wine. I figured..." He trailed off, then rushed to add, "Unless you hate Italian food. In which case, forget I said anything."

Maryan's lips curved despite herself. "Italian is fine."

"Fine?" He groaned. "I'll try not to take that personally."

A small laugh escaped her. "Okay," she said. "Dinner."

He exhaled audibly, the kind of sound that made her realize he'd been holding his breath. "Great. I'll pick you up at six fifteen. Deal?"

"Deal."

"Good. And hey—bring that scarf. It's freezing out."

The call ended, leaving her staring at the black screen, her heart unsteady.

She spent the next forty minutes in restless motion, changing her sweater twice, wiping charcoal smudges from her nails, braiding and unbraiding her hair. The scarf she chose was wool, deep midnight blue. Not modesty, just something to hold onto.

She was slipping on her boots when the phone buzzed again — not Thomas this time, but an international number.

Her stomach dropped. She answered.

It was her father's friend in Berlin, his German fast and breathless. She caught the words as if through fog: her sister's visa had been approved. She was in Turkey. Safe. Waiting.

Maryan pressed her hand to her mouth. Her knees nearly gave way. Weeks of uncertainty, prayers, whispered bargains with God — all collapsed into that single sentence. She could barely find the words to thank him.

When the call ended, she sat on the edge of the bed, shaking. Her sister was free. Alive. With a future. Tears blurred her sight as she whispered, "Thank you. Thank you."

A knock sounded at her door.

Thomas stood in the hallway, hands shoved into his jacket pockets, his grin wide and boyish.

"Ready?"

Maryan nodded, though her body trembled from more than the cold. She hadn't told him about the call yet — couldn't. The news was too new, too raw, fragile like glass. She held it close, warming her from the inside.

Outside, the air bit with February sharpness. The city was glazed in ice, the streets shining under the sodium glow of streetlights. His truck waited at the curb, paint chipped but sturdy.

He opened the passenger door for her. "Not fancy, but it runs," he said.

She climbed in, tugging her scarf closer. The cab smelled faintly of pine from the air freshener dangling by the vent.

They pulled onto the highway, headlights carving tunnels through the dark. Maryan pressed her forehead lightly against the window, watching the cityscape blur by blending into the suburbs.

"So," Thomas said, glancing at her with a crooked smile. "You're officially braver than me."

"How so?"

"You agreed to let a guy you barely know drive you to Bloomington in February. That's practically survival training."

Maryan smirked faintly. "Maybe I like danger."

"Oh yeah?" He raised an eyebrow. "Then you're in luck. We're headed straight for the most dangerous thing in Minnesota: rush-hour traffic."

She laughed, surprising herself. The sound filled the cab, lightening the air between them.

By the time they reached Bloomington, the night had fully settled in, heavy and sharp with cold. The parking lot was crowded, a glow spilling out from tall windows where strings of tiny lights framed the glass. Maryan could already hear the thrum of voices and clatter of dishes as Thomas opened the door for her.

Ciao Bella smelled of garlic and butter, of fresh bread pulled from ovens and basil torn by hand. The lobby hummed with waiting couples, their coats draped over arms, their laughter carrying. A host in black pressed menus to his chest, smiling as Thomas gave his name.

Inside, the dining room was alive. Waiters moved in a practiced rhythm, trays balanced, corks popping. Plates gleamed with pasta in red and gold sauces, bowls of mussels steamed under candlelight. The voices of half a hundred conversations collided, bouncing off brick walls and wood beams.

Maryan felt her chest tighten — the noise, the closeness — but then Thomas's hand brushed her elbow, guiding her through the narrow aisle. He wasn't touching so much as steadying, a gesture light enough to back away from if she wanted. She didn't.

Their table was tucked into a corner, near a window glazed with frost. A small candle burned between them, its flame bending each time someone passed behind.

"Sorry if it's loud," Thomas said, leaning forward as the waiter set down water glasses. "It'll quiet down in a bit."

Maryan nodded, fingers around the cold stem of her glass. The noise pressed in, but Thomas's presence softened it, made it less like a wall and more like background music.

They opened menus.

"You ever had ravioli before." he asked, peering at his.

She shook her head.

"You've got to.. Little clouds. Dangerous, though—eat too many, you'll never get up again."

Her lips curved. "Sounds like a trap."

"Exactly," he said solemnly. "An Italian trap."

The joke loosened her shoulders. She scanned the menu. "I think I'll try it."

"Good choice," he said. "I'm going for the spaghetti and meatballs. Basic, but reliable. Like me."

Maryan smirked. "You call yourself basic?"

He grinned, unabashed. "Basic with a twist. You'll see."

The waiter returned, took their orders, refilled their water. Around them, the room pulsed with motion: forks clinking, chairs scraping, a child laughing too loudly at the next table. Maryan thought of Tehran cafés, of Berlin bars, and realized how much she'd missed the small chaos of people enjoying themselves.

Thomas leaned closer so she could hear him over the noise. "So. Tell me something about you I wouldn't know from just watching you paint."

Maryan hesitated, then countered, "Tell me first."

"Fair," he said, tapping his glass. He thought a moment. "When I was a kid, I wanted to be a pilot. Used to sit outside the airport fence with my brother, watching planes, Thought it was magic. Still kind of do."

"Why not?" she asked.

"The cost, and didn't join the military. So, electrician instead."

Maryan smiled. "That is not basic."

"Your turn," he said.

She traced the rim of her water glass. Her instinct was to deflect, to keep her answers shallow. But the candle flickered between them, steady, patient.

"I used to want to be a doctor," she said at last. "When I was very young. I liked the idea of healing. But it wasn't possible."

Thomas didn't press. He just nodded, his expression open, as if her words belonged to her and didn't need to be pried for more.

The food arrived — steaming plates, fragrant and rich. Maryan's ravaolli glistened dotted with spinach. Thomas's spaghetti came heaped, red sauce clinging thick to the noodles.

"Moment of truth," he said, pointing his fork at her dish. "Tell me if I oversold it."

She speared one, tasted. The pasta melted in her mouth, soft as bread but richer, coated in warmth. She closed her eyes for a second.

"Well?" he teased.

Her eyes opened. "It is... dangerous."

He laughed, the sound rolling easily over the table. "Knew it."

They ate, and as they did the restaurant shifted. Slowly, the crowd thinned, the voices dropped to a softer hum. Chairs were pushed back, coats shrugged on.

Conversation between them began to flow more easily, as if they'd both been waiting for the quiet. They spoke of childhood meals — her mother's stews heavy with saffron, his grandmother's casseroles that could feed a neighborhood. They teased each other about food loyalty, him swearing by cheese curds, her insisting bread was life itself.

And then, deeper still: loneliness, memory, the strangeness of belonging nowhere and everywhere at once.

When she faltered, uncertain of how much to say, he steadied the silence with questions gentle enough not to bruise. When he shared, his voice carried a kind of honesty that made her want to lean in closer.

The candle burned low. The restaurant quieted to a murmur. And Maryan realized with a start that she had not thought of leaving once all evening.

By the time they left Ciao Bella, snow was falling again—fine, steady flakes that caught in the glow of the streetlamps and dusted the parked cars like sugar. Thomas walked beside her across the lot, not rushing, not filling the silence, just matching his stride to hers.

He opened the truck door for her again, a small courtesy that made her pulse tighten. Inside, the cab was warm, faintly fogged from their breath. The heater hummed. He started the engine, and the radio clicked on to an old soul song, low and scratchy.

They pulled out of the lot, tires crunching over salted pavement. Bloomington blurred past—wide streets, shuttered storefronts, the faint neon of gas stations. Soon they merged onto the highway, the city lights stretching ahead like a necklace.

Maryan leaned her head against the glass, watching the snow fall in diagonal streams through the beams of the headlights. Her stomach still hummed from dinner, from laughter, from the warmth of wine and candlelight. And underneath it all, a weightless kind of fear—because it felt too much like happiness, and happiness never lasted.

Thomas glanced at her, one hand steady on the wheel. "So, verdict? On the ravioli. Worth risking a food coma?"

She smiled faintly, not lifting her head from the window. "Worth it."

"I knew it," he said, satisfied. Then, after a pause, softer: "Thanks for coming tonight."

She turned to look at him. "Thanks for asking."

The cab went quiet again, but it wasn't an empty quiet. It was layered—comfort, nerves, possibility. She could feel it radiating from the space between them.

When they reached Minneapolis again, the streets were almost deserted. Snow softened the curbs, muffled the hum of the city. He parked outside her apartment, engine idling.

Neither moved at first.

Thomas drummed his fingers lightly on the steering wheel, then turned toward her. "So… do I get to ask about a third date? Or would that be pushing my luck?"

Maryan's lips curved. "You're very persistent."

"Guilty," he said. "But only with things worth being persistent about."

Her breath caught. The words hung between them, fragile as the snow outside.

She looked at him—really looked. His grin was softer now, tentative, his eyes careful but bright. And for the first time in years, she felt a pull not of duty or danger, but of wanting. Wanting something small, human, ordinary.

Before she could overthink it, before the voice of caution could drag her back, she leaned in.

The kiss was brief, almost shy. Warmth, the faint taste of red wine, the scratch of stubble against her skin. He didn't press, didn't pull her closer, just let the moment exist.

When she drew back, her cheeks burned.

He smiled, slow and stunned. "So that's a yes on the third date?"

Maryan laughed, quietly, shaking her head. "Maybe."

Inside the apartment, the silence felt different—less like exile, more like space. She set her scarf on the chair, pulled off her boots, and sat on the edge of the bed.

The night replayed in fragments: the crowded din of the restaurant, the way his voice softened when he asked about her mother, the candle flickering low, the snow spinning in the headlights, the kiss that still warmed her lips.

And then—her sister.

She pulled her phone from her pocket, stared at the missed call log, the foreign number. The news she had barely let herself hold at dinner pressed against her ribs. Her sister's visa. Turkey. A doorway opening where for months there had only been walls.

Her eyes filled. She pressed her scarf to her face, breathing in its wool and warmth.

For the first time in a long time, the night held both grief and hope, both loss and something that might yet become love.

She blew out the candle by her bedside. The smoke curled upward, a thread fading into the dark.

Chapter 22

The Call

The room was quiet except for the faint hum of the radiator and the soft patter of snow against the window. Maryan had been sitting on the bed with her sketchbook balanced on her knees, though she hadn't drawn in an hour. Her pencil lingered above the paper, hovering in half-shapes she couldn't bring herself to finish.

Then her phone buzzed.

At first she thought it was Thomas. Her heart jumped in that foolish, fluttering way it did now whenever she thought of him. But when she lifted the screen, she froze.

The number was foreign. Not German. Not Berlin. Turkish.

Her breath caught.

Hands trembling, she answered. "Hello?"

For a moment, all she heard was static, a shuffling sound like fabric moving against fabric. Then—

"Maryan?"

The voice was thin, crackling over the poor connection, but unmistakable.

Maryan's entire body went cold and hot at once. "Marineh?"

"Yes, it's me—" the words rushed out, broken by the lag of the line. "I'm here. I'm in Turkey."

Maryan pressed a hand to her mouth. Tears sprang instantly to her eyes. She hadn't realized until that second how much she'd feared she would never hear her sister's voice again.

"Oh, *khoda*, thank God," Maryan whispered. "I thought—I didn't know—"

"I know," Marineh said softly. "I didn't think I would make it either."

They both fell silent, listening to the sound of each other breathing across continents.

"Tell me everything," Maryan said finally, her voice urgent, fragile. "How did you—how did you get out?"

Marineh's breath shook with a half-laugh. "It's a long story. But I'll tell you. I want you to know."

"I need to know," Maryan whispered.

Marineh inhaled slowly, and then her words began to tumble:

"We left at night. Not just me—there were twelve of us. Mostly women, two children. We paid a smuggler, a Kurd from the borderlands. He told us not to bring much. Only water, bread, and clothes we could carry. No suitcases. If you had too much, he threw it away."

"Baba arranged the path, he knew Armin wanted revenge, revenge for the humiliation. But when our mother died ….. " Marineh paused, tears building.

Maryan crying out loud now.

"….When she died, our father, our brave father, saw an opportunity in his grief."

Maryan closed her eyes, picturing it. Her sister, bundled against the cold, walking among strangers with nothing but the clothes on her back.

"We walked through mountains," Marineh continued, her voice hushed. "So high, Maryan. The snow was deep. My shoes were ruined by the second day. The smuggler said to stay quiet. There were soldiers sometimes. Patrols. If they saw us, they would send us back—or worse."

Her voice cracked.

Maryan's throat tightened. "Were you—did anyone—"

"No," Marineh said quickly. "We were lucky. We hid once, in a cave, when lights came down the valley. The children almost cried, but the mothers held their mouths shut. After an hour, the soldiers left."

The line went quiet for a moment, filled only by static. Maryan could hear her sister breathing, and she pictured her crouched in darkness, pressed against cold stone, praying not to be found.

"After that," Marineh went on, "we walked for two more nights. We only traveled in the dark. During the day we hid in abandoned farmhouses or barns. The smuggler brought bread, cheese, sometimes nothing. My stomach was empty, but I didn't care. I just wanted to keep moving."

Maryan clutched the scarf at her neck, the wool damp from her tears. "Marineh, you must have been so scared."

"I was," she admitted. "But there was no choice. I kept thinking of Mama. I kept thinking of you. I told myself, if you survived prison, if you survived the crate, then I can survive the mountains."

Maryan's chest caved. The thought of her sister using her own pain as fuel was unbearable and beautiful at once.

"Then one morning," Marineh said, "we crossed the last ridge. The smuggler pointed down, and there it was—the Turkish side. Just fields and a road. But I wanted to kiss the ground."

"And you're safe now?" Maryan asked. Her voice trembled.

Marineh exhaled shakily. "Safe enough. I'm in Van, staying in a small apartment. There are six of us here, all women. It's crowded, but no one is asking questions. We have mats on the floor, a kettle for tea. It's better than anything I imagined. Tomorrow, I go to the refugee office to register. They said my visa papers are waiting."

Maryan shut her eyes again, tears spilling freely. "I can't believe it. You're free."

"Not free," Marineh corrected gently. "Not yet. But closer."

Maryan sat cross-legged on the bed, the phone pressed to her ear, her scarf bunched in her lap like something to hold onto. Outside the window, Minneapolis was a blur of streetlights and falling snow, but she hardly saw it. All she saw was the image of her sister in some crowded apartment in Van, surrounded by strangers, clutching the phone the way she clutched hers.

There was a pause, the kind of pause sisters understood — silence loaded with something that needed to be said but hadn't yet been touched.

It was Marineh who broke it.

"Maryan…" Her voice thinned. "I should tell you now. About Mama."

Maryan's stomach twisted. She already knew in pieces — a letter smuggled, a whisper from a family friend — but hearing it in her sister's voice made it real in a way it hadn't been before.

"I know," Maryan whispered. "She's gone."

"Yes." A breath trembled down the line. "She died quietly. Baba said she just… stopped. Her heart, he thinks. It was too much, Maryan. The raids, the silence, you being gone. She kept lighting candles for you every night, waiting for news. Then one morning…"

Her voice cracked.

Maryan pressed her palm over her eyes, hot tears spilling. "I wasn't there. I should have been—"

"No," Marineh interrupted firmly. "Don't say that. You would have died too. They would have taken you again, or worse. Mama knew that. She told me once—she said, 'Maryan escaped, thank God. She carries us with her. That is enough.'"

Maryan sobbed softly, the sound muffled in the scarf she held to her face. The memory of her mother's hands, always smelling of flour and rosewater, rushed in so vividly it hurt.

"She was proud of you," Marineh continued. "Even in her last days. She said your art would outlive all of this. That your name would carry her name."

Maryan could barely breathe. "I miss her so much."

"I do too," Marineh whispered.

For a long time they stayed like that, two sisters across continents, sharing silence heavy with grief, the static of the line the only witness.

When Maryan's sobs finally ebbed, she wiped her cheeks and sat straighter. "Listen. You can't stay without help. Turkey is dangerous for refugees if you run out of money. I'll send you something."

"You don't have much," Marineh protested. "You're still living in a one room apartment."

"I have enough," Maryan said, sharper than she meant. Then softer: "Please, let me do this. For you. For Baba. For Mama."

There was another pause, Marineh weighing her words. Finally, she exhaled. "All right. But only until I find work. Some of the women here are cleaning apartments. They say it pays a little."

"You don't have to clean anything," Maryan said fiercely. "Just stay safe. I'll send what you need. You hear me?"

Marineh gave a small laugh, though her voice wavered. "Always the older sister. Ordering me around from across the ocean."

Maryan smiled through tears. "Some things don't change."

"Maryan," Marineh said after a moment, her voice steadier, "I keep thinking... maybe we can see each other. In Germany. I already have the visa. You could come from America. Berlin again. Do you think—?"

Maryan's heart clenched. The thought of seeing her sister after years of absence, of being able to hold her, was almost unbearable.

"Yes," she said quickly. "Yes. As soon as I can, I'll come. We'll meet there. I promise."

Marineh's breath caught. "You promise?"

"I promise," Maryan said, her voice breaking. "We'll light a candle for Mama at the church in Kreuzberg. We'll walk by the river. I'll show you the gallery where I painted. You'll see. We'll be together again."

On the other end of the line, she could hear her sister crying now too, softly but without shame.

"Then I'll hold on," Marineh whispered. "I'll hold on for that."

When the line finally clicked silent, Maryan sat in the dim room staring at her phone. The candle she'd lit that morning had burned down to a stub. Outside, the snow kept falling, endless and quiet.

She felt raw, scraped open by grief and relief both. Mama gone. Marineh alive. A meeting in Germany to anchor them, even if it was months away.

She leaned back against the headboard, the scarf still clutched in her lap, and whispered into the empty room:

"I'll get to you. Whatever it takes. I'll get to you."

Chapter 23

Good Times

The snow had stopped just an hour before, leaving Minneapolis wrapped in a pale hush. The sidewalks glistened with slush, and the air smelled faintly metallic, the way it always did after a storm. Maryan walked slowly down Lyndale Avenue, her scarf wrapped close, the tips of her fingers still stiff from the wind.

The restaurant sat tucked between a record shop and a used bookstore, its sign hand-painted: Luna & The Bear. She'd passed it once before and thought it charming, though she hadn't dared go inside alone. The windows steamed with warmth, and the chalkboard propped outside listed the day's specials in looping script — lentil soup, roasted chicken, apple tart.

When she pushed open the door, the bell chimed faintly.

Inside, the space was small and intimate, all reclaimed wood tables and mismatched chairs. Strings of lights looped across the ceiling beams, glowing softly in the midday dim. The smell of coffee, cinnamon, and bread was immediate, enveloping her like a shawl. There were only a handful of other diners — a pair of students hunched over laptops, an older couple sharing soup — and the hum of conversation was gentle, unobtrusive.

Thomas was already there, seated by the window, his flannel jacket draped over the chair. He spotted her instantly, and his grin widened the way it always did when he saw her — unguarded, a little boyish, as if she were the best surprise of the day.

"Hey," he said, rising halfway as she approached.

Maryan slipped her scarf off, draped it over her chair. "Hey."

"You made it through the storm," he said, nodding at the melting snow outside. "I was worried you'd decide Minnesota winters aren't worth it."

She smirked, settling into her seat. "I already decided that weeks ago."

He laughed, shaking his head. "Fair enough. But you came anyway."

A server appeared with water and menus. Maryan accepted hers with a small nod, though she barely glanced at it. The warmth of the room, the way the light softened Thomas's face, made her throat tighten. She knew what she wanted to tell him today, but the thought of speaking it aloud made her palms damp.

Thomas scanned the menu, his lips moving faintly as he read. "I think I'm going with the roasted chicken. Or maybe the burger. Can't go wrong with a burger, right?"

"I wouldn't know," Maryan said dryly. "I've only had one in my life."

He looked up, eyes wide. "Only one?"

She shrugged, amused by his expression. "It was messy. Too much bread."

"That's blasphemy," he declared, grinning. "Okay, then, I'll prove you wrong. Next time, we're going to the best burger place in town."

"Next time?" she teased.

"Of course," he said, leaning back. "Unless you're sick of me already."

Maryan felt something warm flicker in her chest. "Not yet."

The server returned, took their orders — lentil soup for her, roasted chicken for him — and left them with a basket of bread. The quiet between them was comfortable, punctuated by the scrape of butter knives and the low hum of the café's playlist, some acoustic guitar drifting lazily through the air.

Maryan tore a piece of bread from the basket, more to give her hands something to do than from hunger. She dipped it into the olive oil, watching the swirl of herbs, then set it down untouched.

Thomas noticed. "Not hungry?"

She shook her head. "I am. Just... thinking."

He leaned forward, resting his elbows on the table. "Dangerous habit."

She gave him a faint smile, but her heart was pounding. For days she had rehearsed this moment — how to tell him about her sister, how much to share, whether to hold back. Every version in her head had ended in silence, in awkwardness, in his eyes glazing over. But something about the way he was watching her now — not pushing, just waiting — loosened the knot in her chest.

"There's something I should tell you," she said quietly.

He tilted his head. "Okay."

She hesitated, staring at the candle on their table. Its flame bent slightly every time the door opened, letting in a gust of cold air. "My sister," she began, her throat tightening. "Marineh. She... she escaped Iran."

Thomas's expression didn't change in the way she feared. No flash of discomfort, no polite nod to change the subject. Instead, he straightened slightly, his face intent. "Escaped? How?"

Maryan swallowed. "Through the mountains. With others. She made it into Turkey. She called me a few nights ago."

"Is she safe?"

"For now. She's in Van, with other women. Small apartment. Crowded, but safe enough. She'll register with the refugee office soon."

Thomas exhaled, as if he'd been holding his breath. "That's... incredible. And terrifying. God, I can't imagine."

Maryan nodded slowly. "I wanted to tell you because... it's not something I can carry quietly. Not anymore."

The server arrived then, sliding steaming bowls and plates onto the table. The interruption was jarring — the clatter of cutlery, the cheerful, "Enjoy your meal!" Thomas thanked him, but his eyes never left Maryan's face.

She spooned her soup mechanically, though she didn't taste it. "When she called," she went on, "she told me about the soldiers, the caves they hid in. The children crying. I could hear it in her voice still, like the fear hadn't left her body."

Thomas's fork hovered above his plate, forgotten. "Maryan..."

"She's younger than me," Maryan said, her voice breaking. "She shouldn't have had to do this. None of us should. But I wasn't there. I couldn't protect her. And now I'm here, eating soup, while she is on a mat in a room full of strangers."

Tears blurred her eyes, and she blinked them away quickly. She hated crying in public.

But Thomas reached across the table, his hand stopping just short of hers. He didn't take it — didn't trap her — just let it rest there, palm open, waiting if she wanted it.

She stared at his hand for a long moment, then let her fingers brush against his. The warmth startled her, but she didn't pull away.

"You're carrying all of this," he said softly. "But you don't have to carry it alone. Not with me."

The words undid her more than the memory of her sister's voice.

For the first time, she let herself meet his gaze fully. And in his eyes she saw no pity, no fear — only steadiness, and something deeper she didn't dare name yet.

The steam from Maryan's lentil soup curled upward, carrying the scent of cumin and lemon. She stirred it absently, her appetite gone, though the warmth steadied her hands.

Thomas cut into his roasted chicken but hadn't taken a bite. His fork rested against the plate, his attention fixed on her. It unsettled her, how fully he listened. In Tehran, listening had always been dangerous — it meant someone was measuring your words, deciding how to use them against you. But Thomas's listening felt different, like he was holding out space and asking nothing in return.

Maryan drew in a shaky breath. "When Marineh called… she also told me about Mama."

Thomas's brow furrowed, concern deepening in his expression. He didn't speak, just gave the smallest nod to show he was ready for whatever came.

"She's gone," Maryan said simply. The words landed flat, like stones. "Her heart gave out. Baba said she was lighting candles for me every night. She couldn't bear the silence anymore. She kept hoping I would come back."

Her throat closed. She pressed the spoon back into the bowl, unable to lift it. "I wasn't there when she died. I wasn't there for the funeral. I don't even know where she is buried."

The din of the restaurant seemed to dull around them — the clink of silverware, the murmur of other conversations. It all blurred into a muted hum.

Thomas's voice, when it came, was quiet but steady. "I'm so sorry, Maryan."

She nodded, tears stinging her lashes. "I thought leaving would protect them. That if I carried the danger with me, they would be safe. But Mama… she died anyway. And Marineh, she had to cross mountains to save herself."

For a long moment, neither of them spoke. Maryan could hear her own heartbeat in her ears, faster than it should have been.

Finally, she exhaled, forcing herself to continue. "I'm going to send money. To Marineh. Whatever I can spare. She'll need food, rent, maybe even a lawyer if she wants asylum. I told her not to clean houses, not to exhaust herself just to survive. I'll make sure she doesn't have to."

Thomas's lips pressed together, and then he nodded. "Tell me what you need. I'll help."

Maryan looked up sharply. "No. I can't take your money."

"I didn't mean just money," he said quickly, leaning forward. "I mean anything. Rides to the bank, figuring out wires, someone to double-check paperwork. Whatever it is. You shouldn't have to do it alone."

Her chest tightened. "Why are you doing this? Why do you care?"

He hesitated, as if surprised by the question. Then, simply, "Because it's you."

The words landed in her chest like a stone breaking water, rippling outward. She opened her mouth, closed it again. No one had said something like that to her since before prison, before exile, before the walls she had built around herself had become permanent architecture.

She looked down at her hands, twisting the edge of her napkin. Her voice came out barely above a whisper. "Thomas... I don't know what to do with this."

"With what?"

"With... you." Her cheeks burned. "I've tried not to feel it, but every time I see you, I—" She stopped, the words jamming in her throat.

He waited, not pushing.

She swallowed hard, forcing them out. "I think I'm falling for you."

The confession hung between them, raw and trembling.

Thomas's eyes softened, his mouth curving into a slow, almost stunned smile. He didn't lunge across the table, didn't turn it into a spectacle. He just let out a quiet breath and said, "Good. Because I've already fallen for you."

Maryan's heart lurched. Relief, terror, and something dangerously close to joy tangled inside her.

For the first time in years, she allowed herself to meet someone's gaze without flinching. And she felt the room, the world, steady around her.

The server drifted back to check on them, and Maryan realized her soup had gone cool. Thomas had eaten only a few bites of chicken. Neither of them seemed to care.

"Dessert?" he asked, tilting the menu up like a shield and a dare. "We could call it a celebration. For Marineh making it through."

Her throat tightened. "A celebration," she repeated, tasting the word like something new. "All right."

He studied the chalkboard over the counter. "They've got an apple tart, citrus olive oil cake, and—oh—affogato. That's just gelato drowned in espresso. It's like… dessert for people who can't pick a side."

"Which are you?" she asked.

"A shameless fence-sitter," he said, grinning. "But today? Apple tart. Feels right."

"Apple tart feels like October," she said.

"October can happen in February if you want it badly enough." He raised a hand to the server. "One tart. Two forks. And more tea for the lady, please."

"Bossy," Maryan murmured, but her eyes were smiling.

"Just persistent," he said, softer, and the layered meaning hung there; she didn't swat it away.

They ate in a quiet that wasn't empty. The tart arrived still warm, a glazed fan of apples over a flaky base that cracked delicately under the forks. He nudged the plate toward her. She cut a small corner, chewed slowly, and nodded once as if approving a finished brushstroke. He watched her more than he watched the dessert.

"Good?" he asked.

"Dangerous," she said, and his laugh unfurled easily across the table.

The room around them seemed to filter down into a gentle murmur—the clink of mugs, the low thrum of an acoustic guitar on the café's playlist, a burst of laughter from the students near the back. Outside, the light had shifted to a dim, pewter afternoon. A bus hissed at the curb and rolled on, leaving a trail of wet sound.

Maryan rested her fork. "Thank you for not... looking away."

"I won't," he said.

"You say that like it's easy."

"It isn't." He searched for words and found them without ornament. "But it's necessary."

She felt it again—that sense of steadiness she had almost forgotten a person could offer another. For years she'd braced for the flinch, the hurried change of subject, the moral that tried to wrap horror in a neat bow. He offered none of that. Only himself, the plainness of his presence like heat from a radiator: constant, unshowy, lifesaving.

He took a breath, then lightened the air on purpose. "Okay, serious question. If I fail you on burgers, what's the one food you'll judge me on forever?"

"Bread," she said instantly. "If the bread is wrong, everything is wrong."

"Bread," he repeated solemnly, tapping the table as if making a legal record. "Noted. I will start my training immediately. Step one: stop calling it 'carbs' around you."

"Thank you," she said, pretending gravity. "Heresy is a sin."

His smile tilted. "You know, that's the second time you've called something dangerous today. Apple tart, gnocchi last night. I'm starting to suspect the real hazard is sitting across from me."

She thought about it, then lifted her chin. "Perhaps."

"Okay," he said, still smiling. "Then I accept the risk."

They finished the tart, trading small bites until the plate was a shine of syrup and crumbs. When he reached to set the fork down, his hand brushed the back of hers. It was nothing—a graze, incidental. But she felt it lift through her body like a chord struck on a badly tuned instrument finally finding its key. She didn't move away.

Outside, the thin winter light faded, turning the restaurant windows into mirrors. In their reflection, they were two silhouettes leaning slightly toward each other, a candle's modest fire a tiny sun between them.

"Walk?" he asked. "Ten minutes. We'll pretend it's October. You can tell me if the air tastes like apples."

"Ten minutes," she said, bargaining with both of them. "Then I go back to the museum."

"Deal."

They bundled into their coats. He held the door and the bell rang them out into the cold.

—

The street greeted them with familiar winter noises: the packed-snow crunch underfoot, the heavy hush that made even traffic sound polite, the whisper of wind turning the edge of Maryan's scarf into a small flag. The sky was a dull slab of pewter. Shop windows glowed like little hearths— records, secondhand paperbacks, a lamp store that made the sidewalk glow in pools of amber.

They turned right, away from the busier corner. The block slanted slightly downhill, and she adjusted to the grade without thinking. He kept pace, hands in his pockets, shoulders loose. For all his height, he didn't take long strides that made her chase him; he matched her gait as if he'd practiced.

"What does Berlin smell like in winter?" he asked.

She glanced at him, surprised and pleased by the question. "Metal and coal, sometimes. And baked chestnuts if you're lucky. Wet wool. Cigarettes outside bars. The canal smells dull, like it's sleeping."

"And Tehran?"

A pause, then: "Dust. Diesel. Spices. And orange blossoms if you're in the right neighborhood at night."

He nodded, absorbing, not cataloguing. "Minneapolis smells like road salt and coffee. And pine if you're driving with my dad during December. He overdoes the air freshener."

"You've mentioned your dad often," she said.

"Yeah." He laughed lightly, but fondness tugged at his mouth. "He's a lot. Loud. Good. He comes to every game, even when he pretends he doesn't care about baseball. Says he's there for the hot dogs. He isn't."

"And your mother?"

"Teacher," he said, proud without saying the word.

Maryan's breath fogged between them. "You have a good family."

"I do." He glanced at her. "I know that's luck. And work. And more luck."

They walked past the bookstore. In the window, a cobalt-blue vase held three paperwhite stems. Maryan stopped without meaning to.

"Cobalt Blue," he said, following her gaze. "Favorite color, right? Your mom."

She nodded. The perfume-memory of her mother's hands crowded every part of her for a moment, the way the blue glass bowl on their kitchen shelf had caught morning light in Tehran, the way her mother had turned it to watch the color deepen and change. The ache rose and receded like a wave. She breathed through it.

He shifted closer by an inch. "You okay?"

"I will be," she said—and was startled to realize that, for the space of that moment on the sidewalk, it felt true.

They stepped into the bookstore, pretending it was to warm up, but really because the bell over the door promised a new kind of quiet. The place was narrow, crowded with wooden cases and the sweet dust-smell of old paper. A cat slept on a stack of travel guides as if it owned the concept of movement.

Thomas drifted toward Minnesota history, pulling a book with a watercolor of the river on the cover. He flipped it open. "Look," he said, half-whispering because that's what bookstores ask of you. "Spring thaw. The ice breaks up like plates. It's kind of violent."

"Spring is always violent," she said, running a finger along the spines. Rilke. Hafez in a bilingual edition. A slim book of German photographs of factory windows, repeated panes like prayers.

He glanced over. "Find something?"

She slid the Hafez free. "He's like an umbrella in a storm," she said, lightly, because anything heavier would drop her through the floor. "Also a merciless drunk."

He laughed. "A poet and a menace. My kind of guy." He pulled a book of ballpark photographs and held it up as counterweight. "In the spring, I'll take you to Target Field. We'll get sunburned and eat something terrible on purpose."

"And I will judge the bread," she said.

"Viciously, I hope."

They lingered long enough for the blood to return to their hands. At the register, he bought the baseball book and—without fanfare—the small Hafez volume. When the clerk tried to slide both bags toward him, Thomas nodded at Maryan's. "Separate, please."

Outside, he handed it over. "For you. Not as a metaphor. As a book."

She swallowed. "You don't have to—"

"I wanted to."

She didn't argue. "Thank you," she said, and tucked it carefully inside her coat as if books could be warm.

They stepped back into the afternoon that was already thinking about evening. Streetlights clicked on in a soft chorus. Somewhere a snow shovel scraped like a bow drawn across a too-tall note. The air had shifted colder; the ten minutes they'd bargained with had stretched into forty without scolding either of them.

"I should go back," she said reluctantly. "The museum. I left a canvas like a bad secret on the floor."

"Do bad secrets get better if you leave them alone?" he asked.

"Sometimes they dry enough to touch," she said, surprising herself with the honesty of it.

They reached the corner where they would part—the crosswalk's white lines a ladder painted onto the street. Cars idled respectfully. He looked at her as if he were memorizing this exact frame: her scarf, the tiny plume of her breath, the book-shaped square beneath her coat.

"You told me something big today," he said. "Two big things, actually. About your sister. And about me."

"And about bread," she added, because gravity needs ballast.

"And about bread," he echoed, smiling.

He didn't step closer. She did. Not much. Just enough that the world's noises tucked themselves into pockets and waited. She could smell soap and cold air on his coat. The city seemed to take a slow breath.

"Third date?" he asked, nearly a whisper.

"You're counting?" she asked back.

"Always."

She thought of all the things she had not been able to count: days of hunger, nights in the crate, months waiting for papers, candles burned down to the wick. Then she thought of what could be counted: a first kiss in a parked truck, an apple tart split with two forks, a book handed over because someone had listened.

"Yes," she said. "Third date."

He leaned in. The kiss wasn't a surprise this time. It found them line for line, gentle enough to ask, steady enough to answer. It tasted faintly of apples and black tea. It was quick, because the air was cold and because the street was public and because some things are more lovely when they are short and true. When they parted, their foreheads hovered for a second in a small, unnecessary shelter.

"Go paint," he murmured.

"Go work," she said.

He saluted lazily, a gesture that should have been ridiculous and was instead exactly right. He turned north, she south. After ten steps she looked back. He was looking back too, already raising a hand. She didn't wave—she lifted the Hafez book instead. He laughed, visible even at a distance, then tucked his chin into his collar and walked on.

—

Back in the museum's loading dock, the concrete greeted her with its blunt honesty. The soaked linen lay where she had left it, dark and expectant. The small speaker on the floor still remembered the playlist; a low, old song reached up like a hand. She set the book on a crate and knelt. Her fingers found the charcoal as if they'd been called by name.

She didn't paint the mountains. Or the soldiers. Or the crate's suffocating walls. Not this time. She pulled a stroke across the linen that felt like the first time you find your balance on a moving train. She pressed the heel of her palm into the wet, left the print of a human hand in a field of gray. A second mark, then a third—measured, unafraid. She let the darkness hold the shape of a candle's smoke, a mouth lifted away from a kiss, the spine of a book held close under a coat.

When she paused, the space contained a quiet it had not backed away from. The painting wasn't finished; the ones that hit you hardest never are. But it had a new gravity, the kind that didn't pin you to the floor but steadied your feet.

Her phone buzzed once. A message from Thomas: *Tell the bad secret I say hi.*

She typed back: *It says hello, but it prefers to be called a work in progress.*

Three dots. *Same.*

She laughed. Out loud. Alone. The sound startled a sparrow that had somehow found its way into the rafters. It skittered and then settled, as if deciding it could share this slightly warmer corner of the world.

She thumbed open another thread. *Marineh*: last message pinned at the top, voice note from Van. Maryan listened again to her sister's words, to the breath behind them, to the strength sewn into every seam of that story. She texted: *I told someone about you today. He listened.*

A minute later, a reply bloomed in the blue light: *Good. Keep people who listen.*

Maryan set the phone down gently, as if it could bruise. She reached for the charcoal again and tilted the canvas toward the afternoon, which was now unmistakably evening. Streetlights outside the loading dock door drew long, trembling bars of brightness across the floor. She used them for guides, not cages.

A museum porter rolled past with a cart piled with labeled crates—BAY 3, WEST WING, REHANG. He nodded. "You good?"

"Yes," she said, and heard how new and precise that word felt in her mouth.

Chapter 24

The Quiet Between the Storms

It was slow. Uneven.

Sometimes Maryan recoiled at his touch—not out of fear of Thomas himself, but from something older, deeper. Her body remembered things her voice wouldn't say. Shadows where hands had been. The cold tile floor of the detention room in Evin. The flicker of a bare bulb overhead while she stared into nothing, counting breaths like stitches.

The body, she'd learned, did not forgive simply because the mind wanted it to. Touch, no matter how gentle, could unravel her without warning.

Other times, she spoke in a rush. Her words spilled out between kisses—half-whispers, jagged and unfinished: names of streets in Shiraz, her grandmother's rosewater tea, the girl who didn't return from the march, the tattoo on her cellmate's wrist. She told Thomas about hiding charcoal under her tongue to sketch in secret, about nights when the wind scraped against the shipping crate so hard it sounded like screaming.

Thomas never interrupted. Never tried to thread her fragments into something whole. He just listened.

And when she couldn't find words anymore—when her voice gave out—he gave her silence. Steady, breathable silence.

Once, after she woke shaking from a dream she couldn't recount, Thomas had simply set her sketchbook beside her and said, *Draw it.*

She did.

Tonight was different.

Not easier. But quieter.

They were in his apartment, a loft tucked above a shuttered hardware store near Lyndale. The building itself was old brick, the kind that had survived half a dozen reinventions of the neighborhood. Inside, it smelled faintly of cedar and summer rain. He had left the windows cracked open despite the chill, and the city murmured below — bikes on pavement, the low thud of bass from someone's party, the hum of streetlights that made everything feel slightly electric.

The loft wasn't much: one long room with a kitchen tucked to the side, a bookshelf sagging under the weight of baseball biographies and half-read paperbacks, a battered sofa draped in a quilt his mother had sewn when he was a kid. The bed was pushed against the far wall beneath a skylight patched with condensation. The place wasn't stylish, wasn't curated — but it was lived in. Warm.

Maryan stood at the edge of that bed, barefoot. She looked small. Not fragile — just... new. Like she hadn't decided what shape she was going to be yet. Her hair was damp from the snow, curling against her cheeks, the ends dripping onto her collarbone.

Thomas watched her as though afraid of moving too fast. He always approached her like this. Slowly. Like she was fire. Like she could burn or bloom, depending on the wind.

"Is this okay?" he asked, his voice low, almost reverent.

She nodded. Her throat was dry. "Yes."

He stepped closer, closing the last inches of space between them. His lips brushed her collarbone first, gently, as if to test the ground. Then her shoulder. Then her fingertips. She trembled when he kissed the inside of her wrist. Not from fear. From memory.

He paused, his eyes searching hers, waiting for any flicker of hesitation.

Maryan didn't look away.

"I'm here," she said. "I want to be here."

So he kissed her again.

Undressing her felt like peeling away armor. Every layer was a story. Every scar a sentence.

The burn on her thigh from the slaughterhouse. The jagged white mark near her hip—barbed wire. . The faint line across her collarbone, invisible unless you knew to look, the one she never explained.

She let him see them now, not as confessions but as truths. Evidence of a life lived in survival mode.

When she was bare, she didn't cover herself. She didn't flinch. She just exhaled, slowly, like someone stepping into warm water after a lifetime of cold. Her body was hers, but she was only beginning to believe it again.

Thomas shed his own clothes without ceremony. He didn't pose, didn't perform. He was just there — solid and soft and open, his chest rising with each careful breath.

When they touched, it wasn't urgent. It was careful.

Her fingers traced his chest like she was learning a new language, every scar and freckle its own syllable. He kissed her shoulder again, then the hollow just below her ribs, the curve of her stomach where the ink from a leaky pen had left a faint smear days ago.

They lay side by side for a long time, touching without rush. Maryan rested her head on his chest, her palm pressed to his heartbeat. The steady thump calmed her, reminded her she was not alone in the world, not floating without anchor.

"You're too good," she whispered into the fabric of his skin.

Thomas smiled, brushing her hair back with gentle fingers. "I'm just trying not to screw it up."

"You won't," she said. Then, quieter: "You're not him."

He didn't ask who *him* was. He didn't need to. He knew enough to understand the name belonged to someone who had taken without permission, who had left bruises where tenderness should have been.

Instead, Thomas reached for her hand and held it there, over his chest, his pulse steady under her palm.

When they finally moved together, it was like breathing — tentative, rhythmic, a slow unfolding. She clung to his shoulders, not in desperation, but as if anchoring herself to something real, something present.

At first, she made no sound. Her breath caught, shallow and uneven, as if her body still needed convincing.

But then, just as she began to let go, she exhaled his name — not loud, not dramatic. Just a breath. A confirmation.

Thomas.

The way she said it made him close his eyes, as if he'd been given something rare, something fragile to protect.

When it was over, they didn't separate.

Maryan curled into him, her body still humming, not with arousal but with relief. Relief that her body had obeyed her instead of betraying her. Relief that she had chosen this moment, this man, this tenderness.

She looked up at him, eyes glassy but unbroken. "That felt like... mine."

"It was," he said simply.

A long silence followed. Not heavy — just full.

Then she whispered, "I'm scared of needing this."

He brushed a strand of hair from her forehead, fingers lingering as if memorizing her. "You don't have to need it. Just let it happen."

"I've never had anything like this," she said, the words tasting almost foreign in her mouth.

Thomas kissed the top of her head. "Neither have I."

Outside, rain began to fall — not a storm, just a hush, a soft patter on the roof. The sound threaded into the rhythm of their breaths, steady and quiet.

Maryan pulled the sheet over them and pressed her face to his chest. She listened until his heartbeat and the rain folded into one sound.

That night, she didn't wake screaming. She didn't dream of prison doors or sirens.

She dreamed of birds.
Of olive trees.
Of a future.

Chapter 25

Sled Time

Maryan woke with a start, as though her body knew something unusual awaited her. Her chest rose and fell in a quick rhythm, as though her dreams had ended mid-stride. For a few seconds she didn't remember where she was—her mind flickered with a vision of Berlin rooftops under thin sunlight, then Tehran's courtyard shadows, and finally settled on the plain ceiling of Thomas's South Minneapolis apartment.

The Berlin winter she had just left behind felt far away now, softened into memory. But Minnesota's cold greeted her like a familiar adversary. Through the frosted window she could see pale light filtering through a heavy January sky. It wasn't snowing yet, but the forecast promised flurries by midday—perfect weather, Thomas had said the night before, for snowmobiling.

She had never done anything like it. Back home, the closest she'd come was clinging to the back of her uncle's small motorcycle through Tehran's crowded streets, terrified and exhilarated by the rush of traffic. But this was different. Wide frozen lakes, open fields, and machines designed to glide over snow. It both thrilled and unsettled her.

Thomas was already up, rummaging in the closet for extra scarves, his messy brown hair sticking out in all directions. He glanced at her with a half-smile, arms full of knit hats and gloves.

"You'll need layers," he said, tossing a wool scarf onto the bed. "It gets colder than you think when you're moving. The wind cuts right through."

Maryan smiled at his fussing, touched by his concern. "I survived Tehran's winter prison cells," she said softly, almost without meaning to. "I think I can manage Minnesota."

The words hung in the air. He froze for a second, eyes flickering with something like pain, then nodded. He knew better than to push too far into her past, though he wanted to hold every shadow of it for her.

"Don't worry," he said instead, his voice lighter. "Petey said Mika's bringing an extra set of gear. Her sister's at college, so she grabbed some of her stuff. You'll be fine." He gestured toward the pile of sweaters on the chair. "Just put on a few layers and let's go."

Maryan layered the clothes carefully—thermal leggings, jeans, then the padded snow pants, each zipper and clasp clumsy under her fingers. Leaving Iran, then Berlin, then suddenly standing in a South Minneapolis apartment dressing for something as foreign as snowmobiling—she struggled to comprehend her life. The idea of freedom, particularly for women, had once existed in Iran, but now it was strangled. Freedom here meant absurd, simple things: choosing what to wear, laughing loudly in public, holding Thomas's hand.

Today, with him by her side, Maryan knew her feelings were something much more than freedom. It was longing for love, for the steadiness of Thomas's embrace, for the ordinariness of planning a day.

"Let's rock," Thomas said, suddenly cheerful, slapping his gloves together.

Maryan blinked. "Rock?" she asked.

He chuckled shyly. "It just means let's go."

Her lips curled into a mischievous grin. "Let's rock," she repeated, her accent giving the phrase a musical lilt.

He laughed, and the sound filled the small apartment.

Walking outside, the fresh snow covered the ground in a perfect, crisp sheet. Every step made a crunching sound that seemed louder than city noise. Thomas's old Chevy pickup sat under a powdery coat, icicles hanging from the wheel wells, as though the truck itself was trying to carve out space in the frozen morning.

He opened the passenger door for her, then caught her waist and pulled her in for a quick kiss. She smiled into it, warmth sparking through the cold, then climbed into the seat.

The truck groaned before finally starting after a few tries, coughing up a cloud of exhaust. They pulled out, tires crunching over compacted snow.

Heading down I-35W, the world was hushed under white. Highway signs, bare oaks, suburban rooftops—all softened by the fresh snowfall. A few other cars passed, their wheels cutting narrow paths in the drifts.

Thomas drove with one hand, the other wrapped around Maryan's gloved fingers. She looked out the window, amazed at the vastness. "It is like a painting," she said. "Everything covered, but still alive underneath."

He squeezed her hand, silently reassuring her that this day, this adventure, would not swallow her whole.

The truck turned off the interstate and wound through Lakeville's outskirts, past subdivisions with Christmas lights still strung on gutters, glowing faintly in the daytime, and past sprawling Lutheran churches with parking lots freshly plowed.

"Almost there," Thomas said.

Petey lived near South High School in Lakeville, in a small clapboard house tucked off a trailhead maintained by the snowmobile club. When they pulled into the driveway, they saw him crouched near two sleds, refilling a tank. Exhaust hung in the air.

"Petey! What's going on, man?" Thomas shouted, rushing to open Maryan's door.

Petey looked up, grinning wide. "Just filling up the sled. These things burn oil like crazy." He squinted at Maryan. "But who do we have here? No way she's with you."

"This is Maryan," Thomas said proudly.

"Nice to meet you," Maryan said, her voice careful.

"You're too pretty for Thomas," Petey said with a smirk.

Maryan, not used to American banter, simply smiled politely, unsure whether to laugh or frown.

At that moment, the front door opened and Mika stepped out. She looked like the picture of a Minnesota winter girl—blonde hair, blue eyes, cheeks pink from the cold. Her snow gear matched perfectly in navy and teal, helmet tucked under her arm.

"Hi! I'm Mika," she said brightly, walking over to hug Maryan. "I hope you're ready for some fun."

Maryan let herself be hugged, a little stiff at first, then softer. "I have never done this before," she admitted nervously.

"No worries. It's easy," Mika said with a grin. "Just don't go into the water or hit a tree."

Thomas laughed. "Yeah, you only get to hit the tree once."

Maryan looked between them, confused, but smiled anyway.

Mika grabbed her hand and tugged her toward the house. "Come on, I'll help you with the gear. Boys can handle the sleds."

Inside, Mika laid out snow pants, padded jackets, and gloves. "So, have you done winter sports before?" she asked.

"Not really," Maryan said, fumbling with the zippers. "I come from mountains, yes, but our winters are not like this. Snowmobiles? No. I have painted snow, but never moved through it like this."

"Freedom it is," Mika said simply, fastening Maryan's helmet strap.

By the time they stepped back outside, Maryan was bundled so thoroughly she hardly recognized her reflection in the frosted window. Boots heavy, scarf tight, she felt like a child stuffed in layers. The cold bit at her cheeks immediately, sharp and electric.

"You ready for this?" Thomas asked, pulling his gloves tighter.

She exhaled, her breath a cloud. "Ask me again in an hour."

Engines roared to life, echoing across the field. Mika mounted one machine and motioned for Maryan to climb behind her.

"Hold on tight," Mika said. "Lean with me on the turns. It's easier than it looks."

Thomas and Petey mounted the other sled, grinning as the engines purred.

The first lurch nearly knocked Maryan backward. She gasped, clutching Mika's waist, but then they were gliding forward—fast, cutting across the snow like skates on ice. The wind slapped against her helmet, stinging her cheeks, but beneath the rush of fear came a jolt of exhilaration.

They flew across the field, carving wide arcs, snow spraying high into the air. Maryan let out a startled laugh, then another, until laughter was all she could hear. For a moment, there were no memories of prison cells, no grief weighing her chest. Just speed, and white emptiness stretching forward like a future not yet written.

Thomas whooped behind them, leaning hard into a turn with Petey.

They reached the road crossing and idled, waiting for traffic to clear. Engines rumbled, exhaust fogging the air. Maryan's pulse still thundered.

As they headed toward Lake Marion, she leaned close to Mika and shouted, "This is insane!"

Mika laughed, pulling the throttle harder.

Minutes later, they reached the frozen lake. Petey wasted no time—he whipped his sled into tight circles, spraying snow everywhere. Maryan and Mika laughed, Thomas shaking his head at his friend's antics.

Maryan pulled off her helmet, hair tangled, cheeks flushed. "I didn't think I would like this," she admitted, breathless.

Thomas's face glowed with pride. "Told you. Lakeville's not so bad, huh?"

Petey grinned. "That's just the warm-up. Next stop, the orchard trails."

They rode single-file into a grove of bare apple trees, their branches clawing at the gray sky. The trails narrowed, forcing them to weave carefully. The crunch of treads on snow and the occasional engine rev were the only sounds.

Maryan marveled at the stillness. Snow clung to branches like lace. For a moment, she imagined her mother walking beside her, gathering fruit in summer heat, voices of Tehran markets faint in her ears.

At a clearing, Petey cut his engine. "Good spot for a break." He pulled a thermos from his pack and poured steaming cocoa into paper cups.

Maryan cupped hers carefully, warmth seeping through her gloves. The chocolate sweetness reminded her of Berlin cafés, of moments when she had begun to believe she might survive.

Mika nudged her. "See? Not so scary."

Maryan smiled. "More beautiful than scary." She glanced at Thomas, who was watching her as though she had just painted something only he could understand.

Petey stomped snow off his boots. "We'll head back to the lake. If we're lucky, sunset'll catch us on the ice."

By late afternoon, the sky burned pink and gold. They skimmed out onto Lake Marion, a vast frozen expanse. The ice groaned faintly under the machines, reminding Maryan of its hidden danger, but awe drowned her fear.

The horizon stretched pure white, broken only by distant houses with porch lights flickering on. Tracks behind them etched patterns like brushstrokes across a blank canvas.

Mika let Maryan take the controls of her sled while she pelted Petey with snowballs. Maryan gripped the handlebars, exhilarated, the engine's thrum like a heartbeat beneath her.

Thomas pulled up beside her, helmet visor lifted. "You're amazing," he called. "First time and you're already flying."

She laughed, hair whipping in the wind. "Maybe I was meant for snow after all."

As they regrouped near the center of the lake, Petey checked his watch. "Perfect timing. Let's head back. We can clean up and hit Porterhouse before the rush."

Maryan tilted her head toward Thomas. "Dinner?"

"Porterhouse," he said. "Best steaks in Lakeville."

"Trust us," Mika added. "You'll love it. And it'll warm us up."

The Porterhouse Restaurant glowed warmly on Kenrick Avenue, a refuge from the frozen evening. Inside, the smell of grilled meat and garlic butter wrapped around them instantly.

They stripped off heavy coats and gear, piling helmets in the booth Petey had reserved. Dark wood, white tablecloths, and the hum of diners created a timeless Midwestern comfort.

Maryan sat beside Thomas, across from Mika and Petey. A basket of warm bread arrived, its crust crackling.

"I recommend the ribeye," Petey said. "Though filet never disappoints."

Maryan studied the menu, the terms foreign: ribeye, porterhouse, sirloin. She looked at Thomas. "What do you order?"

"The filet mignon," he said. "But tonight we'll share. Best way."

Wine was poured—red for Thomas and Petey, white for the women. Soon the table filled with sizzling plates. Maryan's steak, tender and dripping with butter, melted on her tongue. She closed her eyes. "This is... incredible."

Thomas chuckled. "Told you."

Conversation flowed easily. Mika talked about her nursing program at Mankato State. Petey told hockey stories and spun jokes about Minnesota winters. Thomas teased him, while Maryan listened, laughing often, her English softening into a rhythm that matched theirs.

At one point, Mika leaned in, her voice gentler. "It must be strange, coming from so far away. To end up here."

Maryan hesitated, then nodded. "Yes. But nights like this make it less strange."

Under the table, Thomas squeezed her hand.

By the time they left Porterhouse, snow was falling in fat, lazy flakes. The parking lot glowed under the streetlights, each flake sparkling as it drifted down.

Petey and Mika headed for their truck, promising another outing soon. Maryan and Thomas lingered by his car, their breath clouding the air.

"Did you have fun?" he asked quietly.

She smiled, snow catching in her dark hair. "More than I expected. Today felt… normal. Maybe even happy."

He kissed her then, slow and lingering, as snow swirled around them.

The warmth of his life, his lips, while the snow fell around them, made for a perfect picture image that no one but Thomas and Maryan got to see.

Chapter 26

Finding Life

The drive back to Minneapolis felt like moving through a shaken snow globe. Streetlights flared into halos; the world was a hush of white and amber. Thomas kept one hand on the wheel and the other threaded through Maryan's fingers, as if the small act could stitch everything together—her laughter on the lake, the heat of the Porterhouse dining room, the strange relief of ordinary happiness. The heater hummed. Their coats rustled. Now and then he glanced over and smiled like he was memorizing her in this light.

She could still taste the faint ribbon of red wine and butter. She could still feel the tremor in her thighs from the snowmobile's vibration, the way it had turned fear into exhilaration. It left residue in her bloodstream, that speed, that daring—something like courage but not exactly, something like hunger.

"Cold?" he asked.

"A little," she said, and then, because the truth would not be kept, "Only on the outside."

He brought her knuckles to his mouth without looking away from the road. The gesture was easy, unshowy, as if it had been part of him long before he met her. Heat bloomed under her skin where his breath touched.

The apartment was quiet when they stepped in, the old radiator clicking awake as if startled. They set their gloves on the radiator cover and stood in that tiny entryway grinning at each other like thieves who had pulled off something improbable. A flake of snow had melted on his eyebrow and left a small wet gleam. She reached to brush it away, and he caught her wrist lightly, not to stop her, but to keep the moment from ending.

"Hi," he said, as if greeting began here.

"Hi," she echoed, as if the day had been only a long preface to this single syllable.

They moved through the ritual of winter—unzipping, unbuttoning, shaking off snow—like two people unwrapping a secret. Every layer gone revealed a new line of him: the curve of wrist where a glove had pressed, the reddened cheekbone where the helmet had sat, the hollow at the base of his throat above his T-shirt. Maryan felt foolish for staring and greedy for staring and unable not to stare. She hung her coat and he hung his and the two coats leaned together on the same hook like they were conspiring.

"Tea?" he asked. "Or... we could just—"

"Just," she said.

It was her voice but it sounded braver than she felt. He waited one heartbeat—long enough to be sure—and then he stepped forward so that the small distance between them collapsed.

The first kiss was not gentle. It had been waiting all day, to be alone, jostling for its chance. It landed with intention, the way a door finds the exact groove of its frame. His mouth tasted like cold air turning warm, like something clean that could still be wild. She leaned into him with a sound that surprised her—half relief, half demand—and he answered it with a low yes against her lip as if he had been waiting to be asked.

The kiss was permission. Permission written and rewritten in a language that needed no words. She rose on her toes and caught his lower lip and felt the moment when his restraint faltered—beautifully, completely—and he brought her wrist to his chest like he wanted her to feel the heartbeat that was taking over his decisions.

They stumbled backward, laughing because they were clumsy with wanting and the apartment was not made for sweeping gestures. Her hip found the edge of the breakfast counter and she gasped, not with pain but with surprise at how alive her body felt—no longer a quiet survivor, but bright, voluble, insisting. He steadied her waist and she steadied his neck and the kiss deepened the way night deepens—incrementally, then all at once, until you look up and the sky has become a different color.

"Tell me if—" he started.

"I will," she said. "I promise."

They moved toward the bedroom because that was the direction their bodies were already going. His hands were sure and unsure at once—confident in wanting, tentative in asking. That duality undid her. When his fingers found her jaw, they paused; when his palm skimmed the line of her shoulder, it lingered long enough to ask again. She answered each time with a tilt of head, with a drawn breath, with the smallest yes that felt as large as a city.

He whispered her name. In his mouth it was two syllables that seemed to touch the ceiling and come back soft. "Maryan." As if the name itself were a pledge.

Her past tried to enter the room with them. It always did, an uninvited guest with a bag of broken stories. But tonight it couldn't find her. Or maybe tonight she couldn't find it. Every time a shard of memory lifted its head—the fluorescent light of a corridor, the slam of a door—Thomas would touch some absolutely ordinary part of her, her elbow, her hairline, the heel of her hand, and the shard would dissolve, ridiculous in the face of such specific attention. He was making a map that replaced the old one.

When they reached the bed, there was a stutter of laughter because the sheets were still tangled from that morning. He tossed the pillow, she pretended offense, he apologized by dragging his mouth over the curve of her cheek to the corner of her mouth, and the apology was accepted with a shiver.

"Look at me," he said quietly, not as a command but as an invitation to be seen.

She did. The room was only lamp-lit, the color of late honey, but she could see everything she needed: the earnestness that made his lower lip tremble when he wanted something he was afraid to take, the reluctance to hurry, the way his eyes brightened in the moments before he kissed her again. She had been starved of that kind of seeing. She had fed herself on imagined kindnesses in the dark. This was not imagined.

The second kiss found a rhythm. Their mouths learned one another, faltered, corrected, laughed, returned. Kissing became its own conversation—exclamation, question, answer, a long dash where breath had to be found. He kissed the corner of her smile and she laughed into his mouth. He kissed the small scar near her eyebrow and she closed her eyes as if a door had opened. He kissed the hollow below her ear and her hands tightened on his shoulders, the sound she made both request and reward.

They separated by inches only to fall back together. Her hands slid under the hem of his T-shirt and he inhaled sharply, as if she had found a truer language. She felt his skin, heat under cotton, and the word mine rose to her tongue like a prayer she had never been allowed to say. Instead she whispered, "Thomas," and he answered, "Yes," without knowing the question.

The bed received them like an accomplice. They sank and rolled and tugged at the trouble of layers until the world was finally simplified: skin and breath and the fierce, fragile border where one person ends and the other begins. He slowed then—so suddenly the air felt warmer— because the slowing allowed them to hear everything: their breath braiding, the soft ticking of the radiator, the distant whisper of snow against the window. He looked at her again in that way that made time behave. "You're sure?"

"Yes," she said, and the yes surprised her with its clarity, its lack of trembling. "I'm here."

He pressed his forehead to hers and the kiss that followed felt like a vow.

They made love the way people do when the past has tried to dictate the script and they are determined to write their own. It was not a performance. It was a reclamation. There were moments of urgency when they clutched and climbed as if the heart could outrun itself; there were pauses so tender they felt dangerous, as if gentleness could bruise. He found the pace that met both needs—a steadiness that held a storm inside it. At intervals he asked without words and she answered without words, and when words were necessary they were small and earnest—"there," "yes," "like that," "I'm okay," "I'm here"—the vocabulary of trust.

Heat unscrolled through her slowly, then fast, then with a ferocity that frightened her until he said her name again, just her name, and the fear turned into something that felt like power. She felt the axis of the room tilt, felt the old map burn at the edges, felt her body insist on being fully alive. When the crest took her, she didn't go silent. She let herself be heard. He was right there with her, tethered, astonished, a quiet sound against her neck where he had buried his face.

After, there was no sudden falling away. They lay wrapped, their breathing trying to find the same gait. He kissed the place above her collarbone as if sealing an envelope, then moved to her shoulder, her wrist, the inside of her palm, as if returning a ring of keys to their proper hooks. Her skin felt newly named.

"Are you okay?" he asked, a whisper in the hollow between them.

She answered by taking his face in both hands and holding it close enough that he had to look at her. "Yes. I'm—" She searched for a word that didn't feel like someone else's. "I am alive."

His mouth softened; something in his shoulders fell away. "Good," he said, and then, "Good," again as if repetition could anchor this in place.

They lay quietly, but quiet did not mean absence. She could feel the echo of everything: the snowmobile's churn, the restaurant's warmth, the stakes of what they had decided without quite saying so. This was not the first time they had touched. But tonight's touch had a fervor that felt like a declaration made to the walls, the window, the snow outside—the whole world a witness.

He rose on one elbow to look at her. "You were glowing on the lake." It sounded like confession. "When you laughed... I thought, if I could give her more of that, I would spend my life trying."

Something bright pricked behind her ribs. It might have been gratitude. It might have been grief turning towards light. "You did," she said. "You are."

He smiled and kissed her forehead as if she were both a beloved and a vow he intended to keep.

They dozed, then roused as if the body couldn't bear to leave this warmth for long, then kissed again—sleepy, unguarded kisses that tasted like yes. At some point she slipped from the bed to fetch water. The floor was cold, and she laughed at herself for tiptoeing. In the kitchen the tiny red light on the stove clock told a time that didn't matter. She drank from a glass and looked at her reflection in the dark window: hair a halo of disarray, mouth fuller than usual, eyes bright like she had been crying and then forgiven. Snow traced soft arrows down the pane, pointing to a night that belonged to them.

When she returned, Thomas was half asleep, the sheet slung low on his hips, an arm thrown toward her side of the bed as if some part of him knew she had left and was bargaining with that absence. She climbed back in, and the mattress accepted her like relief. He turned toward her without fully waking, found her waist with a homing-instinct hand, and pulled her close. The gesture was automatic and therefore true.

"Hey," he mumbled, and the syllable was thick with sleep but full of happiness.

"Hey," she said back, the word warmed by the glass she had held, by the water, by the fact that she got to say hey in this bed in this city in this lifetime.

They kissed again because it was there to be done, and the kiss teased awake what had only dozed. Passion returned, less like thunder, more like a tide that knows what it's doing. He touched her with confidence now—the confidence of familiarity, not entitlement—and she answered him with the same. Urgency gathered quickly, then slower, then quick again as if they were learning the shape of the other's hunger from the inside out.

When they came together this time, it was with a ferocity that surprised them both, a sudden rush that felt like running into warm water at night. She arched and he swore softly—awed, almost reverent—and the room made a sound she had never heard: the sound of two people meeting exactly where they meant to. She held on to him as if a wind might take her, but the only wind was their breathing, and it was safe.

"Maryan," he said again, not to call her back but to meet her where she was.

"Thomas," she answered, and the names completed the circuit.

They lay a long time afterward with their legs in a tangle, the covers a mess, the lamp still on because neither of them had the will or desire to change the light. The radiator ticked softly like a patient metronome. At the edges of the window, frost crystals formed a delicate architecture, as if winter were practicing calligraphy.

She thought of Berlin, of the loading dock at the museum where she had first used charcoal to draw the shape of a new life. She thought of a painting called Ballast, of how weight could be a mercy if it kept you steady on waves. She thought of a blue cross necklace that once pressed cool against her throat; she thought of the way Thomas's steadiness did not erase her past but gave it something to lean against. She thought of the word home and decided she could put tonight beside that word and not be lying.

He fell asleep the way he did—gradually, like a tide going out. She felt the moment it changed: the weight of his arm less vigilant, the breathing deeper, the mouth softening from its careful lines. It made her want to cry, the ordinary beauty of it. She had watched people sleep before for fear they might wake angry. This watching was different. It was the witness of safety.

She propped herself on an elbow just to look at him. The lamp made a pale field on the wall and his profile drew a clean line through it—forehead, nose, mouth, chin. The small nick on his jaw where he had cut himself shaving yesterday. The thin crescent of lash shadow on his cheek. He was not perfect. He was a person. That was the relief.

She felt the tug then—the old superstition staying alive inside her body despite everything she had learned—that happiness was a thing you had to hold with both hands or it would float away. She slid her fingers into his palm under the sheet. At first he did not move. Then his fingers answered, reflexive, curling around hers just enough to make it undeniable.

"I'm here," she whispered, surprise and gratitude wrestling for the right to speak. "I'm here."

The radiator hissed once as if agreeing. The snow whispered at the window, a chorus of tiny audiences. Somewhere downstairs, a neighbor's door opened and closed and footsteps crossed a hallway and quiet returned. Her heartbeat slowed from the high pace of the evening to something sustainable, something that made promises beyond the hour.

Her mind, ever the archivist, tried to catalog each piece of the night, to tuck it into a safe folder: the first kiss at the door, the laughter at the crooked sheets, the way his mouth had said her name, the way she had not gone silent when the crest took her. She wanted to remember the look on his face when he said you were glowing on the lake. She wanted to remember that when offered tea or just, she had chosen just, and what that meant about who she was becoming.

He murmured something in sleep—her name, she thought, or maybe only a vowel that contained it. She lifted their joined hands and pressed her mouth to his knuckles. The gesture was both a kiss and an oath: to return to this exact place in time when she needed to remember that joy had a weight and a shape and a warmth, and that it fit inside her hand.

The lamp hummed. She wondered if she should turn it off. But the light felt like ceremony tonight, like a candle left burning in a window to guide the tired home. She let it be. Her eyes roamed the small room—the sweater thrown over the chair back, the slick of steam on the window, the faint boot-print smudge near the baseboard where she had missed earlier. Evidence that they lived here, if only for now. Evidence of a life.

She thought of her mother, and for once the thought did not arrive armed. She imagined telling her—about the lake, the laughter, the steak, the kiss. About a man who asked with his hands and accepted an answer given with a breath. About how the night ended not with fear but with sleep, and how she held his hand because she wanted to be the one to test the boundary between dream and waking, to make sure it held.

It did. He breathed in, breathed out, and each time his fingers tightened on hers the smallest measure, as if even asleep he was taking her attendance. Present, she wanted to say on each exhale. Present.

Eventually her own eyes grew heavy. She tried to resist because there was a superstition in her that sleep might break the spell. But spells, she remembered, are for people who are powerless. Tonight had not been magic. It had been choice layered upon choice, yes laid upon yes, two bodies insisting that the future would include them both.

She settled onto her back and kept their hands joined, their arms a bridge across the small distance. In that posture, she felt the country she had left, the city she had passed through, the lake where she had laughed, the bed where she had become, all align into a single map. The old map was still in her somewhere, folded with care, the creases deep and permanent. But over it lay this new one, more accurate not because it was precise but because it was generous.

Her last wakeful thought was not a word but a sensation: the pulse in his wrist against her thumb, steady as if the night itself were breathing through him. She let that rhythm be her proof. She let it convince the small frightened citizen inside her that this was real enough to sleep in, and maybe real enough to wake in too.

Thomas turned in his sleep and their fingers slipped, then found one another again with the blind skill of people who have learned that holding is not a miracle but a practice. She smiled at the clumsy perfection of it.

"Real," she said to the ceiling, to the radiator, to the snow scribbling its ink on the window. "Real."

The word hung in the warm light and did not leave.

She closed her eyes and did not let go.

Chapter 27

Tina Returns

Tina told herself a winter break, even if classes were in session, would fix it, or at least quiet it—the gnawing loneliness that had turned every loud, righteous week of campus life into a small ache by Saturday night.

She had lots of hook ups and dates, but nothing to cure loneliness. Thomas Quinn used to be her cure, the only boy who would talk her down, who understood her.

Her friends knew her, but it now seemed superficial, besides friends are not soulmates.

She needed to see him.

She needed Thomas Quinn.

She needed to sleep in her own bed.

She needed familiar.

The house was empty, of course. Her mother's car gone. A couple of glasses in the sink. The hum of the old fridge doing its best. Tina tossed her duffel on the floor of her childhood room and felt the familiar dip of the mattress when she sat. Posters she'd taped up before Madison were still curling at the corners—Nina Simone, a vintage "ERA NOW," the grainy flier from a city council protest where she'd first been handed a megaphone and found out people would actually listen. The carpet smelled like dust and a decade of spilled nail polish. The quiet pressed against her ears and made her want to flee back to the chaos of the dorm, the chanting, the slop of cafeteria pasta, the comfort of somebody always needing something.

She unlocked her phone before her bag had stopped settling.

You around? Need to decompress. She texted Thomas.

She watched the little blue bubble float up and vanish. She set the phone down. Picked it up again. Threw it onto the bed. Picked it up again. Notification pings came for a group thread about canvassing and a professor's announcement about midterms. None for him.

Two hours. A shower she barely felt. A grilled cheese that tasted like cardboard. The first text sat in the thread like a fool.

Hey? Everything ok?

Still nothing.

He was active, though. The little green dot popped up under his name with the cruel cheeriness of a "Smile!" sticker. He'd liked a painting. Tina tapped, more curious than she would admit even to herself.

A square of saturated red and ash-gray. A veiled woman's silhouette, not quite silhouette: the suggestion of a mouth, the bridge of a nose, the eye shaped by the absence of paint. Across her chest, delicate trails of white like missile contrails. Roses bled at the edge of her hijab, inked stems disappearing into charcoal.

Maryan.

The name hit with the sickening certainty of a missed step in the dark. She had to steady the phone with both hands.

She knew the profile picture—she'd known it since that day on the museum steps. The artist. The refugee. The woman who, in Tina's mind, had refused to choose the right words at the right time and had let the crowd applaud her anyway. Tina had rehearsed that argument a hundred times—what Maryan should have said, the courage required to say it, the "both sides" cowardice of reading names without naming the power that ended them. She had plenty of comrades who'd agreed with her, who'd ranted in the comments, who'd said it felt like betrayal. But none of them mattered as much as the green dot under Thomas's name and the little red heart blooming under Maryan's painting with the handle she knew too well.

A blurry shot from the sculpture garden. Snow piled under the spoon, the cherry stem gleaming at twilight. In the foreground, the woman's smile tilted toward the man holding the phone, and he was leaned in, eyes softer than Tina remembered them. The caption was casual and devastating: My favorite human.

Her mouth went dry. She clicked the tags—Thomas had been tagged. Of course he had. He had a grin like an unguarded admission. She zoomed until the pixels fell apart and then squeezed her eyes shut because she could still see what had been written even when she couldn't see anything else.

She let out a sound that wasn't crying and wasn't laughter, a hot broken exhale that tasted like rust. For a sharp second, the feeling surged up—No.

No.

He is not yours—and then it receded under the ordinary facts: they hadn't been together in years; she'd left for Madison, and he'd stayed; they'd tried to be friends and then failed at that too.

He was free.

She was free.

That was the line you tell yourself when you want to be the kind of person who doesn't believe other people belong to you.

And yet.

He should be with someone who knew what he meant when he pointed at the sky in September and said, "Look, the geese are re-routing." Someone who had carved T+T on a damp oak bench with a stolen pocketknife while they were supposed to be at youth group.

Someone who had watched him hold a bat like the bat was an extension of his heart.

Someone who didn't look like fire and disaster in a woman's shape.

She closed the app and reopened it and closed it like a nervous tick. She threw on a jacket and drove. Starbucks was a moral compromise today; so what. The coffee was good and burning and she needed to be holding something that could scald the skin of her mouth into feeling. She took it to Lake Harriet like a pilgrim with an offering and parked near the band shell. The air smelled like thaw and mud and old leaves. March had made everything brown and expectant.

The bench was exactly where it always had been. The carving was still there, worn down but legible: T+T. The + made her ache. A plus sign is just two lines crossing without promise, but they'd called it a plus because they were young and everything might have meant forever. Her fingers traced the groove until she felt splinters lift at the edge.

She texted him again, the last attempt she told herself she would allow.

I need to talk to you.

The message sat beside the others, blue rectangles stacked like bricks around a door that wouldn't open. The lake didn't move.

The sky had that exhausted Minneapolis light that turned everything into a slightly cheaper version of itself and then dared you to love it anyway.

A runner went by in shorts because this city is full of lunatics; a dog shook dirty water across the sidewalk as if baptizing her in more mediocre grace.

The fire started as a coal and then found air. It didn't matter that she knew it was ridiculous. It didn't matter that the rational voice in her head tried to narrate. She had always mistrusted rational voices; they were the ones who explained away the feeling until no one could taste it anymore.

By late evening, the museum's west side was a blunt rectangle against the sky. She knew the route to the loading dock; she'd been there during the protest, the day she'd shouted until her throat was raw and someone had poured water into her mouth and she'd turned and seen Maryan not on a pedestal but at a microphone at the top of the steps with cameras angled upward as if gravity had reversed for her.

A friend in BLM had texted that day, months ago: she's got a space in the dock while she's here. Temporary.

Temporary. The word made something in Tina leap toward it like a starving thing toward salt.

She didn't knock. She pushed the steel door with her shoulder, and it gave, heavier than anything had a right to be.

Turpentine and damp concrete hit her first. The air was warmer than outside and smelled like work. An industrial light hummed; the floor carried the memory of pallets and footprints. The space had been turned into a room by someone who decided a room is simply where you stop moving and stay: a sleeping bag folded near a stack of crates, a kettle on a hot plate, a mug with tea leaves silted at the bottom, an old radio with a piece of blue tape labeled Farsi in Sharpie. Brushes stood in jars throat-deep in cloudy water. A half-finished canvas leaned against the far wall like it had grown there. It was a blood-sunset of red and a shadowed storm of black and ash-gray, jagged sections colliding. The angles looked angry the way a trapped animal looks angry—less rage than the refusal to die.

Maryan was in front of it, barefoot, paint stippled up her calves, wearing an oversized sweater that had once been white. She had a brush in one hand and a jar of crimson pigment in the other. She turned at the sound with an expression that started at surprise and moved quickly to wary.

"Can I help you?" Her English had the shape of another language around it, a gravity Tina always noticed because the voice in her own head had only ever had the one shape.

Tina crossed her arms as if they were a script. "You're dating him?"

For a second, the woman's face didn't change. Then she blinked, frowned faintly. "I'm sorry—who are you?"

She'd seen her. Tina could tell. The day of the protest. The loud one. The crazy one who wouldn't sit down. The woman's gaze took in the details the way artists probably did: the damp ends of Tina's hair from the snow, the scuffed toe of her boot, the way she stood like she wanted to run and punch something at the same time.

Maryan set the brush on a rag as carefully as if it were a living thing. "Who are you?" she repeated.

"Doesn't matter." Tina heard her voice rise into a register she hated—high and brittle. "You know damn well who I mean."

Something like irritation passed over Maryan's face and then went, replaced by that steadiness she'd had on the steps. There was a pause long enough for Tina to take in what she hadn't wanted to take in: a Polaroid tacked to the wall with painter's tape, Thomas's face looking like the air was easier to breathe near her. The kettle's on-switch glowed red. A sleeping bag like someone thought tonight might be another night they didn't go back to your apartment because the painting needed them or they needed the painting.

"Seeing who," Maryan asked, and her voice wasn't mocking, just cautious, like she wanted to be sure she wasn't stepping into a trap.

"You know who." Tina tasted it like a cut in her mouth. "Thomas."

"I didn't know I needed your permission," Maryan said evenly.

It was the evenness more than the words that made Tina's stomach drop. Evenness meant you weren't being taken seriously; it meant you were being managed. She felt the need to bolt and dug her heels into the concrete instead.

"You don't need my permission," she snapped. "You just need to have a conscience."

Maryan's eyes narrowed the tiniest bit, not the American way where people show their offense like a billboard but the slower way where someone draws their strength closer. "Excuse me?"

"You stood up there, on the steps, with the cameras on you and the white people clapping because refugees make them feel compassionate, and you didn't even mention the U.S. bombing," Tina said, the words finally finding the track they'd worn into her tongue. "You condemned Israel for Tehran, fine, but not one word about the drones we sent last fall. Or the sanctions that choke families. You let them clap. Like you were safe. Like you were grateful."

The woman stared at her for a heartbeat. Then she set the pigment down, its glass clink precise, and held Tina's gaze like you would an animal that might bolt.

"I buried friends in Iran," Maryan said, each word pulled clean. "I smuggled myself out in a crate. I watched my father bleed. You think I am grateful?"

"You sounded like it," Tina spat before she knew she'd chosen the words.

Silence arrived in a slab. Even the humming light seemed to hum more quietly.

When Maryan spoke again, the volume of her voice had dropped far below Tina's. "I am allowed to choose my moments," she said. "My grief is not a public service."

It should have shamed Tina, and maybe a small part of her was shamed, but the rest of her was already reaching for the next thing because the momentum felt safer than stopping. "You're with him," she said, and heard the nakedness in it and hated herself and went on anyway. "You're letting him in. And he doesn't even understand any of this."

"You're wrong about him."

Tina laughed, a short bark that hurt her own ears. "No. I'm wrong about you. I thought you were one of us."

Something like a sigh moved through Maryan's body. She stepped closer but not into Tina's space, just enough to soften the angle. "You think 'us' is simple?" she asked. "A side? A slogan? I live between borders. I have died between them."

The room felt hot. Too tight. Tina's coat suddenly itched. She wanted to strip it off and couldn't give that much ease to this woman.

"I stood up," Maryan went on, "and named every victim I could remember. Iranian. Israeli. Palestinian. I refused to be a mouthpiece for your purity tests."

Tina flinched before she could stop herself. "So, my causes are the problem now?"

"I did not say that."

"You didn't have to." Tina could hear herself turning cruel to keep from turning small. "You already picked your side."

Maryan tilted her head like she could see the fissure running behind Tina's eyes and was deciding whether to touch it. "I didn't steal him," she said gently.

"This isn't about him," Tina said, and her voice betrayed her by shaking. "This is about you." Then honesty took the wheel and made her a liar. "And it's about him."

They stood like that long enough for the smell of turpentine to settle into Tina's clothes. Somewhere above the dock, footsteps crossed and crossed again—someone locking doors for the night, someone deciding not to come down here and ask two women if everything was all right because nothing in either of their faces said they wanted a witness.

"You want to tell me something," Maryan said at last, and it wasn't a challenge; it was an invitation. "Say it."

Tina felt it like a push to the brink. The words that had driven her all the way here gathered, not a chant now but a plea disguised in anger.

"He's using you," she said.

The sound of it shocked her. She hadn't expected it to come out so bald.

"You are convenient. You're paint under his nails and a sad story at his back. It's winter and he's lonely.

You'll be a season.

He won't stay."

The words flushed the air between them. Tina swallowed the bile that rose and told herself it tasted like truth.

Maryan didn't move right away. Then she wiped her fingers on the rag like a ritual and looked at Tina as if cataloging the injuries that would make someone choose a blade like that. "I'm not convenient," she said without heat, which somehow made it heavier. "I am difficult. I am the opposite of convenience. He knows that."

Tina's throat burned. "Men like to think they know things."

"And women like to think they can save men from themselves," Maryan said, not unkindly. "I will not apologize for the fact that he is kind to me."

"You think kindness lasts?" Tina heard the way the shape of her own life poured into the line and couldn't find the brakes. "He's a good guy, sure. He's Minnesota nice and holds doors and says please and thank you. He'll show up to your show and smile and tell everyone how proud he is. But he doesn't stay. Not when it's hard. Not when it gets ugly. Not when it means choosing you against the world he's actually in."

Maryan's face didn't crumple; it didn't do anything so easy. It went still in that way that said a person loved themselves too much to let you rearrange them. "He has stayed," she said. "In the night, when I shake so hard I could break my own ribs, he stays. "

Tina had nothing for that except the bench at the lake and the memory of a boy who had promised to love her forever and then loved her for a while and then didn't know how to love her in the way she needed when the world kept expanding and she kept choosing it. She knew the details didn't map. She knew she was comparing weather systems like they were interchangeable.

She took a breath that felt like scraping the barrel. "He didn't answer my texts."

Maryan blinked, genuinely thrown. "I don't—what?"

"I came home," Tina said, and now she heard how young it sounded. "I texted. I needed—" The word stuck. "Never mind."

Maryan's gaze softened without collapsing. "I am sorry you are lonely," she said. "Truly. But I will not apologize for not performing my grief the way you want, or for loving someone you think should have been yours."

"Love?" The word knifed its way out. "That's a big word for a secondhand couch and a Polaroid."

"You barged into my studio to tell me you know what will happen to my life," Maryan said, and the smallest smile pulled at the edge of her mouth. It was not a kind smile, and it did not need to be. "I think I'm allowed one big word."

Tina's eyes burned. It felt unfair that the woman had the better lines even in the place where Tina thought she was strongest. "You don't even live here," she said, petty and hating the pettiness. "You're going to Berlin. Or wherever. He belongs here. You'll leave, and he'll—" She stopped. The sentence finished itself anyway in the slice of air between them: and he'll be fine, and I'll still be alone.

Tina wanted very badly to say something that would make time rewind. She wanted to ask a question that would split Maryan into pieces easy enough to fit into a category. She wanted to hurt her in the exact way she felt hurt. The urge felt ridiculous and enormous, and she recognized it for what it was: the old injury flaring, the weather changing, the part of her that had never forgiven Thomas for not being able to follow wherever she led him at seventeen closing its fist around a new set of facts.

"You really think he'll stay?" she asked finally, and it was almost a whisper. Not a taunt. A dare she wished the woman would take and then fail.

Maryan considered the red on her brush, then set the bristles against the canvas and made a single, unhurried stroke that changed the entire balance of the piece. "I don't know," she said. "But he is here now. And I am here. And that is a life."

The gentleness of it almost did Tina in. She pressed her nails into her palms until the little half moons burned. "He's using you," she said again, softer, as if saying it kindly would make it truer. "He's lonely. You're…you. You're a story that makes him feel like a better man. He's not built for your storms."

"You do not know his storms." The first hint of anger crept into Maryan's tone, not hot, not wild—controlled, the way a person who has learned to be precise with force has to be. "You know your version of him. I know mine. We are both right and we are both wrong. But I will not let you make me a prop in your grief."

Tina felt the breath leave her like someone had opened a door inside her chest and winter had come in.

On the wall, the Polaroid tilted slightly under the tape. Thomas's smile did not change. The red on the canvas deepened into a color that was not blood and not sunset but something in between, a thickness that might hold.

"Please leave," Maryan said, the words clean. Not a shout. A boundary.

"I see his posts, we are still friends, he calls me to check on me and make sure I am OK, I have seen his burn through girls like you, girls who are lost, girls who are not wanted. Believe me, as a woman, he will break you and throw you away." shouted Tina.

"Please leave, now." Maryan said with more urgency.

Tina lifted her chin because the only armor she had left was her posture. "One day," she said, and now she could hear how cruel she sounded and there was nothing she could do to stop it, "you'll see I was right."

"Maybe," Maryan said, and the assent was so unexpected, Tina blinked. "Maybe you will be. And if you are, I will survive it. I always do."

The fire in Tina's chest flickered, confused by the absence of a proper enemy. She turned on her heel because leaving was the only win she could claim. The hallway's concrete smelled like mop water and echo. Her boots made that hollow ringing sound that had always made her feel like she was bigger than herself. In the car, her hands shook—anger, shame, hunger, the need to tell someone what she'd done, the certainty that anyone worth telling would tell her she'd made it worse.

She drove to the bench. By then the lake had gone slate. The carving was just black lines in the low light. She sat and remembered a night senior year when she and Thomas had sat with their knees pressed together and told each other where they wanted to live in five years—she'd said "anywhere there's a fight," and he'd said "here." She had laughed into his shoulder and told him she would drag him into the world and he had kissed her damp hair and said "good luck," not as sarcasm but as honest blessing.

They had both believed they could be currents and not rocks, and then the water had had its say.

She texted him again, because the part of her that refuses to die refuses to die.

Never mind. Don't call. I shouldn't have.

She watched the delivery receipt pop and then turned the phone facedown and tried to be a person who did not wait.

Chapter 28

Splinters in the Paint

It was late when Maryan texted Thomas.

Can you come by the studio?

She stared at the message until the blue ticks appeared, then tucked the phone under a rag as if it could burn her hands if she held it too long.

The loading dock behind the museum was quiet, the kind of late that makes a big building sound like it's sleeping. A single halogen bulb flooded the concrete bay in yellow light, pooling in the middle and thinning at the edges. The air smelled like turpentine and damp cardboard, a scent she privately called *honest*. Unfinished canvases leaned against the cinderblock walls like a quiet jury: tall, raw, some stapled to cheap stretcher bars, some pinned to foam. A kettle ticked on a hot plate; somewhere above her, a door clicked and then clicked again, the security guard making his rounds.

Maryan had her sleeves rolled past her elbows. Black gesso smudged her palms and the crooks of her fingers; a streak of charcoal ran from wrist to mid-forearm where she'd wiped at an itch. She paced a neat rectangle between a crate and the back wheel of a dolly, chewing the side of a thumbnail until her jaw ached. She didn't know if she was ready for what she'd asked for. She didn't know if readiness was even a thing a person like her ever got to feel.

She heard the growl of his truck before she saw it, a familiar engine note that her body recognized faster than her mind. Headlights hit the loading-bay door and slid away. The engine cut. A moment later, the door creaked open, the heavy kind of creak that metal doors do when they've been doing their job for decades.

"Hey," he said, stepping inside and bringing March cold with him.

His baseball cap was backward, which meant he'd been working late; he always flipped it to keep it from hitting ducts when he was up on a ladder. Dust clung to the toes of his boots, a gray halo at the edge of the rubber. His maintenance jacket smelled like winter air and a little like pine from the freshener in his truck. There were two small crescent-shaped slices on his knuckles, new.

Maryan looked up, tried to read his face, tried to gauge whether *now* could bear the weight of what she was about to lay on it. He looked tired and open in the way he always did when he came straight from a job: all the pretending plucked off, only the person left.

"Hey," she replied.

He walked toward her with his arms open—tentative, offering, not assuming. "You sounded... serious."

She nodded. Serious was the cheap word for the kind of heaviness that had settled on her chest. She stepped into his hug and let herself rest in it for one heartbeat longer than she should. His chin touched her hair; his hands were careful at her back. She felt the warmth of him as information: *you're not alone*. She knew better than to mistake information for outcome.

He pulled back and smiled the small smile he used when he wanted to tilt a room toward kindness. "What's going on?"

Maryan turned away and walked to the easel as if her feet had been assigned there. The canvas on it was primed, nothing more—an emptiness she'd prepared as a stage for the conversation. Her fingers ran along the raw pine of the stretcher bar like you'd run a hand along a guardrail while crossing a narrow bridge.

"I wanted to talk to you about something that happened… " she said.

Thomas leaned against the work table, palms braced behind him, the pose of a person trying to give someone else the floor. "Okay."

She took a breath, shallow first and then deeper, found the courage she hated and also loved herself for. "Tina came to see me."

He blinked. "Tina?" The name sharpened his tone instantly; she watched the muscles in his jaw wake up. "What the hell for?"

Maryan kept her voice level. Her own training in detonation and control had been harsher than his. "She wanted to warn me. About you."

He straightened. "Warn you? What, like I'm dangerous now?"

"She said... a lot of things," Maryan answered, feeling her throat get tight. "That I shouldn't trust you. That I was being used."

Thomas laughed, bitter and low, without humor. "Used. That's rich, coming from her."

"She thinks you're just with me because I'm different," Maryan went on. "Because I'm... convenient for your guilt."

His face flushed quick, color rising under winter-pale skin. "Bullshit."

Maryan held up a hand, the universal sign for *don't aim that at me*. "I'm not saying she's right. I'm telling you what she said."

He ran a hand over his jaw and started to pace, a short line past the dolly and back. "She texted me today. Out of nowhere. Said I was embarrassing myself." He let out a humorless snort. "Like I should still be with her, like she owns me."

Maryan frowned. "Did you tell her about us?"

"No." He shook his head. "I didn't have to. She probably figured it out when she saw your photos."

Maryan swallowed. The thought of being seen through a camera's rectangle made her feel both exposed and stubborn. "She also said that you'd never stay with someone like me," she added quietly. "That I'd just be another story you told your friends later."

He moved closer, his face going softer, eyes reading hers like a page he didn't want to skip. "Do you believe any of that?"

"I don't know what to believe, Thomas." She met his eyes because not meeting them would be an insult to both of them. "I know you've been good to me. Kind. But this world—your world—is not my home. It never will be."

Thomas rubbed the back of his neck, the move he did when he wanted to slow himself down. "I'm not asking you to live in my world forever," he said. "I'm just asking for right now."

Maryan's fingers pressed into the canvas edge until the pine gave a little. "And I'm telling you... I won't be here forever."

Silence stretched, thin at first and then taut.

"You're leaving?" he asked finally, the word landing heavy in the middle of the room like a dropped tool.

"Not yet," she said. "But yes. Eventually. I need to go back to Europe. To my sister. To Berlin." She heard the apology in her voice and hated it. "It's where my work has meaning. It's where I'm connected."

His jaw tensed. "So what have we been doing here? Playing house until you disappear again?"

"No," she said, too quickly, and then steadied. "I've been trying to find something good. Something alive in the middle of all this grief." She swallowed. "And I did. With you."

"Then why walk away?"

"Because it's not real."

"It *is* real," he said, stepping toward her, palms out. "Whatever Tina said—whatever she thinks she knows— she doesn't get it. She never did."

Maryan took a step back and felt the cool metal of the easel bump her hip. "And maybe you don't either."

It hit him like a slap. His face hardened, not cruel—just braced. "So this is about your art. Your purpose." His voice moved to the safer ground of sarcasm. "And I'm just what, a warm body until you get back to your real life?"

She felt the snap rise in her like a wave she couldn't stop. "You think this is easy for me?"

"I think it's convenient for you to leave before it gets hard."

"I've already lived through hard!" she snapped, her voice cutting against the concrete. "This—this is survival. I have to keep moving or I'll disappear."

He stared at her, and when he spoke again his voice had lost its edge. "You know what I hear?" he asked. "I hear fear. That maybe, if you stayed, this could be something real. And that scares you."

Her hands curled into fists without command. "You think you're the only one who's real here?" she whispered, then louder: "I have buried people. I have escaped a shipping crate. I have stood in front of crowds and spoken the names of the dead. *Do not* talk to me about fear."

He looked away, pain flicking across his face like shadow. "You're doing it again," he said softly. "Running."

"And you're doing *your* thing again," she answered, cold now, the anger dropping in temperature to something more dangerous. "Trying to fix something you don't understand."

"I've tried to understand you, Maryan. Every day since we met." His voice frayed. "You shut down. You disappear."

"And what would *that* look like?" she demanded. "Telling you about prison? About what happened to my mother? About how I still wake up expecting sirens? You think you can hold that?"

"I could've tried." His mouth trembled, just once. "If you'd let me."

They stood there, breathless—the air in the dock turning thin as if someone had climbed thirteen floors and opened the door at the top to a different pressure. The halogen hummed. A truck rumbled somewhere far away. A drip ticked into the slop sink with patient accuracy.

Finally, Maryan said, very quietly, "Thomas... I love that you tried. But this... this was never meant to last."

He shook his head once, sharp. "No. Don't you dare say that. You don't get to decide for both of us."

"But I do," she whispered, the truth cutting her throat on the way out. "Because I'm the one who has to keep surviving."

A long silence folded itself neatly between them.

He stepped back. His jaw went tight; his eyes shone the way eyes do when a person is doing the dignity math in their head and deciding which way to go. "Then survive without me," he said.

And just like that, he turned and walked out.

The door shut with a sound the building had made a thousand times and never for this reason.

—

Maryan didn't cry right away.

She picked up the nearest brush—too big for detail, too soft for priming—and dragged it across the canvas. Black, thick, violent. The bristles chattered a little against the tooth of the gesso and left a ridge that looked like a small mountain range.

Then another line. Then another.

The sound of bristles and breath built into a rhythm. Her shoulders found the old work posture, the one that belonged to nobody, not even her. The muscles below her shoulder blades began to burn in that way that told her she was alive and doing something about it.

Paint ran down her wrist and pooled in the hollow of her elbow. She ignored it and pressed harder.

Only after the paint bled onto her skin, after the first lines had dried into an ugly, necessary geography, did she let herself slide down the wall and sit on the concrete. She sat with her knees up and her head back and waited for the ceiling to blur.

She had chosen survival.

It still felt like losing everything.

—

When the tears came, they weren't cinematic. They were the small, stubborn kind—salt, heat, breath hitching now and then like her body was trying to remind her it had limits. She wiped them with the hem of her T-shirt and then with the back of her hand and then let them fall and evaporate because the dock's air was dry enough to drink them.

Her phone vibrated where she'd thrown it. She didn't move. It stopped, started again, stopped. The third time it hummed longer and then quit.

Eventually she stood, because standing is sometimes the only way to finish a thing. She cleaned the brush until the water ran gray-then-clear and laid it across the jar like a bridge. She poured hot water over a teabag and let it sit until the liquid went dark. When she took a sip, it scalded her tongue in a way that felt righteous.

She looked at the door. It looked back.

She turned the music on—not loud, not loud, not as if she were trying to drown out thoughts, just enough to remind the air that someone had stayed to keep it company. A woman's voice, old and low, slipped into the space between things.

The phone buzzed a fourth time. She checked it—not because she wanted to, but because she didn't want to lie to herself about wanting to.

—I'm outside. Can I come back in? —T

She stared at the words until they blurred. Then she typed, erased, typed again.

—Not tonight. Please.

A minute. Two.

—Okay. I'm sorry. I shouldn't have said that. I'm just—
—It's okay.
—Do you want anything before I go? Tea? Food? To yell at me where I can hear you?
—I don't want to yell.

—Okay. I'm going to leave you alone. I'm here. But I'll leave you alone.

She put the phone face down and listened to the particular way his truck started, the note of it, the way it idled for a second longer than it needed to, then pulled away.

She made three more marks on the canvas. Wiped one with the flat of her palm. Made a fourth that didn't belong, then left it anyway.

She lay down on the sleeping bag without unrolling it and stared at the triangle of light on the ceiling until the edges turned soft.

—

Thomas drove without the radio, same way he did leaving Tina's that night long ago.

The truck made its usual clicks and rattles: the seatbelt buckle tapping the side of the seat, the plastic bag of work gloves sliding and sliding back again, the coin in the cupholder he kept meaning to remove. He kept his hand at ten and two like a teenager because he needed the discipline of it. The city went by, unconcerned—storefronts shuttered, a pizza place still lit, a bus at a stop with two people in parkas looking like a single shape.

His mouth kept forming the thing he wanted to say and then he kept not saying it because saying it to an empty cab would make it loose in the world with nowhere to land.

At a red light he thumbed a text he didn't send: **I'm not leaving.** He thumbed another: **I will book the flight to Berlin.** He deleted both because both sounded like promises made to win an argument and he didn't want to win an argument. He wanted to meet a life where it stood.

He turned the truck toward Lyndale out of habit, then changed his mind and took Lake instead, then changed it back. At home, the loft felt like a witness; he didn't ask it to be. He showered too hot, stood with his hands against the tile and the water beating the back of his neck, the word *survive* sounding like a place he'd never been and a place he had never left.

He left his phone on the counter. He made tea because that's what he knew how to do in the presence of pain. He didn't drink it. He sat on the floor with his back to the couch like a man who'd forgotten how chairs worked. The apartment smelled like cedar and laundry detergent and the faint, sweet ghost of the donut box he'd thrown away this afternoon.

Then survive without me.

He hadn't meant it like a weapon. He could hear how it had sounded like one. He could see it now, the way she would have heard it through a history he couldn't fix, the way *without me* would push against a staircase of other *without me's* stacked below it—mother, country, freedom, all of them stairs that had dropped out from under her feet while she was still on them.

He pressed his palms together hard enough to make a line of heat at the base of his thumbs. He breathed the way the physical therapist had taught him after he'd wrenched his shoulder last winter—count in, hold, count out—because the body, unlike the mind, liked instructions. He thought of the first time she had said his name like a confirmation and felt something in his chest loosen cruelly.

The phone buzzed.

He looked at it like it might bite.

—**I need some space,** the message read. **Please.**

He understood space as a thing you leave between live wires so they don't arc and set the whole wall on fire. He understood it as air in a room when too many people are breathing too hard. He understood it as the distance a batter needs between himself and the plate to keep from crowding the strike zone. He understood it as love. He tried to.

—**Okay,** he typed. **How do you want it to look? Do you want me not to text at all? Or do you want one text so you know I'm here but I'm not asking you for anything?**

He watched the three dots appear and disappear.

Chapter 29

Thresholds

The fight with Thomas, Maryan told herself, was for the best.

Repeating it gave the sentence a handle she could hold. With the exhibit winding down, the thought that had been waiting at the edge of every day stepped into the center: I need to go back to Berlin. To Marineh. To the work that began before Minnesota and will go on after it.

So she did what she'd trained herself to do when the heart got noisy—she narrowed the field of vision. She shut down every corridor of thought that didn't lead to canvas, paper, pigment, the slow, unshowy labor of showing up. It wasn't denial so much as triage.

Survive now; explain later.

The atrium at the Minneapolis Institute of Art, which had been a small city for months, was finally exhaling. Friday's rush had thinned to a hush. Light fell through the gauzy, clouded skylights in long, slanting panels that made dust look ceremonial. Volunteers rolled up the freestanding signs and leaned them in obedient triangles against the wall. Curators with soft voices and gloved hands straightened labels, nudged frames a hair, spoke to each other in the tender register people save for newborns and paintings. A photographer on the far side of the gallery crouched and stood, crouched and stood, the shutter stitching a private rhythm into the room.

Maryan stood off to the side with her hands tucked under her elbows, not quite hugging herself. She'd stopped counting attendance around the third week, when numbers had begun to feel unrelated to anything that mattered. The wall labels bore her name now—MARYAN DARYA—in an elegant serif that made everything look older than it was. Even printed, even formal, the name sometimes floated a few inches off the wall, like it belonged to a safer version of her who lived elsewhere.

Chelsea found her in that twilight between public and private, clipboard tucked beneath one arm, a red scarf knotted at her throat like a small flag. Chelsea was the kind of woman who made difficulty look like a choice, whose lipstick obeyed the line of her mouth no matter the hour.

"We're preparing final records for the close," she said, scanning the room with a curator's part-proud, part-bereaved gaze. "It's been a powerful season, Maryan. Turnout exceeded our expectations."

"Thank you," Maryan said, which was the right sentence for the moment. The other sentence sat just behind it: I don't know what to do with praise that doesn't require me to kneel.

Chelsea hesitated, then stepped closer, lowering her voice the way people do when they mean something. "I've been meaning to ask. Would you be open to donating a piece to the permanent collection?"

Maryan blinked, a bodily pause as her mind rearranged the furniture. "One of mine?"

"Yes. Only if you're comfortable." Chelsea's smile was steady, not coaxing. "It could be a smaller work, or something that didn't sell. But your voice belongs here. It would mean a lot to keep part of this exhibition in the city, for good."

The phrase *leave something behind* opened a door inside Maryan's chest she hadn't realized was latched. The idea of claiming space not temporarily but on purpose, indefinitely, made the room tilt. She glanced around the gallery the way you do when you're trying not to cry— cataloging light, lines, floor, exits.

She didn't answer. Chelsea, bless her, didn't press. "Think on it," she said, and drifted away in that museum-witch way of disappearing without ever looking like she'd left.

In the hour after closing, the building changed dialects. Public noise gave way to maintenance music: the purr of a vacuum, the soft *shff-shff* of a dry mop gliding over stone, the hiss of a radio in a pocket. The chemical tang of floor wax rose and layered itself over the museum's older smells—wood, paper, human breath.

Maryan walked alone, letting the gallery reorder her pulse. She stopped in front of one of the older pieces—a charcoal on heavy paper framed in inexpensive black wood. The staff had mounted it beside one of her newer color works, and visitors often treated it like a sketch, an aside. It had never been that for her. It had been the opposite.

The drawing had been born in the loading dock on a day that had begun in ordinary gray and then become a hinge. The same day a maintenance guy with a backward cap and a careful mouth had asked if the song on her speaker meant what it sounded like it meant. The same day she had drawn until her wrist cramped and her stomach protested and still she couldn't stop. Lines climbed the paper like scaffolding, then decided to be a body—rooted, open, a weight that steadied rather than sank.

She hadn't named it until days after the fight, when language returned with its small compass. The word had come like a whisper she didn't want to trust; she'd looked it up to be certain it belonged.

Ballast: heavy material placed low in a vessel to improve its stability.

The definition struck her with ridiculous, devastating clarity. It was such an unromantic word for what he had done simply by existing where she could reach him. Thomas had anchored her without binding. He had seen her grief and not turned it into a project. He had not asked to be the reason; he had been content to be a fact. When she cracked, he had not tried to glue her into a shape she no longer recognized; he had sat with the pieces and learned the dangerous patience of not rearranging.

That afternoon in the dock, as she tore at the paper with charcoal, everything that had been bubbling below the spoken world—fear, hope, desire, loneliness, the older griefs that made new ones ring—had found a mark to live in. The figure at the center wasn't him, not literally; she wasn't interested in likeness. But its stance—slight forward lean, arms low, spine sure without rigidity—was a sentence her hand understood. Around the shoulders she had smudged with two fingers to suggest weight, not as burden but as gravity. If people read rescuers in the drawing, that was their language. She had drawn balance.

Now, under the soft museum lights, with the building exhaling around her, she realized she could let it go. Not because it had stopped mattering—because it wouldn't. Because it had done its job so completely it no longer needed to be hers alone.

Maybe leaving it here was another kind of ballast. Maybe the city deserved the weight of this steadiness as much as she did. Maybe claiming space was not only standing on steps with cameras pointed up but also letting a quiet work in a quiet corner alter the angle of a stranger's day.

She found Chelsea near the registrar's office, scarf loosened, clipboard marked with fresh checkboxes. "I've made a decision," Maryan said.

Chelsea's eyebrows lifted. Hope looked good on her.

"The charcoal on the east wall," Maryan said. "The day I met someone who... reminded me how to stand again. I'd like to donate it."

"Ballast," Chelsea said, the name a confirmation. "It's beautiful." She softened the administrative with warmth.

"We'll complete the paperwork, reframe if needed, catalog, store it properly. And we'll show it again. I promise."

"Thank you," Maryan said. She meant more—thank you for making a place in the world where my work can live without me guarding it, thank you for not asking me to translate—but she had learned to let gratitude be a small thing when it needed to be.

Back in the studio—the loading dock that had become a sanctuary by accident—she sat cross-legged on the concrete, hands stained dark again. Light came in dusty at the high windows. The distant growl of delivery trucks made a pulse she'd come to rely on. Her sketchbook lived on her lap, its pages holding quick, disobedient lines: bodies moving, faces blurred, barbed wire that could have been music staffs, the idea of flight, the idea of home, the outline of a man drawn with negative space.

She hadn't heard from Thomas in over three days. Not since the fight. Not since she'd told him the thing that was true and still sounded like betrayal: that someday, inevitably, she would leave.

She had said it cold. She wished she'd said it better. He had gone quiet in the way that meant he was doing long math inside, then he had nodded at some invisible point and left. The apartment door had clicked shut with the softest kind of finality. She had stood there listening to the absence, and then she had gone back to her canvas because that was the lever she knew how to pull.

With a fingertip she traced a smear at the bottom of the charcoal drawing on the wall—her own fingerprint, pressed into the paper months ago and now preserved under glass as if to say yes, a real person made this with their real hands. She'd thought, early on, about cleaning the edges, making it museum-neat. She hadn't. The fingerprints were the argument.

Visitors had stood in front of *Ballast* for long stretches and made their own weather. Some cried; some took notes; one young woman had left a folded slip of paper beneath the frame. Maryan had picked it up and read only the first line—*Thank you. I didn't know I was allowed to feel this way*—and put it back. The rest wasn't for her. Response is a collaboration you don't get to direct.

Chelsea's sentence replayed in her head—*Your voice belongs in this place*—and for the first time, Maryan didn't flinch. Maybe belonging, for her, would always be a verb and not a noun. Maybe the museum could hold the artifact while she carried the living thing out into the weather.

She stood to go, then paused at the threshold and looked back one last time. Part of her, the young part that doesn't die, hoped he'd walk in right then, sheepish grin, hoodie he refused to retire, eyes doing that careful scan for her shape. He didn't. The gallery kept its dignity. The air held.

She let the longing pass through her without letting it take anything on its way out. She turned toward the work that still needed finishing before travel, toward the paperwork that would make the Berlin residency real, toward the wire transfer receipts folded carefully in her bag for Marineh. She chose the line she'd written in charcoal in the margin of a canvas where no one would see it unless they dismantled the whole: *I choose breath.*

The gallery was empty. The painting would stay. She would not. Between those facts, something steadied. She felt it— not triumph, not relief. A ballast settling low in the hull so the vessel could turn its bow toward the ocean again without capsizing on the leaving.

Chapter 30

The Color of Forgiveness

Thomas stood in front of the jewelry counter at a small boutique store on 50h and France. The shop was quiet, scented faintly with sandalwood and rosewater. Outside, the sky had turned that uncertain color between gray and blue, threatening rain. Inside, the lights were soft, golden, casting warm halos on the glass displays.

He didn't know what he was looking for. Not really.

He had walked past this store twice before finally stepping inside. Something had tugged at him—intuition maybe, or just desperation. He hadn't heard from Maryan in three days. She hadn't blocked him, not exactly. But she hadn't responded either. And in those silences, she became a ghost. Just another chapter in someone else's tragedy.

The clerk was middle-aged, wearing thick glasses and a tailored charcoal suit. She watched him patiently as he circled the cases, eyes moving from one glimmering display to another. Gold chains, silver lockets, Baltic amber, tribal turquoise. All beautiful. All meaningless.

Then he saw it.

It was simple. A small cross, enameled in cobalt blue, hanging from a delicate silver chain. The color stopped him. The exact same blue color he had seen in her paintings, her mother's favorite color—the one she said she sad inspired her to dream.

The clerk noticed him stop.

"That one?" she asked, approaching quietly.

"Yeah," Thomas said, swallowing. "That one."

"It's handmade. From a studio in Thessaloniki. The enamel work is old-school—glass over sterling silver. Cobalt blue is the most difficult to fire without cracks."

Thomas didn't care about Greece or firing techniques. All he could think about was Maryan's face the last time they spoke. How she wouldn't meet his eyes when she told him about Tina confronting her. How her voice had trembled—not from fear, but from conviction—when she said she needed to go back to Europe. That their time here, together, might need to end.

She hadn't asked him to wait.

She hadn't asked him to follow.

She had only said, "You deserve someone who stays."

Thomas pulled out his wallet. "I'll take it."

"Gift box?" the woman asked.

He nodded, then hesitated. "Do you have a little card?"

She handed him a folded one with a watercolor print of Berlin on the front. He stared at the blank space inside for a long minute, then wrote only four words:

You're my world.

The apartment building where Maryan lived was one of those older converted industrial buildings, all exposed brick and tall windows. Her unit overlooked a narrow alley and a shared rooftop garden that only bloomed in spring.

Now, as he climbed those same stairs, box in his pocket, he felt like he was walking toward a border.

Either he'd cross it and find her on the other side—

Or he'd find a wall that couldn't be climbed.

He knocked.

No answer.

He knocked again.

Still no answer.

He almost turned around, almost walked back down the stairs, thinking maybe this was stupid, maybe she wasn't home, maybe she didn't want to see him. Maybe she'd already left. Maybe—

Then the door opened.

Maryan stood there in a loose t-shirt and jeans, barefoot, a smudge of black charcoal on her cheek. Her hair was down. Her eyes were rimmed red, like she hadn't slept. But she wasn't angry.

Just tired.

"Thomas," she said, her voice small.

"I had to come," he said.

She didn't reply.

He stepped inside without asking. She didn't stop him.

Her apartment was dim. The windows were open, letting in the summer air. A few half-finished canvases leaned against the walls—strange pieces, dark and geometric, far different than her usual human forms. One looked like a cracked doorway. Another, a silhouette crumbling into dust.

He reached into his jacket and pulled out the box.

"I got you something."

Maryan didn't move.

"It's not much. I mean—it's kind of a symbol, I guess. But I saw it and… I thought of you."

She took the box slowly, opening it in silence.

When she saw the necklace, her breath caught. She didn't say a word, but her fingers curled around the tiny cobalt cross like it was made of bone.

Then she looked up at him. Her eyes shimmered.

"You remembered."

"I never forgot."

Maryan held the necklace in the palm of her hand for a long time, the cobalt cross catching the dying sunlight slanting through the window. It glowed like something alive, something impossibly fragile, like her.

She didn't speak right away.

Thomas stood in the center of her living room, awkward in his own skin, unsure if he should sit or just keep standing there like an idiot. He wanted to reach out to her, but he didn't want to scare her off. Not again.

Finally, she spoke.

"This color," she said softly, brushing the chain between her fingers. "It was everywhere in my mother's house. On the tiles in the kitchen. In the little ceramic dish she used to keep her wedding ring. It's the blue of the mosques in Isfahan. The domes. The sky just before sunrise."

Thomas said nothing.

She touched the cross again. "I don't know what to say, Thomas, its perfect."

Thomas stepped closer. "Maryan... I don't know what the future holds for you. Or for us. I'm not asking you to promise anything. I just need you to know that I love you. I'm not afraid of your past, and I'm not afraid of what's next. If you go back to Europe... I want to be part of that too."

Her jaw tightened.

He could see her shoulders go rigid, as if preparing to hold back an avalanche.

"Don't say that," she whispered. "Don't make this harder."

"Why does it have to be hard?" he asked. "Why are you already packing this up like it's over?"

"Because it has to end sometime, Thomas. I'm not from here. I'm not staying here. And you—" she turned to him, eyes brimming, "—you have a whole life here. Your family, your future. You can't follow me across the ocean just because you gave me a necklace."

"That's not what this is," Thomas said, stepping closer. "This isn't about guilt or fixing you or proving something. This is about how I feel when I'm with you. Like I finally understand what it means to choose someone. Even when it's complicated. Especially when it's complicated."

Maryan shook her head. "You don't know what it's like. You think loving me is enough. But love doesn't open borders. It doesn't erase the pain I carry. It doesn't make the nightmares go away."

He reached out and touched her arm gently. "Then let me stay in the nightmares with you."

Her breath hitched.

"You remember when I told you about the container?" she said, voice cracking. "How I almost died in that wooden box? I couldn't breathe. For three days I didn't know if I would make it. But even worse was coming out and realizing no one knew who I was. I had to prove I was real. That I wasn't some lie smuggled across borders."

"You don't have to prove anything to me," Thomas said.

Maryan stood across the room, her body taut with resistance, her voice trembling even as she tried to sound resolute. "I cannot stay in America. I am not a refugee here. I am not a citizen here. I am a nobody here."

Thomas didn't flinch. He didn't back away. "We'll figure it out together," he said softly. "We will fight the demons together."

She let out a sharp breath, half-laugh, half-sob. Her arms folded tightly across her chest like armor, but it was slipping. The vulnerability had cracked through already. He could see it in her eyes—the flicker of exhaustion, the ache for someone to hold the weight with her.

Walking slowly toward her, Thomas placed his hands gently on her hips and pulled her close.

Maryan didn't resist.

Her forehead dropped to his chest, her breath warm against his shirt. For a moment, they just stood like that— her breathing jagged, his slow and steady as if trying to lend her some of his calm.

"You don't understand," she murmured into him. "You've never had to run. You've never lost your language, your land, your mother's scent on a pillow."

Thomas didn't try to answer that. He didn't pretend to understand her pain. Instead, he ran his hands up her back, over the curve of her spine, grounding her in the present. In him.

"I don't need to understand everything," he said. "But I can be here. I *am* here."

She looked up.

Her eyes, rimmed red, searched his face—his jawline, the scar by his eyebrow from a childhood fall, the gentleness that lived in his eyes only when he looked at her.

"You're stupid," she whispered, her voice catching. "You'll regret this."

"Maybe," he said with a faint smile, brushing a strand of hair from her cheek. "But not tonight."

And then he kissed her.

It wasn't a kiss of hunger or frenzy. It was reverent. A kind of asking. His lips moved slowly against hers, tasting salt and history, grief and hope. She kissed him back with a sharp need that surprised even herself—a need not for escape, but for anchoring. For witness. For being seen.

His hands slid beneath the hem of her shirt, fingertips gliding over the scar tissue along her ribcage. She flinched—not from pain, but memory.

"I'm here," he whispered again, steadying her with both hands. "With you."

She nodded. Just once.

As she raised her arms to let him remove her shirt, the cobalt cross necklace he had given her swung loose around her neck, the color catching the low lamplight. He paused, his lips brushing the center of her chest, just above the pendant.

"This," he said, pressing a kiss there. "This means you're not nobody."

Maryan swallowed hard.

They moved together slowly, a rhythm more sacred than sexual. The bed creaked softly under their weight, but neither noticed. Thomas undressed with quiet care, watching her the whole time, not like a man who wanted something from her, but like someone grateful just to be allowed close.

She pulled him down to her, her palms sliding over his back, her thighs wrapping around his hips. Her body, once braced for survival, now moved with intention. She wanted this. Not as escape, not as distraction—but as reclamation.

Their lovemaking was quiet, punctuated only by the sounds of breath and sheets and the city faint outside the window. Sometimes she clung to him, other times she seemed to drift, eyes closed, as though feeling her body for the first time in years. He never hurried her. He matched her pace, slowed when she slowed, deepened when she pulled him closer.

And when her tears came—quietly, suddenly—he didn't stop.

He held her tighter.

"I'm sorry," she whispered, a hand covering her face.

"No," he said, brushing her hair back gently. "Don't be. You're safe."

Afterward, they lay together, their bodies still entangled, the cobalt cross resting just below her collarbone like a seal.

Thomas traced his finger across her shoulder, down her arm, until his hand met hers and held it.

"I still might leave," she said, voice hoarse.

"I know," he said.

"But I might stay for a little longer."

He kissed the top of her head.

"That's enough."

They didn't need to talk about the future that night. The immigration status, the art grants, the train tickets, the time difference between Minneapolis and Berlin. All of that would return in the morning.

For now, all that mattered was this: she was not alone in her grief. She was not invisible in her love.

And in Thomas's arms, Maryan, for the first time in a long time, felt like somebody again.

Thomas broke the silence first. "Do you remember that day we got lost driving around Lake Harriet? It was supposed to be a ten-minute trip. Took us an hour and a half."

Maryan smiled. "I remember. I kept pointing out houses I wanted to live in."

"And I kept saying we couldn't afford them," he said, laughing. "Even the ones with sagging roofs and paint peeling off the porch."

"You said you'd fix one up for me someday."

"I still would," he said. "If you ever came back."

Maryan's voice turned soft. "You really would, wouldn't you?"

Thomas didn't answer right away. "I already started fixing things, you know. Not a whole house, but my dad's workshop. I kept your paintbrushes. They're in a mason jar on the shelf."

She blinked away new tears. "You kept them?"

"I couldn't throw them out," he said. "They still smell like turpentine and burnt paper."

"Those were my Berlin brushes," she whispered. "The ones I used for the exhibit you came to in secret."

"I didn't come in secret. I just didn't want you to feel obligated to talk to me."

"You were there?" she asked, stunned.

He hesitated. "Yeah. I stood in the back. Wore a Twins cap so no one would recognize me. Watched you give that speech. Watched people cry."

She sat slowly on the studio bench. "Why didn't you tell me?"

"Because you looked... free. Powerful. Like you didn't need me anymore. And honestly? I didn't want to make it about me."

Maryan exhaled. "I wish I'd known."

"I left you a note."

She sat up straighter. "What?"

"In the guestbook," he said. "I signed it T.Q. You probably thought it was a student or something."

She covered her mouth. "That was *you*? It said, 'The weight we carry is worth it if it's carried for love.' I thought it was some poet."

"I'm no poet," he said with a nervous laugh. "I just remembered you said once that art needed to carry something real. I figured maybe love was heavy enough."

She was quiet for a long time. Then: "Do you believe in fate?"

Thomas's voice gentled. "I didn't. But after you? I'm not so sure."

"I used to think fate was just the excuse people gave when things went wrong."

"And now?"

"Now I think maybe it's what we call the things we can't undo. Like loving someone who isn't staying. Or leaving behind a painting that carries your whole heart."

He was quiet. "Would you have painted *Ballast* if we hadn't met?"

"No," she said without hesitation. "That piece only exists because of you. Because of how you didn't push. Because you saw me as a person, not a project. Because you waited."

"I wasn't waiting," he admitted. "I was holding on. There's a difference."

Maryan closed her eyes, letting the truth of that settle. "Still. You were my ballast."

"And now?"

She froze.

Then softly she said "Forever."

Chapter 31

The Return

Maryan sat cross-legged on the floor of her apartment, surrounded by piles of crumpled packing paper, half-filled boxes, and canvas bags bursting at the seams. The air smelled faintly of turpentine and old paper—the familiar scent of charcoal sketches and oil paints left drying on her studio shelves. She picked up a torn sketch from the floor, one she had made during a restless night months ago, before the grant, before the exhibit, before she knew she would be leaving all of this behind. The lines were hurried, jagged, like she had been trying to wrestle the night onto the page.

The walls felt both too big and too small. Too big because memories clung everywhere—the corner where the sunset light turned golden against the hardwood, the narrow kitchen where she had made tea while talking politics with Thomas, the window overlooking the cracked sidewalk where the first snowfall had caught her by surprise. Too small because she could already feel the emptiness that would come after the last box was taped shut and the last canvas rolled.

Her throat caught. "I can't believe this is happening," she whispered, the words absorbed by the apartment's silence.

From the hallway came soft footsteps.

Thomas appeared in the doorway, hands in his pockets, eyes tired but steady. His presence had a way of making even silence less sharp.

"Hey," he said quietly.

Maryan looked up and tried to smile. "Hey."

He walked in and lowered himself beside her, careful not to disturb the fragile piles. His jeans brushed against a roll of bubble wrap, and it popped loudly in the stillness. They both laughed, the sound small and necessary.

"Are you ready?" he asked.

She shook her head. "No. How do you even get ready to leave your whole life?"

Thomas reached out and took her hand. His fingers were calloused, warm, grounding. They always were. She thought of the way he held wires steady when repairing museum lights, of how those same fingers traced her shoulder in the middle of the night.

"You don't have to have it all figured out," he said. "You just have to take the first step."

Maryan swallowed hard, feeling the weight of that truth. She didn't know if she had steps left in her.

Her gaze drifted to a small charcoal sketch pinned to the wall—an untitled piece that reminded her of Ballast. It showed a lone figure walking against a storm, the lines bending around it like wind, but the figure moved forward anyway, unsteady yet upright.

"Remember this one?" she asked Thomas.

He nodded. "I do. You said it was about learning to carry the weight without breaking."

She sighed. "I'm scared I'll break."

Thomas squeezed her hand, his thumb brushing the space between her knuckles. "You won't."

Before she could reply, there was a knock at the apartment door.

Maryan stood and opened it to find Chelsea, the museum's art director, framed against the hallway light. Her short blonde hair was tucked behind her ears, and she carried a slim wooden box tied with a ribbon.

"Maryan," Chelsea said warmly. "I brought you something."

Maryan blinked, surprised. "What is it?"

Chelsea stepped inside, smiling. "A little something to remember us by. From the museum."

Maryan untied the ribbon. Inside was a handmade ceramic tile painted with an abstract swirl of blues and blacks—a miniature homage to *Ballast*.

Her throat tightened. "It's beautiful."

"I thought you might want to keep it," Chelsea said softly. "Even if the painting is leaving."

Maryan's eyes shimmered. "Thank you."

Chelsea reached out and squeezed her arm. "We're all going to miss you. You've left something important here, Maryan. More than you realize."

"I have to meet the next batch of artists, but Maryan you are special. You will always have a second home here. Please keep in touch." Said Cheslea.

After a few hugs goodbye, Cheslea smiled and walked out.

Maryan glanced at Thomas, who stood quietly by the wall, his gaze steady on her. She realized then that she wasn't just packing up belongings, she was preparing for her future.

For the first time in a long time, a future felt possible.

The sky was heavy with low, swollen clouds as Maryan and Thomas drove toward Lake Harriet for one last walk. The air outside was thick and cool, smelling of wet earth and fallen leaves—a scent that always carried memories, even for her, who had only lived in Minneapolis a short time.

Maryan sat quietly beside him, her fingers nervously tracing the seam of her jacket. The city passed in blurs: brick storefronts with neon beer signs, sleepy sidewalks where bundled children dragged sleds, the green-gold stretch of parkland where she and Thomas had spent countless hours walking, arguing, dreaming.

At the lake, they parked near the bandshell. The water lay still under the gray sky, ripples spreading slowly like secrets told too softly. The bare trees leaned toward the shoreline, their branches skeletal, their roots clutching earth that was already hardening with frost.

They found the bench—the one by the water's edge where Maryan had once confessed her fears and Thomas had told stories about his grandfather's fishing trips.

They sat side by side, shoulders nearly touching, the silence between them heavy but not uncomfortable.

Maryan watched the ripples chase across the water's surface. The wind tugged at her scarf, and she pulled it tighter, a small shield against the ache in her chest.

"Do you remember when we first came here?" Thomas asked quietly.

Maryan smiled softly. "You tried to teach me about ice fishing."

He chuckled. "And I was so confused why the fish didn't freeze."

They both laughed, the memory warming the gray afternoon.

For a while, neither spoke. The only sound was the water lapping against the rocks, and the distant cry of a gull.

Finally Maryan turned to him, her voice almost lost to the breeze. "I'm scared."

Thomas reached out and covered her hand with his. "I know."

"I don't know if I'm ready for the 'after,'" she whispered. "Leaving feels like tearing away part of myself."

Thomas nodded slowly. "But sometimes we have to leave to find the parts we didn't know were inside us."

She squeezed his hand. "Promise me we won't forget this place."

"We won't," he said. "Because we're not really leaving, are we?"

"No," Maryan whispered. "We're just starting somewhere new."

Thomas's hand slipped into his pocket. For weeks he had carried the weight of a small box, feeling it press against his thigh during late-night drives, museum days, and mornings when he'd watched Maryan wake with hair tangled across her face. He had rehearsed words in his head—half speeches, half prayers—but standing here, with Lake Harriet rolling quiet before them, he realized he didn't want speeches. He wanted honesty.

"Maryan," he said, his voice catching slightly.

She turned, eyes deep and searching.

He slid off the bench and onto one knee, the cold earth pressing through his jeans. He pulled the small velvet box from his pocket and opened it, revealing a simple ring, a band of gold with a modest stone that caught the gray light like a flicker of fire.

Maryan gasped, her hand flying to her mouth. "Thomas—"

He looked up at her, eyes steady. "You are my ballast, Maryan. You've taught me what strength really is—not the kind that muscles carry, but the kind that keeps you standing when storms try to knock you down. You've shown me love isn't about fixing the past, but building the future together. I don't want to imagine a life without you. Not here, not in Berlin, not anywhere. Will you marry me?"

The world seemed to still—the gulls, the ripples, even the clouds paused as if waiting.

Tears slid down Maryan's cheeks. She shook her head once, not in refusal, but in disbelief. "I never thought—" Her voice broke. "After everything, I never thought I'd get to choose love."

Thomas reached for her trembling hands. "Then choose it. Choose us."

Her lips trembled into a smile. "Yes."

He slid the ring onto her finger, his hands shaking as much as hers. She pulled him up into her arms, and their kiss was fierce, desperate, sealing the word that had changed everything.

Yes.

The wind whipped across the lake, scattering leaves into the air like confetti.

Chapter 32

Love Is In Season

The first thing Maryan heard was the radiator's soft ticking, the sound of heat nudging its way through the old pipes of Thomas's apartment. A pale light pressed against the curtains, hesitant, as though the January morning wasn't quite sure it wanted to arrive. She lay very still, eyes open, listening to the rhythm of his breathing beside her.

Thomas was still asleep, one arm flung across the quilt, his chest rising and falling in steady waves. She let herself study him the way she might study a painting—slowly, noting the textures, the imperfections, the quiet beauty. The stubble on his jaw had grown dark overnight. His lips were slightly parted. A small crease ran across his cheek from the pillowcase. Ordinary details, yet to her they were extraordinary, the proof that he existed here, warm and alive, within her reach.

She rolled onto her side, bringing her face closer to his shoulder. The faint scent of soap and wood lingered on his skin. She pressed her lips there lightly, not enough to wake him, but enough to anchor herself in this moment.

Today was the day.

The word repeated itself in her chest like a drum. Today she would leave Minneapolis, leave this apartment, leave Thomas—at least for now. Berlin waited, with its galleries and grant obligations, with the studio space she had fought for and the curators expecting her arrival. This was the next step, the logical step. But logic did not quiet the ache behind her ribs.

She closed her eyes. In another life, she might have chosen to stay. But life had never given her the privilege of staying. From Tehran to Shiraz, from a shipping crate to Berlin, from the museum in Minneapolis to this small bedroom—her story had always been one of leaving.

Beside her, Thomas stirred. His brow furrowed as though he were dreaming something complicated. Then he blinked awake, his gaze hazy until it landed on her.

"Hey," he murmured, voice thick with sleep.

"Hey," she whispered back, smiling despite the heaviness in her chest.

He reached for her, pulling her against him. Their bodies fit together in the easy, unthinking way they had learned over weeks of nights and mornings. His hand slid into her hair, his lips brushed her temple.

"You've been awake a while," he said.

"I wanted to remember," she admitted.

He pulled back enough to look at her. "Remember what?"

"Everything. The way the light looks in this room. The way you breathe when you're dreaming. The sound of the radiator. I don't want to forget."

His eyes softened. "You won't forget. And you don't have to. I'll be with you in two weeks. That's nothing."

Two weeks. She repeated the number like a mantra. But to her, days had always stretched long when measured against absence.

They stayed like that for a while, wrapped in silence, the clock on the nightstand ticking forward. Finally Thomas kissed her cheek and sat up. "We should get moving. Don't want to cut it too close."

Maryan nodded, though her body resisted the idea of moving at all.

Together they dressed slowly, deliberately, as if dragging out every minute. Maryan folded the last of her clothes into the suitcase, smoothing the fabric even though she knew it would wrinkle again on the plane. Thomas made coffee, the smell filling the kitchen with a comfort that already felt like nostalgia. They ate toast in near silence, breaking it only with small smiles across the table.

Her eyes caught on the small ceramic tile Chelsea had given her, the miniature homage to *Ballast*. It lay wrapped carefully in her carry-on. That, too, was a tether— something to remind her that what she had built here would not vanish.

When the last bag was zipped, they stood in the doorway, coats on, boots laced. Maryan turned in a slow circle, her gaze sweeping across the apartment. The cracked window frame. The mismatched mugs drying by the sink. The scuffed floor where Thomas's toolbox had once left a mark. Every detail felt like a farewell.

"I don't want to go," she whispered.

He took her hand, squeezed. "You're not leaving me, Maryan. You're just… going ahead. I'll catch up."

Tears stung her eyes, but she nodded.

They stepped out into the cold, breath pluming in white clouds. Thomas carried her suitcase down the stairs, his movements practical, efficient, but she could see the set of his jaw—the way he was holding himself steady for her sake.

The truck was already dusted with snow from the night before. He brushed the windshield clear with his sleeve, started the engine, and loaded her suitcase into the back. Maryan climbed into the passenger seat, hands folded tight in her lap.

As they pulled away from the curb, she pressed her forehead to the window, watching the neighborhood slide past—the convenience store on the corner, the café where they had shared coffee after long nights in the studio, the mural painted on the brick wall down the block. Each one felt like a small goodbye.

The highway stretched out ahead of them, a gray ribbon lined with snowbanks and flickering billboards. It was early enough that traffic moved lightly, but the sky was already thick with clouds that promised more snow by evening. Maryan kept her gaze fixed on the horizon, though her reflection in the glass kept catching her eye—her dark hair tucked beneath her scarf, the small gold ring on her finger catching faint light.

Thomas's hand found hers across the console. His grip was steady, even while he kept his eyes on the road. She let her thumb rest against his knuckle, memorizing the texture of callus there. The same hands that strung wires in the museum. The same hands that had steadied her the night she cried over her mother's death in Berlin. The same hands that had lifted her chin at Lake Harriet when he asked her to marry him.

Neither spoke for long minutes. The silence between them wasn't empty—it was heavy, alive, filled with things they didn't want to say too soon.

Finally, Thomas cleared his throat. "You nervous?"

Maryan smiled faintly. "Yes. But not about the flight."

"Berlin?"

"Berlin, the studio, the exhibit... all of it. It feels so big." She paused, her voice thinner. "And leaving you here feels even bigger."

He squeezed her hand, eyes still on the road. "Two weeks. That's all. I'll be there before you've had time to figure out the train system."

She laughed softly, the sound cracked by tears. "You make it sound simple."

"It is," he said firmly. "It has to be. Because I'm not letting this"—he lifted their joined hands—"slip."

The hum of the tires filled the cab. Outside, the snow blurred into a curtain of white along the fields, the trees etched like ink against sky. Maryan leaned back into the seat, closing her eyes for a moment, trying to fix the feeling of him beside her, the sound of his voice, the way Minneapolis looked in winter.

As they neared the airport, the skyline appeared behind them in the rearview mirror—the faint outline of towers and church steeples fading into haze. It struck her then how many places she had left behind: Tehran, Berlin once before, now Minneapolis. Each goodbye had hurt differently. This one, though, was not only sorrow. It was threaded with joy, with hope, with the terrifying possibility that she could have both love and art.

The exit for the airport came too soon.

Thomas guided the truck into the lanes, following the signs toward Departures. The traffic thickened—cars dropping off passengers, shuttles pulling in and out, luggage carts rattling across the pavement. The terminal loomed ahead, glass and steel gleaming even under gray light.

Maryan felt her stomach tighten. She clutched his hand tighter as they pulled to the curb.

He parked, shifted into neutral, and turned to her. "We'll walk in together."

She nodded, though her throat was too tight for words.

Thomas carried her suitcase with one hand, the other free so he could hold her fingers as they entered the terminal. Inside, the airport buzzed with movement—families juggling strollers, business travelers tapping at phones, voices echoing in half a dozen languages. The air smelled faintly of coffee and disinfectant. Announcements crackled overhead, boarding groups called like clockwork.

They moved slowly, as though time might bend around their steps. Maryan glanced at every detail—the banners for Minneapolis tourism, the ceiling strung with harsh lights, even the polished floors that reflected the scurry of shoes. She wanted to remember this place not because airports were beautiful, but because this was where the line between before and after was being drawn.

At the airline counter, Thomas set down her bag. He stood beside her as she checked in, answering the clerk's polite questions, accepting the boarding pass printed in a neat rectangle of paper. Maryan slid it into her jacket pocket, her hand shaking just slightly.

With her bag tagged and sent away, they were left with only her carry-on. The final stretch of togetherness lay ahead: the walk to the security line.

Maryan's chest felt as though someone had looped wire around it and pulled tight. She reached for Thomas's hand again, gripping it like a lifeline.

"Hey," he said softly, leaning down so only she could hear. "Don't disappear on me. Not now."

She swallowed and nodded. "I won't."

They walked slowly toward the TSA checkpoint. The line stretched long, travelers queuing with weary patience, trays stacked for shoes and laptops. A uniformed officer directed traffic at the rope barriers. The scent of coffee was stronger here, mixed with perfume and the faint metallic tang of machinery.

When they reached the point where only passengers could continue, Maryan stopped. The rope between them and the waiting line felt like a wall.

Thomas set her carry-on down and turned to face her fully. His eyes, steady all morning, now shimmered with unshed tears.

"This is it," she whispered.

"For now," he said quickly. "Not forever."

Her breath shook. "What if something happens? What if—"

"Maryan." He cupped her face in his hands, his thumbs brushing the damp corners of her eyes. "No what-ifs. Two weeks. I'll be in Berlin before you've had a chance to miss me properly."

She gave a choked laugh. "I already miss you."

"Good," he said, his smile trembling. "Then you'll be waiting."

He leaned down and kissed her, there in the middle of the busy terminal, surrounded by strangers who hurried past without pausing. The kiss was fierce, desperate, as though it might carry them across the ocean. She clung to him, her fingers digging into the back of his coat, memorizing the exact shape of his shoulders beneath the fabric.

When they pulled apart, both were crying.

"You promise?" she asked.

"I promise." His voice cracked, but the words were solid. "Two weeks."

She nodded, pressing her forehead to his for one last moment. Then, with trembling hands, she picked up her carry-on.

The TSA agent gestured her forward.

She took one step, then another, turning back after each as though she might run to him again. Thomas stood rooted behind the rope, watching her with a steady, breaking gaze. When she reached the conveyor belt, she glanced back once more. He lifted his hand, palm open, and she lifted hers in return.

The line moved. She placed her bag in a tray, slipped off her shoes, and passed through the scanner.

When she emerged on the other side, she turned again, searching across the distance. Thomas was still there, still watching, his figure small against the sea of travelers. Their eyes locked one final time before a wall of people passed between them.

Maryan pressed her hand to her chest. Her tears did not feel like sorrow. They felt like joy, like proof. She was not leaving him behind. She was carrying him forward.

As she walked toward her gate, she whispered to herself: *Two weeks. Just two weeks.*

And for the first time in all her years of leaving, she believed in the promise of return.

Chapter 33

The Build Begins

Waking up in Berlin, in Thomas's arms, was something Maryan had never dared to imagine—not in the Minneapolis apartment with its humming radiator and scratchy curtains, not in the intervening weeks of quiet, negotiated space, not even in those wild moments of longing when a person lets themselves picture a life too tender to speak aloud. But here it was, ordinary and unastonishing in the most astonishing way: the low, steady hum of old radiators clanking back into warmth, the smell of bread from the café down on the corner drifting up like a daily benediction, the diffuse winter light filtering through gauzy curtains and flattening the world into a soft lithograph.

Ordinary. And the ordinariness felt revolutionary.

Thomas stirred beside her, the weight of his arm slipping heavier across her waist, his breath switching registers as a dream let go. He mumbled something half-remembered— maybe a joke he'd meant to tell her last night and forgot mid-sentence—and she smiled into the pillow. He'd taken to Berlin's rhythms with a humility that surprised and steadied her. The city, with its post-industrial grit and fluent melancholy, could press too hard on people. She had seen it. Berlin's ghosts were not shy; they didn't hide their names. She had worried they would weigh on him, a boy from the plains whose life's map had been drawn with big skies and straightforward distances.

But Thomas, true to form, had simply nodded at the old and marveled at the new. He learned to hold both without commentary. He carried a paper map in his pocket as if to honor a past self and a transit app on his phone to honor the fact that life gets easier when you let it. He learned the U-Bahn lines not by color but by the names that felt good in his mouth: Kotti, Südstern, Hallesches Tor. He bought day passes and never abused them. He tried to tip in places where tipping wasn't a thing, then learned not to, and laughed at himself without pride. He listened more than he spoke, which in Berlin is a form of fluency.

He left in a week. They both knew it. She could already feel the goodbye tracing its outline in her chest, a seam being basted before the real stitching began. But seams are what hold things together; she reminded herself of this as she slid out from under the blanket and padded barefoot into the kitchen.

The kitchen was two meters by three and somehow contained four lives: the present tense of a kettle and two mugs, the recent past of a drying rack, the long ago of her own earlier years in the city, and the stubborn future of a stack of forms she and Thomas had been wading through. Civil paperwork. Consulate forms. Questions about dual citizenship, translations, witnesses, registrars, appointments made months in advance and then rearranged in weeks because a person's life did not always consent to the state's calendar. The bureaucracy of love.

In Germany, marriage wasn't just vows and rings; it was also documents—birth certificates translated and stamped, residence registrations, proof of legal freedom to marry, appointments at the Standesamt that felt like buying train tickets into a future you had already promised each other. With Thomas's travel schedule and visa constraints, they'd had to persuade the clerk at the Bezirksamt Charlottenburg to look at their file with kinder eyes. The woman—square glasses, hair that had given up on style in favor of authority—had squinted at the pile across her tidy desk, then begrudgingly offered a date: March 17.

Two weeks away. Maryan had called it too soon. Thomas, the absolute menace, had called it perfect timing. In the end, she didn't resist. Her past had taught her not to wait for perfect conditions; the ship leaves whether or not you feel ready, and learning to step aboard while your hands are still shaking is as good a definition of courage as any.

He adapted while she painted. Thomas made calls from her kitchen, his knee bumping the cabinet door with the rhythm of an old song. His father—quiet but supportive— arranged his ticket with a kind of Midwestern efficiency that made Maryan want to hug him on the spot. Quincy, Thomas's older brother, offered his vacation days without hesitation, lacing a joke through the offer: "Fine, I'll come supervise," which meant I want to be there. Petey, the youngest, who had never left the U.S., responded with a string of question marks and then a line that made Maryan laugh out loud: *Do they let you bring peanut butter in your suitcase or is that a crime?*

Maryan watched it unfold like a play she never would have written for herself. Her life—once shattered in a shipping crate, then reassembled into motion and survival—was now being pieced together with faith and phone calls and the kind of family logistics that looked like ordinary magic. There is a kind of love that doesn't announce itself as romance; it shows up in texts about layovers and offers to carry an extra duffel and reminding you to bring an outlet adapter.

Outside, Kreuzberg stayed gray in a dignified way. Drizzle. The rumble of the U-Bahn overhead, like a neighborhood heartbeat. Spätis with their long-necked beers and gummi candies and clementines stacked in crates by the door. A florist bucket of tulips, too early and therefore absolutely necessary, puncturing the sidewalk with color. Men smoking under awnings and women pushing prams and a professor-looking person in the same thrift-store coat she'd once owned, all of them threading the gridlike without telling the city what to be. Berlin's unofficial slogan—*poor but sexy*—had always bored her. The truth felt closer to *broken but brave*.

Two days later, her phone buzzed with an Istanbul number. She flung the brush into a jar as if throwing it could somehow move the signal faster.

"*Marineh?*" she said, breathless.

"I got the visa," her sister's voice answered through a thousand kilometers and a handful of bureaucracies. "For Germany. Just three months, but I got it."

Maryan closed her eyes, clutching the phone to her chest like a relic, let the relief rush through her ungracefully. Tears did what tears do when they decide to be kind: they arrived fast and didn't require explanation.

Thomas looked up from the kitchen table, where he had been sorting translated documents into stacks with paperclips and good intentions. "Good news?" he asked, not assuming, not requiring the world to arrange itself into his idea of hope.

"She's coming," Maryan whispered. "Marineh's coming."

Thomas's grin unfurled across his face like something he'd been holding back for politeness and could finally let loose. "Then we'll wait to get married until she's here."

Maryan blinked, practical even inside gratitude. "But she doesn't arrive until the eighteenth…"

He nodded, already solving. "Then we'll move the date."

"You can't stay that long," she said automatically, defending him against his own generosity.

"I'll change my flight," he said, shrugging as if the laws of airline rebooking had been passed with him in mind.

She shook her head, the old impulse to apologize already forming. "Thomas, you don't have to keep—"

He stood, crossed the small room in two steps, and cupped her face. "Stop telling me what I don't have to do," he said, gentle but immovable. "I want to wait for your sister. This isn't just your marriage, it's ours. If she's part of your heart, then she's part of this."

She kissed him because there are sentences you answer with your mouth or not at all.

They spent the next morning in the Standesamt's waiting room with a stack of forms and a hope they tried not to call hope. The clerk who called their number wore the exact same square glasses as the first clerk at the Bezirksamt; Maryan wondered if the frames were part of the uniform, a way to remind citizens that the state expects you to see clearly before you ask for anything. The woman glanced at their file, then at the calendar, then back at the file. "March seventeenth," she said, tapping the date. "This was difficult."

Maryan could see Thomas physically hold himself back from saying *we know*. He had learned how to make himself smaller inside institutions and larger on sidewalks; she loved him for that.

"We need to move it," Maryan said, and there it was: the risk. She explained about her sister, the flight, the temporary visa, the distance that had shaped their lives for too long already.

The woman pursed her lips in a way that might have meant no in another universe. Here, strangely, it meant wait. She left them with a poster about the city's civil services and disappeared into the back. When she returned, she had a new sheet of paper with a blue stamp that made the whole document look authoritative. "The eighteenth," she said. "Ten in the morning. Bring the same documents. Bring your witnesses. Bring yourselves on time."

Thomas nodded, grateful as if the woman had offered him shelter instead of a bureaucratic adjustment. "*Vielen Dank,*" he said, careful, pleased.

The woman's mouth softened. "*Gern geschehen,*" she said. You're welcome.

They walked out into cold sunlight and bought a paper bag of still-warm Brötchen from the corner bakery because some moments require a carb. On the way back, Thomas called his airline, endured an AI voice and a hold music symphony, and emerged victorious with a new departure date and the kind of fee that makes you swear and then shrug because money is not the only thing with a clock attached to it. He called his father next. "We shifted," he said. "Are you good with the eighteenth?" Through the line, Maryan could hear a man who did not love airports say, "We're good," and felt herself like the city feels when spring pushes under the door.

They spent the days in between living like people who had known each other for years and like people who had met last week. Maryan painted in the mornings, lines that were less careful than she was used to, marks that let the charcoal speak first. Thomas fixed the window latch that had stuck since 2019, put felt pads under the chair legs, swapped the dying bulb in the stairwell for an LED, taught the neighbor kid how to oil a squealing hinge and earned a lifelong ally who would bring them pastries the day after the wedding with the seriousness of a diplomat. He learned to say *"Entschuldigung"* in a way that made strangers forgive him for any number of small sidewalk crimes.

At night, they walked without destination: down along the Landwehr Canal, over Admiralbrücke where guitarists played for coins that clinked like gentle rain, past the Turkish grocer where the oranges piled like little suns, past the anarchist bookstore with a window full of pamphlets printed in a dozen languages. He pointed at parts of the city she had stopped seeing from familiarity, like a person at a museum reminding you that the painting you pass by daily is a wonder.

They went to Neukölln to buy rings from a goldsmith who worked in a tiny studio at the back of a courtyard. The bands were slmple—thin, plain, a little imperfect. "Exactly like us," Thomas said, delighted, and the goldsmith laughed, because humor and humility translate.

They chose flowers the day before the ceremony because tulips had crashed the party of winter and Maryan loved their stubbornness. The florist wrapped them in paper the color of old paperbacks and tucked in a sprig of rosemary—"for remembrance," she said, as if Maryan didn't already know that all art is built with rosemary.

Thomas's father and brothers arrived on a Wednesday afternoon with rumpled hair and the look of men who had just negotiated a series of metal corridors designed by people who hadn't met each other. The arrivals hall at BER was a threat of noise, but then there they were, and Thomas's body did that involuntary thing a child's body does when it spots home in any form: it straightened and softened at once. Introductions were handshakes and then hugs and then jokes: Quincy bowed to the city as if it were a person; Petey held his passport out dramatically as if expecting someone to snatch it back; their father, who had the hands of every carpenter who ever decided that wood deserved care, looked around and said, "So this is Berlin," the way men say *so this is the Grand Canyon.*

They went for currywurst and ate it standing because that is the rule. They took pictures on the bridge because that is the law. Thomas's father asked a stranger to take a family photo, and the stranger did that thing where they take six "just in case," and everyone smiled the way people smile when they cannot believe what their lives have done.

On the morning of the eighteenth, the sky did not commit to blue but it thought about it. Tulips stood in a jar on the table like a chorus of small yeses. Maryan tied her hair back with a strip of cobalt cloth she had embroidered, the same thread she had used on the collar of the white tunic dress she'd sewn at the studio in a long afternoon with

Sahar's laughter and a playlist of Armenian songs breaking and mending time by turns. The dress was simple—the shape of a promise you don't adorn because what matters is inside it. Thomas wore his only suit, the one he'd worn at Quincy's graduation, and it fit him better now because love and winter will do that to a man.

Marineh's flight from Istanbul landed at eight. She walked through the glass doors into the hall carrying a bag that looked too light and a strength that had never weighed less than a mountain. For a second, the sisters paused because the eyes have to confirm what the heart already knows, and then they closed the distance as if they had invented running. They held each other at an angle that would have broken a weaker roof. Maryan felt her sister's ribs through her coat and the miracle of breath between them. *"Joonam,"* she said into Marineh's hair. *"Azizam."* Mine. My dear. I'm here. You're here. We're here.

They took a cab that smelled like pine cleaner and new beginnings to the registry office, a small Standesamt with wide windows and bare white walls that had seen everything and therefore saw this gently. The officiant wore square glasses because of course he did; his suit was the color of good asphalt; his plan was efficiency wrapped in politeness. He spoke a clipped Berlin German that Thomas only half caught, and Maryan whispered translations against the edge of his sleeve because certain intimacies should be performed for a single audience.

Witnesses stood where they were told. Quincy cracked nervous jokes under his breath and Petey took pictures like a tourist with reverence. Thomas's father held the program as if it might tell him the right time to breathe. Sahar and Cem leaned together in the back, shoulder to shoulder, and Maryan thought: this is scaffolding made visible, a little forest of uprights keeping the structure from collapsing while the cement sets.

The rings went on without drama. The *ja* came out of their mouths and echoed around the small room as if multiplying. The officiant nodded with the satisfaction of a man whose job is to stamp meaning onto moments and keep order; he shook their hands like a father, and it felt right. They kissed—soft, certain, the kind of kiss that understands ceremony and gratitude— and for a suspended moment Maryan forgot what grief had taught her to remember first: borders, bombs, displacement, doubt. It was only them. This improbable bridge between lives that had no reason to be connected and yet were.

Outside, Kreuzberg offered its reluctant sun and the sound of bicycle bells and the sight of a woman walking a dog who clearly wanted to attend. They stood on the steps with their tulips and their relief and let a stranger take a photo because in Berlin strangers are an entire extended family you haven't met yet. Petey threw a handful of the tiny paper hearts Chelsea had snuck to them in Minneapolis—she had mailed a care package ahead, because that is the kind of person she was—and they floated on a small moving wind like the city had thought to clap quietly.

They walked to the Landwehr Canal and leaned on the railing in the place where couples lean without any instruction. A swan did its unbothered swan business. Quincy made a speech about not falling in. Marineh squeezed Maryan's hand so tightly it almost hurt—a wonderful, human, proof-of-life kind of pain—and murmured, "Mama would have liked him," and Maryan nodded because this was the sentence that would keep the day from floating away.

That night, they returned to Maryan's old studio above the tailor's shop, the one that smelled like dust and thread and the lives of clothes that had been made to fit people who were still becoming themselves. It was a small party and an ample one. There was wine and halva and salatim and a tray of börek that an elderly neighbor sent up as if she had been assigned the role of *auntie* by a benevolent casting director. Someone tuned a guitar and played Armenian folk songs that made the room lean toward them; someone else put on Dalida, because exile loves a torch. Thomas danced in that way that makes you love a man more for not pretending to be good at what he is bad at. Sahar laughed so hard she slid off the low couch, caught herself with the grace of a former gymnast, and demanded another glass because falling well is as important as not falling at all.

Maryan sat at the worktable that had seen her through winters and visas and the blank terror of blank paper. She opened a sketchbook to a fresh page, and her fingers traced a few easy lines, the kind of marks a hand makes when it is allowed to be a hand and not a translator. Beside her, Thomas dozed in an old chair, the celebration wearing off him like sunset that doesn't ask permission. The lamp made a soft cone of light; everyone else became silhouettes with voices. She wrote in the margin of the page:

We build by showing up. Even in winter. Even in exile. Even with no instructions.

She set the book down with the care you give a fragile object when you are trying to teach yourself that love is not a fragile object. She turned and tucked a blanket around Thomas's shoulders because everyone deserves a domestic miracle on their wedding night: to be covered by a person who knows the length of your body and chooses a blanket that fits.

Later that month, he flew home to Minnesota. Airports make theater out of leaving; they always have. They did not make promises they could not keep in the gate area; they did not stage a tragedy for strangers; they did the quiet work instead. He held her face with both hands and said, "I'll be back before you have time to kill the plant," and she said, "The plant will outlive us both," and then he said, "Text me when you get back on your bike," because he had learned that the small verbs are the ballast.

The security line ate him with its snaking patience and spit him out at the other side into the geography of screens and duty-free. She stood until she couldn't see the cap anymore and then stood longer because leaving is not a single act. On the train home she did not cry because crying on the U-Bahn is a cliché she will avoid if possible. She looked at other people's faces instead, the way Berlin teaches you to, and found in them a mirror she could hold for a few stops.

Something had shifted. He wasn't returning alone in spirit. They were already discussing residencies and time split between Berlin and Minneapolis, and the idea didn't terrify her the way it would have last year when love felt like a trap disguised as a song. She had been offered a year-long fellowship in Leipzig—access to a bigger studio, a printshop, a kiln she had no idea how to use and therefore wanted badly. He was looking into conservation and construction jobs in Europe, the kinds that let a man with good hands make old things last longer. They started using phrases like "when you're here next" and "we'll figure it out" instead of "goodbye." In a city built on the faith that you could knock down a wall and not be swallowed by the absence, this felt like a reasonable bet.

The world remained on fire. Israel bombed Rafah. Protests unfurled in Tehran. Students marched in Washington with handmade signs that let love and fury share a page. Walls were still up. Borders were still enforced. The news did not become kinder because she had found a husband and a registrar had stamped a certificate. But Maryan had begun to believe in something deeper than protest or painting, something that did not replace either but held them both. She believed in scaffolding. In the quiet act of choosing. In returning to a room because you said you would. In a man who carried a box not with a ring, but a question: *Do you want to keep doing this with me, even when the instructions run out?*

Her answer had been yes not in the cinematic way—no balloons, no out-of-season fireworks—but in the reliable way. Yes in mornings that had to be built with coffee and paperwork. Yes in afternoons where a form asked for a document you couldn't produce because the country that issued it no longer issued anything. Yes in evenings where the right thing to do was sit on a step and peel an orange and hand a segment to a sister who had been stamped for entry only temporarily and was still more permanent than anything else in her life.

In Leipzig, a week after she signed the fellowship letter, she found a scrap of paper in the pocket of the coat she'd been wearing the day they went to the registry office. She pulled it out and recognized Thomas's handwriting, clear and slightly leaning like a man who is moving forward and wants his letters to come too. It read:

I will not fix your fear. I will stand next to it.

She folded it and tucked it into the inside seam of her wallet. Not as a talisman, not as a memory. As scaffolding.

The kind of sentence you leave in the walls when you rebuild a room so the house will remember what it was supposed to hold.

On a Tuesday, she biked to Treptower Park and back, just to make her muscles remember a kind of work they'd paused while the bureaucracies rearranged themselves for her life. The sky was a dignified gray again. The willow trees dipped their hair into the water because someone had to perform spring's costume fitting. She parked the bike on the balcony and texted him, as promised: **home.**

Good. he wrote back. **I fixed the loose outlet in the hall. Your plant made it past the danger week.**

I knew it would, she wrote.

I didn't, he wrote. **But I wanted to.**

She set the phone down and turned the ring on her finger without thinking, the metal warm because bodies are proof of physics. She looked at the small pile of forms still waiting on the table—residence permit extension, fellowship tax paperwork, an email from a curator who wanted a studio visit—and she felt the old panic stir, then settle. Panic had always been the first responder. Now it wasn't the only one.

She pulled a new sheet of paper across the table and wrote at the top: *Build list.* The list was unromantic: frame two drawings, answer Sahar's email, order charcoal, call Marineh's landlord about a letter for her file, ask the fellowship administrator about access to the printshop on

Mondays, fix the squeak in the chair. She added one that made her laugh and blush in an empty room: buy better weatherstripping for Thomas's dad's back door, bring it in May.

At night, the radiators hummed like old men telling stories at a table you're allowed to sit at as long as you don't interrupt. The café downstairs kneaded tomorrow's bread. The city filtered itself through the curtains. If the world outside was a bonfire, then inside she could keep a candle lit and know it wasn't weakness. She could love the person she had become who believed that showing up counts and that survival is not the opposite of tenderness and that marrying a man in a room with square glasses and tulips was not an act against her politics but an act for her life.

They were not done leaving; no one ever is. There would be flights to miss and emails that arrived in the wrong tone and nights when two cities did not talk to each other gently across time zones. There would be headlines that made the act of going to the studio feel inadequate and therefore necessary. There would be days when the plant decided to be dramatic despite everyone's best efforts. There would be mornings when the text read **good morning** and felt like a small, shared country.

When she finally crawled into bed, Berlin breathed its slow, contradictory breath: big and intimate, harsh and generous. She lay with her palm over her sternum, feeling the steady drum that had once been a stranger and was now the oldest friend. She thought, not with bravado but with the matter-of-fact faith of someone who has walked across borders and survived the counting of days:

We build by showing up. Even in winter. Even in exile. Even with no instructions.

In the morning, the bread would be warm, the light would be indecisive, the emails would arrive, the plant would keep trying, the city would remember its ghosts and make room for its children. In Minnesota, a man she loved would put on his boots and drive to a job that made things last longer. At noon his phone would buzz with a picture of a drawing-in-progress and he would not ask *what is it?* He would say *keep going,* which is the best thing a person can say to another person who is trying to make something that wasn't there before.

And she would.